SHADOWS HOLD THEIR BREATH

SHERRY ROBINSON

Also by Sherry Robinson

Blessed (2019)

Echo Her Lovely Bones (forthcoming 2022)

(*Echo Her Lovely Bones* was previously published
under the title *My Secrets Cry Aloud* (2009))

SHERRY ROBINSON

SHADOWS HOLD THEIR BREATH

A NOVEL

Shadelandhouse
MODERN PRESS

Lexington, Kentucky

Published in the United States of America by:
    Shadelandhouse Modern Press, LLC
    Lexington, Kentucky
    smpbooks.com

First edition 2022

Shadelandhouse, Shadelandhouse Modern Press, and the colophon are trademarks of Shadelandhouse Modern Press, LLC.

Library of Congress Control Number: 2022933725
ISBN: 978-1-945049-28-6 (paperback)
ISBN: 978-1-945049-29-3 (e-book)

Book and cover design: iota books
Cover art: Annelisa Hermosilla
Author's photograph: Michelle Giles Morgan

For Glenn

SHADOWS HOLD THEIR BREATH

ONE

1

KAT HUNTER WAS ABOUT TO DO THE UNTHINKABLE—the unforgivable.

In the morning, her daughters would wake, scramble from their cozy beds, and hurry down the stairs in their flannel footed pajamas, hoping to find a fire already crackling in the oversized kitchen fireplace and hot chocolate warming on the stove. It had become the Saturday ritual on cold autumn and winter mornings—the girls' giggles filling the kitchen until it was time to huddle in the den under a fuzzy blanket to watch cartoons. Sometime later, David would come down, showered and ready for a few hours at the office, expecting a muffin or piece of toast and a kiss goodbye as he headed out the door.

But tomorrow morning the girls would find an empty kitchen. There would be no fire, no hot chocolate. There would be no mother. There would be only confusion and tears.

For weeks, Kat had been wondering what to do. She had been a stranger in her own body for a long time, inhabiting the life of Mary Catherine Hunter but strangely apart from it. Her parents had named her Mary Catherine and to everyone except her sister-in-law, Beth, that's who she was. Loving wife and mother. Dutiful daughter. Devoted friend. It was

Beth, though, that began calling her Kat—a name she chose while trying to free Mary Catherine from the bonds of tradition, especially the kind of tradition Kat had been immersed in growing up. Yet even the free-spirited Beth, whom she'd met in college, couldn't shake loose the traditions that had been so deeply embedded in Kat's life. But Beth did manage to sow a seed of restlessness in Kat, a disquiet that remained buried under the surface for years, even after Beth was killed in Vietnam. It didn't matter that the war was over when Beth had been killed or how selfless she had been while she was there. Her death six years earlier had wallowed out Kat's insides and left nothing but a dark and empty shell.

Barely six months had passed after Beth's funeral when everyone, except maybe Beth's mother Betty, had seemed to accept Beth's death, as tragic as it was, and move on. Kat was surprised—though perhaps she shouldn't have been—that David had dispatched his grief just as quickly as he did any difficult emotion. "I loved Beth, but she's gone, and dwelling on it won't bring her back." That's all he had said when Kat asked him how he wasn't also falling apart. "Beth wouldn't want us to stop living because of her," he added. Kat didn't have any doubt that David loved his sister, though she wondered how he would have had any idea what Beth would want. His conversations with Beth had rarely moved beyond the weather or the girls, since the siblings seemed to realize their differing views on the Vietnam War—and just about everything else—wouldn't be resolved through mere words.

So, Kat began to live a lie, pretending that everything was normal, that she was normal. She was the wife and mother and friend she had always been. Except she wasn't—not really.

Over the years, whenever her grief surfaced unexpectedly, through inconvenient tears or a catch in her voice when someone might mention anything remotely related to Beth, she recognized the disapproval in her mother's eyes. She saw David's shoulders stiffen, as if he just wished she would be done already. She even sometimes heard a slight irritation in Betty's voice, a response that surprised Kat more than anyone else's reaction. No one said why they no longer wanted to see Kat's grief—maybe it was because they didn't understand why she was grieving so much for a woman who was only related by marriage—but Kat knew her grief made them uncomfortable.

She tucked the grief deeper, making the sinkhole that had formed inside her finally begin to collapse, sucking her marriage, her friendships, her joy into its depths.

Kat remembered the moment she decided she would leave her family. That morning started normally, and any thought of leaving was safely buried in her mind. She dropped Jenny and Lizzie off at their elementary school and stopped by the grocery for milk and eggs. She made the beds, smoothing the sheets and tucking under the corners, while she waited for her mother to pick up Kris. She had asked her mother to watch Kris for the afternoon, using some flimsy excuse, which was met with her mother's usual acerbic response.

"Of course, I'll watch Kris for a few hours, though I don't really understand what you do with your free time. If you ask me, you'd do well to use that time to *really* clean your house."

Kat had not asked her—would never have asked her mother for the opinions she always offered, because her mother had a way of making even a compliment sound like criticism. It was the way she pulled her lips tight as she spoke. As a pastor's wife, her mother was accustomed to a level of self-control in public, but at home, she was quick to drop any civil pretense. Instead, she constantly reprimanded Kat for failing to understand what was expected of a preacher's daughter. The whole family's reputation was at stake, and Kat had come dangerously close in college to damaging that reputation with a pregnancy out of wedlock. A rushed marriage and an early miscarriage were the only circumstances that saved her mother from having to face a shocked congregation—

and the only way her mother could ensure her reputation would remain intact was for Kat to pour herself into her marriage and to raise well-behaved children.

It was little wonder, then, that Kat couldn't tell her mother the reason she wanted some time alone, without a two-year-old under foot, was to read more of *The Feminine Mystique*. Her mother would have called it a disgrace for Kat to read that book, since, in her opinion, it advocated tearing down everything that God had intended for women. Even David would have wondered what she found lacking in her own life to make her want to read it. So, Kat had been sneaking at night to read a chapter or two.

Beth had first mentioned the book before she went to Vietnam. "You obviously haven't read *The Feminine Mystique*," Beth had commented at the time. "It's a myth, Kat, the whole feminine fulfillment thing. Like Friedan says in the book, education and a career, that's where it's at for women." Kat dismissed Beth's comments at the time and had all but forgotten about the book, but when she saw the young nurse at the library, her pigtails cascading over a stethoscope, reading to the children, Kat saw Beth there instead, in her white uniform, a stethoscope around her neck, and her long red hair pulled back in a single braid and topped with a small white cap. As the young woman read about doctors and nurses to the children, Kat could hear Beth's voice—the way the vowels were elongated in certain words, giving the sense of a Southern gentility that made Beth's habit of cursing all the more shocking.

When the nurse finished reading, Kat helped the girls pick books, but when she was at the desk checking them out, Beth was still on her mind. It wasn't until she was almost out the door, the girls carrying the books they'd selected, that she thought about *The Feminine Mystique*. She lifted Kris onto her hip and told Jenny and Lizzie to wait on the stone bench beside the great marble staircase near the exit. She looked for the book in the card catalog and then found it on the shelf. At the circulation desk, she nearly changed her mind, afraid of what the librarian would think when she saw the title. But the woman didn't seem to notice as she removed the card in the back of the book and stamped the return date. She didn't even seem to notice Kat's hands shaking when the book was handed back to her.

As Kat read the book, she saw herself in a great number of the women described within the pages—plenty of other women who were also plagued by the question "Who am I?" It was a simple enough question on the surface. For a long time, her answer would have been "I am a mother." She had wanted children, and she had loved her daughters—she *did* love them. Hadn't she given up college with only a semester left so she could raise a family? Hadn't she thrown her whole self into the roles of wife and mother? Now, with her mother watching Kris for the afternoon, Kat was determined to finish the book so she could find answers.

After putting the tea kettle on the stove, she sat down at the kitchen table with the bright orange book in her hands. She felt the full weight of the thick book. It had not been easy to read, with its dense psychological and sociological descriptions. She had skimmed some sections that didn't seem to have relevance. She was not a sex seeker, after all. Yet in other places, certain words rose like specters off the page. *Trap. Terror. Escape.*

They hovered—even beckoned her.

Was she trapped, she wondered. Had she forfeited herself, as the book suggested, in pursuit of some idealized, and false, feminine role? Beth would have thought so.

The final chapter promised a new plan. Was this why Beth wanted her to read the book? A plan. An answer to the questions that unsettled her. Yet she didn't make it past the first page of the chapter. Not even the first paragraph, really. *It's frightening when a woman finally realizes that there is no answer to the question 'who am I' except the voice inside herself.* Her chest tightened. How could she hear that voice when she wasn't even sure if there was a voice inside her at all? A singular voice, anyway. *Her* voice. Too many others competed for attention. David pleading for the Mary Catherine he had married to come back to herself. Her mother criticizing her for being too loose with her ideas. Beth arguing she was too rigid. The girls begging her to play with them like she used to. They all wanted her to be who they thought she should be.

But who was she really?

The tea kettle began to whistle, so she laid the book on the table. The words still echoed in her head, though, as she pulled a mug, the one she'd picked up at the arts and crafts fair at the beginning of the month, from the cabinet and glanced out the window. *It's easier to live through someone else than to become complete yourself.* Is that what she had been doing—living through someone else? Had she been living at all? She felt so empty.

Out the back window, everything seemed to be dying. The garden only had a few final remnants left to give—a couple of heads of cabbage, a little bit of spinach, a small patch of broccoli, and potatoes to be dug and stored for the winter. Not far from the garden, the girls' playhouse was decaying from six years of weathering and eventual neglect. The door was dangling from its hinges and several shingles were missing from the roof. Even the trees at the back of the yard that formed the small, wooded refuge had transformed to their autumn browns and yellows, readying to shed their leaves and remain bare and dormant for winter.

She set the kettle on a cool burner and pulled her sweater from the hook beside the door, feeling the sudden urge to walk in those woods that had always settled her spirit. The October air was chilly. It tingled against her skin, bringing goose pimples to the surface of her arm. She slipped her arms through the sweater and pulled it tight around her as she moved past the garden and the playhouse. Under the canopy of the trees, she breathed in the earthy scent of the leaves. The path to the old pond was familiar—should have been familiar—but she became disoriented. Her eyes searched for something recognizable, some intimate sign of memory. Then she saw it. The tree stripped bare of a section of bark. The initials carved deep into the trunk.

D.E.H. + M.C.H.

She stared at the initials for a long time, trying to conjure the young woman who had fallen in love, who had given up everything to be his completely. David was a good man. Even she couldn't deny that. But he was so different from Beth. Kat could see that the first time Beth invited her to meet her family when they were in college. Beth was so much more of a free spirit than her brother. But wasn't that what she loved about David? His dependability. That no matter what happened to them, his answer was always, "We'll make it work."

Only it hadn't worked—not the way Kat ever planned, anyway.

―――――――

Her breath began to come in desperate gasps as she imagined the decades stretched out in front of her. The restlessness, the disquiet that Beth had planted in her had finally germinated and was longing to sprout, to be nourished, to bloom. Her heart pulsed relentlessly in her chest and throbbed in her ears. For a moment, she considered picking up a rock and scratching out her initials. Instead, she turned toward the house. The leaves crunched under her feet as her pace quickened. Out from under the trees' canopy, Kat felt the raindrops for the first time. By the time she reached the kitchen, she was shivering from the cold rain. She paused at the tea kettle before heading upstairs and running the tub full of steamy water.

She stripped off her clothes and left them in a damp heap on the bathroom floor. The water stung when she first stepped in, but she let the warmth seep into her skin and settle in her body. For a while, she lay motionless, letting one of her arms float to the surface of the water. She studied its buoyancy—how strange the feeling was for it to be both heavy and light at the same time. Two opposite feelings inhabiting the same body. She recognized the dissonance—had tried to explain it to David for months.

"You haven't been yourself lately," David had said as he took a sip of his coffee. He didn't look up from the blueprints that were spread across the kitchen table.

Kat watched him, waiting for him to continue. When he didn't, she finally spoke.

"What do you mean?" She knew how strange she had felt, but she had often wondered what he had noticed.

"You seem distant...quiet. You used to talk non-stop about the children, about the women's club, about, well, everything that happens to you."

"I thought that bored you to tears," she said with a half laugh.

"Well, I guess I didn't listen to *every* word." He gave her one of his sideways grins. "Seriously, though. Is anything wrong?"

"I'm not sure I can put it into words." She wasn't trying to be evasive. For weeks—months actually—she had tried to put a name to the feeling. "I wonder sometimes if I should just get away for a while. Be by myself." She waited to see how he would respond, but her comment seemed lost among the details of the blueprint he was studying.

"Are you unhappy with something?" he said, again with his eyes focused intently on the blueprints. Then, as if something had suddenly registered with him, he looked up at her. "Are you unhappy with me?"

"I'm not unhappy, David. But I'm not happy, either. Does that make sense?"

David stared at her, his expression a mixture of confusion and irritation. All she could do was stare blankly at him. Finally, he shook his head and turned his attention back to the blueprints. Nothing more was said, yet something between them had changed, as if her marriage had fully crumbled into the sinkhole inside her.

David was not wrong. Her answer didn't make any sense, even to her. But as she watched her arm float, almost as if it was detached from her, she was beginning to understand how she could be full of love for her children and empty of any emotion at the same time. A few years before, she had found the papers, tucked away in the attic of their one-hundred-fifty-year-old house, of the women who had lived in the house before Kat. She had read what Gracie, who had lived there just twenty years before her, had written. Gracie had wondered if the women who would live in the house after her would ever understand what it felt like to be empty. When Kat had first read the pages, she hadn't understood what Gracie meant. She couldn't understand the despair and certainly not the desperation that led Gracie to consider suicide.

The recollection of Gracie, who sat in that same tub while contemplating death by slipping her head under water and never reemerging, caused Kat to jerk upright. Kat had also once considered death, had even briefly formulated a way to do it. At the thought of it now, though, she pulled her knees to her chest, a shiver causing her to pull tighter. But just as Gracie had decided not to kill herself, whatever other consequences that meant, Kat knew she would never have been able to do it, either. Yet Kat realized that she couldn't stay in that house, not with her mind so confused. That's the moment she began to develop her plan to leave. She wouldn't leave for long, she told herself. She could never be away from her girls for too long. But she would go away somewhere—she didn't know where—away from everyone. Maybe her mind would finally be quiet enough to hear her own voice above the echoes of others—the one that would tell her who she really was.

She spent the next few days planning—putting meals in the freezer, washing the girls' clothes, digging up the potatoes and putting them in the root cellar. At the bank, she withdrew a few hundred dollars from the savings account they used for summer vacations. She knew she shouldn't take the station wagon. David would never be able to transport the girls in his sports car. So, when she was in town to go to the grocery, she stopped by the bus station to look at prices and routes, though she still hadn't decided exactly where she was going. Every time she stopped somewhere, she had to buckle and unbuckle Kris from the seat beside her. The little fingers from her growing-too-fast girl wrapped tightly around Kat's neck as she lifted the child out of the car. Joy and despair lying side by side in her heart. Dissonance.

When the night finally came, the night she had picked to leave, she let the girls help her make rolls for dinner, and, for once, she wasn't chastising the girls for covering themselves with flour or for creating a snowy trail across the kitchen floor. Instead, they laughed at each other, at their funny faces covered in the white dust. Even Kris, who was really too young to help, was allowed to pound the dough with her tiny fists. And when David smiled and told the girls how proud he was of them for helping, she saw their eyes twinkle. They'll be okay, she told herself. She knew David would take good care of them while she was gone.

After dinner, she gave Kris her bath, blowing the bubbles off her hand, and she laid out Jenny's and Lizzie's pajamas. By the time she put Kris to bed at eight, the other girls were in the den ready to watch *Diff'rent Strokes* while David worked at the kitchen table. The girls loved to wait for the moment when Arnold would cock his head and ask Willis the same question he asked in every episode. Then the girls would giggle, sometimes repeating the line to each other. Kat watched the girls, who were so absorbed in the show that they didn't notice her wipe away a tear. When the show was over, she hugged them so tight that Lizzie cried out.

"You're hurting me, Mommy," she squealed.

"Sorry, honey," Kat said as she loosened herself from the girl. But she was still tempted to hold onto them extra long when she tucked them into bed.

When she went back downstairs, David was still bent over his blueprints and T-squares. He rarely took a night off to watch a television show with her or just sit and talk. She missed the early days of their marriage, before he became so ambitious for promotions, when they would do something mindless—but at least together. She went back to the den and picked up a book that was on the end table. It didn't matter that she read the same paragraph over and over. The activity was more about passing time until David went to bed. Finally, he poked his head in the door.

"I'm going upstairs," he said. "Are you coming up soon?"

"I'll be up in a little while. I want to finish this chapter."

He came over to the couch, leaned down, and kissed her forehead.

"Good night," he said. She knew he'd be asleep when she finally came to bed. He always fell asleep as soon as he laid his head on the pillow, even if he had a book in his hand.

When the house was quiet, Kat removed the orange-covered book from the desk drawer, where it was hidden under folded sheets of wrapping paper. Tucked in the middle of the book were several pieces of lavender stationery. Like the other women who had lived in the house before her, Kat had written her story on those pages. She intended to leave it in the small lap desk in the attic with the other women's letters.

She laid *The Feminine Mystique* on the desk. Gently, she nudged her wedding band over her knuckle. Inside the band was inscribed *D.E.H. & M.C.H. Forever.* She wondered now if she truly understood what that pledge meant. If she *was* able to find the answers she sought, would she even still want to be married to David? The thought scared her, and she started to put the ring back on her finger. But when the gold glistened in the lamp light, she instead lifted a small square of pastel blue tissue paper from the drawer and placed the ring on it. With two quick folds of the paper, the ring was hidden from view.

Is it that simple, she wondered.

She picked up the folded tissue paper and slipped it into her pocket before grabbing the book. On the stairway up to the bedrooms, she was careful to avoid the places that usually creaked under her weight. The moonlight streaming through the window at the end of the upstairs hall cast strange shadows on the walls. When she reached the attic door in the hall, she turned the knob with a slow, deliberate motion. The hinges, original to the house, made a low moan as she eased the door open, and she paused to make sure no one was coming out of the bedrooms. She laid the heavy book on the first step up to the attic then turned to her and David's bedroom. If David was awake, she didn't want him to ask about the book.

Their bedroom was dark except for moonlight filtering through the window sheers. David's silhouette was stretched the length of their bed and she could hear his light snore. She pulled the tissue paper from her pocket and rested it on the dresser before creeping back to the door. She paused, wondering if she should leave David a note beside the tissue paper. But what would she say? She didn't know where she was going or when she'd be back. She told herself that she would call when she got to where she was going, let David know she was safe, and tell the girls how much she loved them, that she would be coming back as soon as she could.

In the attic, she pulled the cord on the bare bulb that hung in the middle of the room. In the dim light, she picked up the old walnut lap desk, the one containing the letters from the women who'd lived in this house before her, and crouched with it on the top step, pressing her feet firmly against the second step. She pulled a pen from the desk, pressed the top to release the nib, and scribbled a few more lines on the lavender pages.

As I sit here in this attic, I know now what I have to do. I have been wrestling with this for weeks, but I can't live this way any longer. Tonight, I took off my wedding band. I've wrapped it in tissue and left it on the dresser. My finger looks bare, but it looks more normal to me than it has in a long time. I hope David can forgive me. I hope the girls can forgive me. God, the girls. I love them with all my heart. But I can't be the mother they need me to be. I can't be the wife David wants me to be. I can't be the daughter my parents want me to be. I cannot even be the woman Beth wanted me to be.

I have to find the woman I want to be—that I need to be. So, Mary Catherine will stay here. She will linger in their memory, in the myth of who she tried to be. It will be Kat who will walk out that door. I hope she can find the peace she has been searching for. I hope that when she walks back through that same door, she will finally be whole.

When she finished writing, she put the pages and *The Feminine Mystique* in the compartment of the lap desk with all of the other pages that had been left there years before and she returned the desk to its place by the chimney.

Her purse and the two small suitcases she had packed earlier in the day were waiting for her inside the attic near the steps. She slung her purse over her shoulder and picked up the suitcases. She eased the attic door open and stepped cautiously into the moonlit hallway, carefully closing the door, cringing again at the low moan of the hinges. As Kat was about to turn and slip down the hall toward the staircase, she heard a noise behind her. Was it David's feet creaking against the floorboards in the bedroom? What would she say if he saw the suitcases in her hands? She held her breath and waited until she heard the sound again, exhaling only when she realized it was a branch rubbing against the side of the house.

Down the hall, she stopped at Kris's bedroom door. Kat had never been the mother Kris deserved—the mother she had been to her other two daughters. Even when Kat was pregnant with Kris, she had been consumed with images of Aunt Beth doting on her new niece—something Kat knew would never happen. The urge to rush in and scoop Kris into her arms almost made her set the suitcases down. Kat had never considered taking the girls with her. How selfish would that be to take the girls away from their school and their friends, even if it was just for a little while? No, this journey to sort out her confusion was meant for her alone. Anyway, she told herself as she descended the stairs, she would be back soon and her daughters would have a better mother. She had to believe that.

Before walking out the front door, Kat looked back up the stairs one more time. Then she headed into a light rain to the taxi waiting for her at the end of the long driveway. At the bus station, she purchased a ticket for the next available route—the one to Birmingham. When the Greyhound left the Lexington station, Kat rested her head against her window, listened to the rhythm of the tapping rain, and finally let suppressed tears trickle down her cheeks.

2

THE BUS PULLED INTO THE LOUISVILLE STATION at nearly eleven. Through the rain-spattered bus window, the cars glistened under the streetlights, washed free of their road-weary grime by the rain. Kat squinted to see them lined along the curb. They looked like shiny beads against a black-draped neckline.

An hour or so in Louisville and then another three until Nashville before transferring to another bus. Birmingham wouldn't be her final destination, but she hadn't yet determined what it *would* be. She had a friend who moved to Mobile the year before. Maybe she could stay there for a while—or there was a cousin in Sarasota, or maybe she would eventually pick a place she'd never been before. Some place where she didn't know anyone and where they didn't know her. The destination didn't matter anyway.

Kat watched as several passengers filed off the bus. They scurried to the safety of the awning and into the waiting arms of family or friends. Kat turned her head away, pushing hard against the pain that stuck in her throat. She buried her face in her hands.

"Are you alright, Miss?" She looked up to find the bus driver standing in the aisle, and she managed a slight smile.

"I'm okay. Just tired."

It scared her that she could become so accustomed to lying. The man smiled at her, unaware of her pretense.

"These trips can make for a long night," he said. She nodded at him, at his small talk. "You have time to go into the station for a bit, if you want to. Just put the Seat Occupied card in your seat."

"I'm fine. Thanks, though." She squirmed in her seat and was glad when he moved to the front of the bus. In the quiet, she listened to the melancholy tapping of the rain, a sound she had grown to hate. The only other sound was the snoring of a man a few rows back.

Kat reached down into her purse and felt for Beth's letters, the ones Beth had sent from Vietnam, the ones Kat had tucked away in the top of her closet at the same time she had tucked away her grief. But she needed them now. She needed to feel close to Beth. Her hand moved from the letters to the muffin she had purchased from the vending machine at the Lexington bus station. She pulled it to her lap and unwrapped the cellophane before pinching off a piece from the top of the muffin and popping it into her mouth. She let it dissolve a bit, giving the taste of apple and cinnamon a chance to linger on her tongue, before swallowing.

She looked out the window again, at the empty walkway in front of the building. Images flashed in her mind. The girls curled up in their beds, blankets pulled tight—except for Lizzie, who always seemed to fling the covers over the side of the bed, no matter how cold it was. The girls were everything to her. Why weren't they enough to make her stay?

She was glad when the bus began filling again with people. She wondered if she'd be without a seatmate, like she was on the first part of the trip. Men and women—even a couple of children—passed her row, until there were no more people coming down the aisle. She wasn't sure if she was relieved or disappointed. Determined not to let the unbearable silence be filled with her thoughts again, she reached into her purse for the Walkman that David had given to her as a birthday present. She had forgotten that a Bee Gees tape was still in it until she heard "How Can

You Mend a Broken Heart" blasting through the headphones. She pulled the Walkman to her chest, letting it hang there a moment before sliding the headphones from her head and clicking the cassette off. She bent over and placed it back in her purse.

"Whew. I thought I wasn't going to make it," a pretty girl said as she plopped down in the seat beside Kat. She was talking to herself mostly, but she glanced at Kat and smiled. She took a couple of deep breaths before tucking her oversized purse at her feet.

"I was running late," she continued, but this time clearly focused on Kat. Her smile pushed dimples into her soft, round cheeks. "My mother says I'll be late to my own funeral."

Kat stared at the girl—her dark brown eyes, her pale skin, and her hair the color of turmeric. It could have been Beth staring back at her. She shoved back at the memory.

"Well, it looks like you made it just in time," Kat said. The bus eased backward with several loud beeps. As it began to roll forward, the interior lights shut off. The girl kept talking, although she lowered her voice.

"I'm glad I made it. Jake—that's my boyfriend—he would have killed me if he had to wait for me to catch the next bus."

"He's waiting for you in Birmingham?"

"Birmingham?" She looked startled. "No, Nashville. Is Birmingham where you're headed?"

Kat made a quick affirmative sound.

"What's waiting for you there? Or should I say who?" Though Kat couldn't see the girl's face very well, she was sure there was a smile to match the lighthearted tone in her voice.

"No one," she said too quickly. "I mean, nothing's waiting for me. Birmingham's not even my real destination." Kat stumbled over the words.

"So, what's your real destination?"

"I'm not sure." Kat looked out the window at the stream of headlights coming toward her on the other side of the interstate. She knew how ridiculous it sounded.

"Not sure? Now that sounds like an adventure in the making."

"I suppose." She turned her attention back to the girl. "I just needed to—"

The words caught in her throat. Of course, she couldn't tell this stranger, no matter how friendly the girl was, why she didn't know where she was going. "I just needed a change," she finally said.

"I understand completely. That's exactly what I needed—a change. Jake and I are headed to Gatlinburg with a dream. He's an artist, and he says it's been his dream to live among other artists and learn from them. He asked me if I wanted to go with him and I said, hell yes."

"That's his dream. So, what's yours?" Kat remembered the conversation just the week before, when her mother-in-law Betty said that women of her generation didn't have the opportunities to pursue their dreams like modern women did.

"To be with him, of course," the young woman giggled. "Seriously, I think life is meant to be lived spontaneously. Does that sound crazy?"

"No, not crazy at all," Kat said softly. "I had a friend once that believed the same thing. In fact, you remind me so much of her."

"You aren't friends anymore?"

Grief ambushed Kat, as it sometimes did. It lay in wait until it thought she was comfortable, until she believed she could remember Beth without the heavy weight of sorrow.

"Are you alright? Did I say something wrong?"

Kat stared at the gray silhouette sitting beside her. She hadn't even noticed that she had sucked in her breath and held it deep in her chest.

"No. Nothing wrong," Kat said as she exhaled. "It's just that my friend died several years ago."

"I'm so sorry."

They both fell quiet, and Kat again rested her head against the window. The distant murmur of other voices mingled with the hum of the bus. Grief settled in and became a too familiar pulse in Kat's body. She drifted off to sleep, allowing a hazy dream to creep in. When she woke, she couldn't remember the dream, or even where she was at that moment. Then she heard the murmured voices again and saw the girl under the tiny circle of the reading light.

"How close are we to Nashville?" Kat asked.

"About thirty minutes, I think." The girl's voice wasn't cold, but it didn't carry the same warmth it had before. She closed the book she was reading and turned her body toward Kat. "Listen, I'm sorry about earlier," she said.

"Sorry about what?" Kat was surprised by the genuine troubled expression on the girl's face.

"I shouldn't have pried like that. I mean, you don't even know me. Mom's always telling me that I start talking before I start thinking."

"There's nothing to be sorry about, honey. It's just that even though I lost my friend several years ago, it's still quite painful sometimes." Kat reached over and took the girl's hand, as if by instinct. It was a maternal gesture; one she had used many times with her own girls. She pulled her hand back but looked into the brown eyes staring back at her.

"I'm so sorry. Is that why you needed a change?" the girl asked.

"More or less."

"But you don't have a specific plan?"

Kat shifted in her seat. "No, I don't," she said.

"Then why don't you come to Gatlinburg with Jake and me?" Kat scanned the girl's face and saw the same authentic smile as when the girl first sat down. "I know it sounds crazy. I mean, I know we just met. But isn't life meant to be lived spontaneously?"

Kat studied the girl. It was as if Beth was speaking to her. *Just do it. I found myself in Vietnam. It's time for you to find yourself, Kat. Take a chance.*

"Are you sure your boyfriend won't mind?"

"He'll be cool with it." She waved her hand with an air of confidence. "It's settled, then? You're coming?"

"Call me crazy, but why not." Kat leaned back and laughed— something she hadn't been able to genuinely do for quite some time. This *was* crazy, but it felt strangely like something she was supposed to do.

"Then I guess we ought to know each other's names." The girl smiled, her dimples presenting themselves again. She stuck out her hand in an exaggerated formal gesture. "I'm Molly Fisher."

"Nice to meet you, Molly. I'm Kat Turner." Her maiden name came gliding out of her mouth before she even realized it. She glanced down at the bare spot on her left hand then looked again into the shimmering brown eyes. They reassured her.

Kat knew this girl was not Beth—could never be Beth. Yet grief had chosen its path. How it would use Molly or what it might become because of her was still unknown. Perhaps grief would only take on a mask, as it had done many times before, to make her believe it had moved on. Or maybe it would finally loosen its grip on her and allow her to find peace.

Despite the uncertainly, or maybe even because of it, when they arrived at the Nashville station, Kat gathered her purse—with Beth's letters safely inside—hugged her coat tight around her body, and followed Molly off the bus into a cold wind.

3

November 3, 1972

My dear Kat,

I'm finally here in Vietnam. Such a long flight and then a grueling 17-hour ride from Saigon to the clinic, which is about two hours south of Da Nang. Didn't get much sleep on the trip, and only a few hours since we got here. Seems like land mines are going off around here at all hours of the day and night, or military trucks are rumbling down the street. The team I'm with, Dr. Michaels and Dr. Winslow and another nurse, Carrie Hernandez, seem to be taking it in stride. Hell, it's not like we didn't know what we were signing up for.

It's raining like hell today. They say it's the rainy season here, so what's a girl to do? You know what rain does to my hair—I mean, right now it would rival Danny Kaufman's 'fro. You remember him from college? Anyway, I just braid it and go on. After all, it's not like my hair's what's important here. I mean, we're better off than the refugees, especially as far as shelter goes. We're set up at a small clinic in Quảng Ngãi near a couple of the camps. Solid roof over our heads and bunks to sleep on in the back of the clinic, so the rain is only a nuisance most of the time.

You wouldn't believe how these people are living. I saw poverty in Guatemala, but this goes beyond poverty. The camps are really just shanties or bombed out houses. It's mainly children and the elderly— most of the older boys and men are either dead or fighting somewhere, their families waiting every day for news of them, good or bad. They're prepared for both.

I've always hated goddamn war, especially this fucking one. (We Americans have no business being here.) Now that I'm here, though, and see what it's done to the people, I hate it even more. War has made them fight over scraps from trash heaps dumped by American bases. At least we're doing something for them, right? I know how you feel about our soldiers, so I'll just ignore that disapproving look you're probably giving me right now. HaHa.

It's the children, though, that break my heart. I saw several children pounding tin cans flat, flies buzzing all around them, and I asked the interpreter what they were doing. She said they can get a dollar for every hundred pounds. It's not that they are working to help their mothers and grandparents that bothers me as much—that kind of thing has been going on for centuries. No, when it gets to me—I mean, really gets to me—is when I see the children playing, when their laughter spills across that wasteland. It's then I realize that this is all they've ever known. They were born with fucking war all around them. Their whole lives, nothing but fucking war. So they play and laugh like they aren't living in a house made of bamboo, scrap metal, and damn cardboard boxes.

For our first visit to the camps, we focused on meeting the families and basic wellness checks. I met a woman who was living with her mother and three of the cutest children you've ever seen (besides Jenny, of course). The older woman's face bore the deep lines of years of war and burdens, but she had small gold studs hanging from her ear lobes. I guess they were one of the few remnants she had from her life before war. The interpreter told me that the woman's husband had been a fisherman and they had lived in a village by the coast. He was killed in the war a number of years ago and her daughter's husband is off fighting now. So, after the government resettled them in this camp, they depend on each other. Small comfort, I'm sure.

This woman's children were shy at first but they got curious about my red hair. They wanted to touch it, especially the youngest, a little boy named Gian, who's about four. He kept saying "con khi, con khi" and his sister, half hidden behind her mother's leg, was giggling. I looked up at the interpreter. "Monkey," she said, a big grin on her face. So I made a monkey sound and Gian crawled up in my lap and tried to make the sound, too, until even his mother was laughing. That's when Dr. Winslow appeared at the door and gave me a stern look. "We're here to examine their health, not to play," he said. He's such a prick. All business and no compassion.

Yesterday, Carrie and I went back to the camp to check on a few people with respiratory issues, especially one older man who was very weak. He had refused to go to the clinic—many of the people here are wary of anything that resembles a hospital. The best we could do was monitor his condition and encourage him to take the medicines we brought.

I was with him when a loud explosion shook the building. When my ears stopped ringing, I heard the screams. The old man looked up at me. There was no alarm in his eyes—just fucking resignation. I rushed outside and saw Carrie several yards away bent over someone. When I got closer, I realized it was Gian. His sister had triggered a land mine—she was already dead—but shrapnel had ravaged Gian's leg and face. Carrie had taken off her jacket and wrapped it around his leg. I yanked mine off and held it against his face.

Carrie and I held onto him like that all the way back to the clinic, about 15 miles. Dr. Michaels met us at the door and rushed him back to one of the exam rooms. I started to follow, to assist Dr. Michaels, but Dr. Winslow caught me by the arm. "Let Nurse Hernandez do it," he said. "She has more experience." He thinks that just because I'm 25 I don't know anything. "Let go of me," I shouted at him. "I've worked in a goddamn emergency room, you asshole." You know I don't put up with that kind of shit.

It's not all bad, though, Kat. Gian is going to be okay. He's going to lose sight in his left eye, but he's a fighter. After he woke up from surgery, he looked up at me and reached out to touch my hair.

I know this all sounds horrible, and it is, but please don't worry about me, Kat. Because I know that's what you're doing, even though I told you not to before I left. I saw you try to hide your tears before I got on the plane, trying to be brave for me. But, I want you to know that there are moments of serenity here, even in the middle of a war, even with what I've already seen, just a week in country. Last night, I woke up in the middle of the night and I couldn't get back to sleep. I was lying in bed listening to my own breathing and staring into the murkiness of the room, except for a thin strip of moonlight coming through the window. It was then that I thought I heard singing. I sat up, trying to figure out if I was imagining it, but when I was sure it was real, I slipped out of bed and noticed Carrie wasn't in her bunk. I opened the door to our room and walked toward the singing.

The door to one of the rooms was cracked open a bit, and there was Carrie rocking Gian in her arms and signing a lullaby. "I heard him crying," she whispered when she saw me. "He was scared."

Watching Carrie comfort Gian made me think of you—the way you sing to Jenny when she gets scared. Remember that time last summer, when that thunderstorm came. The wind was so fierce we thought the roof was going to come off. Jenny didn't want to go to bed, but you promised her everything would be okay and you carried her to her room. I watched you through the door, rocking her and singing to her. Your voice was so comforting that she fell asleep there in your arms. You kept rocking her until you were asleep, too. I think it's the only time in my life that I've ever wished I was a mother—to experience a peaceful moment like that.

Anyway, tell that brother of mine I said hello. I doubt he's fretting about me the way you are. I'd tell you not to worry, but I know you too well to do that. So, I'll just encourage you to concentrate on your family. Unlike me, you were born to be a wife and mother. How many days now until your new little one arrives? I'm sorry that I won't be there for its arrival, but when the baby does arrive, sing a lullaby from Aunt Beth, won't you?

We're heading to Da Nang in a little while for supplies. I'll be okay, my dear friend—you are more than a sister-in-law to me, you know. I'm doing what I was born to do, which is to be a goddamn non-conformist in this fucked up world.

Above all else, Kat, don't forget to take care of yourself until I can see you again in person.

Lots of love,
Beth

4

JAKE MALLOY WAS NOT HANDSOME in a conventional sense, with his narrow—almost gaunt—face and his long slender nose. But when he smiled, his whole face transformed into a pleasant warmth. As soon as Molly saw him, she dropped her suitcases and ran to meet him. His smile broadened as he opened his arms to receive her, and the way she melted into him, for a moment becoming one body, made Kat stop.

Was it young love that made their eyes stay locked and their fingers intertwined even when they pulled away from the embrace? Was it the newness of a relationship that seemed to endow them with the ability to tune out everything and everyone else around them? Kat might have believed that, except she couldn't picture her and David ever looking at each other that way, even before they were married—and they certainly were never that uninhibited in public.

Molly glanced in Kat's direction and pointed. When Jake turned his face toward Kat, she could see the confusion on his face. He looked back at Molly and gave his head a slight shake, but she cocked her head and stared at him with doe eyes while she talked. Her hands moved like flowing water as she occasionally motioned in Kat's direction. Finally, Jake nodded, and Molly flung her arms around his neck.

"Kat Turner, this is Jake Malloy," Molly said when they came to where she was standing. "He's the best boyfriend in the whole world."

"Nice to meet you," Jake said. His smile seemed forced, but Kat pretended not to notice.

"Sorry to be a bother," Kat said, avoiding a direct glance at him.

"It's no bother," Molly quickly said as she gathered her luggage. "Jake, can you help Kat with her bags?" Kat let Jake pick up the luggage and followed him and Molly outside the bus station. She wondered if this was another bad decision in a long string of bad decisions.

When they got to Jake's light blue Blazer, he crammed Molly's suitcases into the back then moved a guitar case and some art supplies to the middle of the back seat before stacking Kat's suitcases on the seat.

"Sorry about the cramped conditions," Jake said as Kat climbed into the back seat. "If I'd known we were going to have company, I would have tidied a bit." He glanced at Molly.

Kat settled into the seat, gently moving aside a plastic tub of paint brushes. As the SUV moved through the dark night, she dozed. Along the way, she heard snatches of conversation between Molly and Jake. Their words were mostly muffled, but even through her sleepiness she recognized a sharp edge to Jake's voice.

She woke up just as they were entering Pigeon Forge. A few streaks of bright yellow broke through the heavy gray clouds that hung close to the mountaintops. Kat peered out the backseat window of the Blazer as they drove down the main road. The shops and motels rushed by almost too quickly to make out what they were. She had been to Gatlinburg only once, about ten years before. Back then, she barely noticed Pigeon Forge, which was mostly farmland, although she did remember seeing The Old Mill and Pigeon Forge Pottery on the end of town nearest Gatlinburg.

"Are you hungry?" Jake's voice fell backwards from the driver's seat. At first, Kat didn't know if he was talking to her, but then she could see his eyes in the rearview mirror staring directly at her.

"Sure," she said, though she wasn't sure she was.

Jake pulled into the Pancake and Breakfast House and Souvenir Shop, where the sloped roof promised forty-five types of breakfast. After Jake stepped out of the SUV and stretched his long legs, he pushed the seat forward and held out his hand for Kat. She scooched toward the front seat, careful not to upset the suitcases, art supplies, and guitar case crammed beside her. She was grateful for Jake's hand as she made her way down the small step beside the driver's seat and the big one out of the vehicle.

Whatever he and Molly had talked about on the drive seemed to have softened his mood. His pleasant smile had returned, and it was the first time that Kat noticed the deepness of blue in his eyes. When Molly came around the side of the SUV, Kat felt as if her cheeks must be burning, as if she had been caught in a tryst.

The restaurant was busy, full of tourists who had come to these valley towns in autumn to view the vivid reds, yellows, and oranges that painted the Great Smoky Mountains. While they waited for a table, Molly and Kat wandered through the souvenir shop. Shelves of coffee mugs and trinkets. T-shirts emblazoned with mountains or black bears.

Souvenirs were oddities, Kat thought—the collecting of them, that is. What would make a person pick up a snow globe, for instance, with a lumbering black bear and Smoky Mountains, Tennessee, etched somewhere on it? Or even containing something as emblematic as the Statue of Liberty or the Eiffel Tower? At home, it would sit on a shelf somewhere only to collect dust, but rarely would it ever make its owner pause long enough to revive the memories or emotions it was supposed to evoke.

Wedding rings were much the same way. Kat looked at the bare spot on her finger again. Until she slipped it off and left it on the dresser the night before, when she left David and the girls, her wedding band had been on her finger from the moment she had taken her vow in a church more than a decade earlier. Yet in all those years she had barely even noticed it as she went about her daily routine. She had never—even though she knew what taking it off meant—looked at it and connected it to any emotion she should have felt.

"The table's ready," Molly said as she came around to the aisle where Kat stood blankly staring at a row of meaningless trinkets.

A pretty, brown-haired waitress, in her salmon-colored smock and white slacks, showed them to a booth along the front windows and handed them menus. She was soon back with a pot of coffee and ready to take their order. Kat knew she needed to eat. She had eaten very little the night before as she watched her girls chatter away at the dinner table. Even the muffin she'd had on the bus was only half-eaten. Despite nothing sounding particularly appealing to her, she finally ordered a stack of pancakes and a side of bacon.

She glanced at her watch. The girls would be up by now.

When she looked up, Jake and Molly were staring at her. She shifted uncomfortably in her seat and wondered if she should say something.

Jake spoke first. "So, Molly tells me that you're a lost soul."

"Jake!" Molly gave his shoulder a push, then focused on Kat. "He didn't—I didn't mean it like that."

"It's okay. You're not wrong."

"We're all lost at one time or another, I suppose. It's a product of being human." Molly gave a shrug. "Anyway, we're glad you decided to come along with us, aren't we, Jake?"

"Of course, we are." He smiled—another forced smile—before stuffing a forkful of waffle in his mouth. He looked down at his plate and swirled a bit of waffle in the syrup. "So, I'm guessing you don't have a place to stay, since this wasn't the place you were actually going," he said without looking up. Kat wasn't sure if it was sarcasm she heard in his voice.

She shook her head, then uttered a quiet no. It hadn't occurred to her what she would do when she got there. The truth was, although she had developed the plan to leave, she hadn't gone so far as to think about what she would do when she got to wherever she ended up—not where she would stay, or how long she would be away, or what she would do when her money ran out.

"After breakfast, Jake's got to call Rusty, the man who's going to apprentice him. Rusty's supposed to set us up with some place to stay. If you'd like, Jake could ask him if he knows somewhere for you, too." Jake stared at Molly, and Kat saw irritation in his face.

"Would you?" she said, glancing at her pancakes. "That would be so kind."

"Of course, we'll do it, honey," Molly said as she reached across the table and placed her hand on Kat's arm. Kat had no idea how old Molly was—twenty-two, maybe twenty-three, she guessed—but at that moment, Molly could have been much older, gentle and wise beyond her years. It was almost as if God had brought the two of them together for a divine purpose, if Kat still believed God worked that way.

She wanted to believe in divine intervention, like she did when she was younger. She had believed everything her father had preached from his pulpit. Be good and God will reward you—that was the message implicit in nearly all of his sermons. She had been good—had tried to be anyway. Until she met David. Sleeping with David and getting pregnant before they married was certainly not good—her parents made sure she understood that. But God had already punished her for the transgression by taking the baby before it could even breathe life. Her mother never let her forget this fact, even while she claimed that forgiveness meant that transgressions were erased from the ledger.

Kat's ledger would always have this black mark—she sensed that— and now she had added to it by abandoning her girls, even if it was just temporary. But she had a ledger of her own for God. He had taken her first child from her, punishing it instead of her, and he had taken Beth, even though she was doing something so selfless. Perhaps God had led her to Molly. But it was just as likely coincidence that put them together on that bus. Whatever it was, as she watched Molly chatter on about how she and Jake met at an arts fair in Louisville that spring, Kat felt a dizzying electricity, as if she was cresting the first big incline of a roller coaster, ready for the curious mix of panic and anticipation of a single exhilarating moment, before plunging toward whatever lie ahead.

———————

Jake and Molly decided to browse in a nearby bookstore since Rusty couldn't meet them until eleven. Kat stayed back, pretending to browse again in the souvenir shop. "You all go on," she told them. "I'll be okay." She knew they probably wanted some time without her tagging along anyway, since she had been an unexpected companion on the trip. More importantly, Kat knew she needed to make a phone call. Jake had used a phone booth on the corner just up the street from the restaurant. As soon as Jake and Molly were out of sight, Kat headed to make the call she had been dreading all night.

She pressed herself against the wall of the phone booth. Her feet felt rooted to the floor as she stared at the black box in front of her. It should have been a simple task. Drop the coins in the slot and dial the number she had called hundreds of times before. Of course, this was different. *I don't know if I can do this*, she whispered, as if she was begging some invisible judge to spare her the horrendous sentence he had just handed down. Yet it had to be done, and she knew it. She took a step forward and drew in a deep breath before picking up the receiver. As the phone rang, she considered hanging up. Then she heard his familiar voice.

"David? It's me, Ka—Mary Catherine."

"Mary Catherine? Where are you? Are you alright?" His voice had a quality she had never heard before.

"I'm okay," she said, her breath coming out in a little puff along with the words.

"You don't sound okay. What's going on?"

"I just needed to get away—to think, to figure some things out."

"You're not making any sense. What have you got to figure out? Is it us? Is it me?" His voice exposed his exasperation, like it sometimes did with the girls when he was trying to work at home.

"I think it's me mostly."

"Then why did you take off your goddamn ring?" It was full fledge anger now. The only time Kat remembered David using language like that was a couple of times when he'd had too much to drink. Her body tensed.

"Are the girls alright?"

"Of course they're not alright. They were hysterical this morning because their mother left without saying a word. Kris kept calling for you, and I couldn't calm her down."

The words pierced Kat. Kris's face came clear in her mind—the big brown eyes full of tears, the tremor in the tiny voice. How many times had Kat scooped Kris into her arms and held her tight until the sobs slowly slipped away? But now Kat was not only the reason for the tears, she wasn't there to provide the comfort. She had vaguely imagined the scene—tried to avoid picturing it, actually—but hearing it described, hearing what she had done to her babies, made her body tremble.

"Did you hear me? The girls are devastated. I finally had to call Mom, who ended up taking them to her house. You've made a mess here, Mary Catherine. When are you coming home?"

"I don't know."

"You don't know? After what I just told you, you don't know?"

"It's not that simple, David. I wish it was." The phone beeped. She was out of time. "I have to go. I'll call back in a day or two."

"Don't bother. Don't bother coming home, either."

"David, don't—"

The phone went dead. Kat clutched the receiver in her hand, not able to move, as if she, too, was now dead. Her marriage was over. Though she had somewhere in her consciousness been aware that her actions would have that effect, the certainty of that fact was suddenly—painfully—real.

Our choices always have consequences, her mother told her the day Kat miscarried her first child. She had hated her mother for her inability to provide comfort rather than judgment.

Heavy gray clouds were again gathering in the western sky. Kat hung up the receiver, laid her head against the wall of the booth, and watched the clouds crawl toward her. She listened to her breaths. The deep inhale that bore with it a whisper of mourning. The slow and lingering exhale that carried the weight of consequences yet to come. She feared she might not ever be able to go back, but moving forward seemed just as impossible.

As she stepped out of the phone booth, she heard Beth's words on the wind. *I can't feel helpless anymore.* Beth chose to sacrifice herself in Vietnam so she wouldn't feel helpless. Kat sensed she would have to make a sacrifice, too, and it would have to be a choice, a choice she alone would have to make.

5

KAT HAD BEEN AWAY FROM HOME FOR THIRTEEN DAYS. Thirteen days of sitting alone in her sparse studio apartment over the garage behind Rusty's house. Thirteen days of dying inside without talking to her girls. The first week, she had called the house every night. At first, David hung up as soon as he heard her voice, then he stopped answering the phone altogether. When she tried on Saturday morning, she wasn't too surprised that her mother answered the phone.

"David's at work," her mother said, her voice icy and distant. The sound of it awakened the old pattern. Kat pictured her mother on the other end of the line. The familiar tension that started in her mother's face and travelled to her arms, held tight in her body and in her legs, with the knees locked in a rigid stance. The image dropped Kat back to high school, when she had grown accustomed to the glaring eyes and accusing finger as she tried to explain herself. Now, even in her thirties, she still had a tendency to wither at her mother's scathing rebukes.

"I might have guessed he'd be at work," Kat said, hearing the bitterness in her own voice. She twisted the phone cord around her finger and tried to soften her voice. "He won't talk to me."

"What did you expect? He's hurt and angry—and he has a right to be. You can't just walk away from your family and think there won't be consequences."

"Of course, I knew there'd be consequences." The words sounded worthless, even to her. Had she really considered everything before she left? "Mom, please let me talk to the girls."

"David said that if you called, I was not to let you talk to them. He's right, you know."

"He's not right. He hasn't even been willing to listen to me. At least let me talk to Jenny. She's old enough to understand."

"Understand what? I'm in my fifties, and I don't understand."

"Please, Mom. They're my babies." Her fingers went numb as the phone cord tightened around them.

"You gave up the right to say that the moment you walked out."

"What does that mean?"

"Just what I said. No woman who can leave her children can ever claim to be a mother. You created a gaping wound in those girls, and we're just now getting them calmed down. There is no way that I would let you talk to them right now."

Kat didn't remember anything else that was said before the call ended. Her thoughts had stopped as soon as her mother mentioned a gaping wound—a wound Kat was responsible for inflicting.

After she hung up the phone, she pulled a picture from the dresser drawer. At first, she couldn't bring herself to look at it, nearly slipping it back into the drawer. Then she caught a glimpse of the only face fully visible. Jenny, with her shoulder-length blond hair dripping wet. Her round cheeks made fuller by her broad smile. Lizzie's back was to the camera, but her hair was also dripping with water. Both girls were reaching toward their baby sister, who was standing in the grass just outside the wading pool, urging her to come in. Kris, with her soft brown curls tumbling haphazardly around her face, was looking up at Jenny with a smile that glowed white in the sun.

It was one of Kat's favorite pictures of the girls—not like the stiffly posed pictures they did every year at the Olan Mills Studio.

She remembered the day the picture was taken. The oppressive August heat, just three days before the new school year, had Jenny and Lizzie begging to pull out the wading pool, even though both of them were really too big for it. They shrieked as they took turns spraying each other with the water hose while the pool was filling up. Even after the hose was turned off, they poured buckets of water over each other, sending even more shrieks into the air. Kris, who had been playing with blocks in the cool grass, finally decided to see what her sisters were doing. When she hesitated at the edge of the pool, Jenny and Lizzie stopped and held out their hands for her. That's when Kat captured the moment with the Nikon 35mm camera she'd gotten for Christmas.

But it was what happened next that endured in Kat's memory.

"Come on in, Kris. It's okay," Jenny said, taking hold of the tiny hand. Kat could still recall the tenderness in her eldest daughter's voice. Kat watched as Kris eased her leg over the plastic edge of the pool, squealing as she plunged first one leg and then the other into the cold water. Jenny tried to lead her across the pool, but Kris pulled her hand free.

"I do it," she said, her mouth pursed in determination. But two steps in she slid on the slick plastic bottom of the pool, landing in a big splash.

The next frame always replays in slow motion. The camera dropping to the grass. The three—maybe four—steps to the pool. The frantic plunge to sweep Kris into her arms. Two white ribbons of water drenching Jenny and Lizzie.

The scene, when it resumes normal speed, is filled with laughter. Kat is now standing in the middle of the pool, with Kris cradled against her chest. Water curls down her legs from her khaki shorts while her wet cotton shirt clings to her body. The girls' faces glisten in the hot August sun. Something in their eyes causes Kat to lower Kris back into the water and then to sit down beside her. Kat reaches for a bucket, fills it with water, and dumps it over her own head. She slings water from her hair, spraying droplets on the girls as they clap and shriek with delight. Kat hands the bucket to Lizzie, and the girls take turns pouring water on Kat. She remembers everything. The laughter that floats in mid-air above her like hummingbirds. The water that shimmers like crystals on summer-baked skin. The wet earth that stings her nostrils. The tiny fingers that cup Kat's face and turn it to meet the girl's glittering brown eyes.

Kat would have held onto that moment—the euphoria of it—if she could have, like capturing a butterfly and putting it in a jar to admire its beauty.

But butterflies don't survive long in glass jars.

The weight of grief suffocated everything until all that was left was a faint echo of joy. She was tired of the heaviness, tired of the smothering pain that seemed to overwhelm every other emotion. She studied the photograph. The curve of Kris's face, the angle of Lizzie's arm, the drip of water from Jenny's hand. She wondered if she would ever feel again as she had that day—the giddiness of abandonment to the moment, of letting go of all her inhibitions. It had never been who she was. But now she had a deep longing for it.

At seven o'clock, the room was still dark—the murky kind of gray just before dawn that transforms the familiar into strange contours and shadows. Even though Kat had been living over Rusty's garage for two weeks, she was still getting used to the layout of the room, especially once the lights were out. Kat squinted, trying to decide what a particular contour was across the room.

It was the lava lamp, she finally decided.

The lava lamp belonged to Rusty's son, who used to live in the apartment when the boy was in high school. He was away now at the University of Tennessee, studying engineering, but he left the apartment just as it was. The lava lamp. The daybed. The old television set. The oak table and two ladder back chairs. Even the kitchen was mostly stocked with Corelle dishes, pots and pans, and silverware. She was grateful that the apartment was furnished, even with eclectic items like the lava lamp and the bead curtain that separated the living space from the efficiency kitchen. The apartment was slightly out of step with time, which was oddly comforting to Kat.

She rolled to her side and snuggled the covers tight against her chin. She knew she needed to get up because Molly would be there soon. She had seen Molly only a few times since arriving in Gatlinburg. Molly had been immersed in her job at Rusty's glass shop, doing some light office chores. When she wasn't working, Molly was settling into her apartment with Jake, just next door to Kat in a house that Rusty had divided into two apartments. She and Kat did make a couple of trips together to the store in Sevierville for sheets and towels, kitchen supplies, and shower curtains. Kat had been frugal with her purchases, since she was still living off the money she'd taken from the vacation account—not that she had ever been extravagant. For her, making her new temporary home was in the small touches, like the basket of pinecones she had collected from behind her apartment that now decorated her dinette table.

Kat yawned and finally sat up, reaching for the lamp behind her head. The room came into focus—the cozy brown paneling, the bright green shag carpet, and the orange and brown curtains. It wasn't home in so many ways, but she had grown accustomed enough to it to feel at home there.

She yawned again and threw off the covers. The room was chilly, so she turned up the thermostat and waited until she heard the baseboard heaters turn on. Then she laid out her gray corduroy slacks and the pink turtleneck sweater David had given her last Christmas. She tried not to think on that as she showered. Tried not to think about what she had done to him or what would happen next. She had spent too much time dwelling on that already.

After she dressed, she lifted the covers and pillows off the daybed and laid them neatly on the shelf in the closet, then she replaced the wedge-shaped bolster against the wall to form a couch again. It wasn't the most comfortable couch for visitors, but Molly didn't seem to fret too much over things the way Kat did. "It's just a place to park my ass for a while," she said when Kat had her over right after she moved in. Molly had kicked off her shoes and sat cross-legged on the hard couch as if that's what everyone did.

Kat was still smiling when she started the coffee, trying to imagine herself sitting cross-legged like Molly. Sometimes Kat felt ancient next to her, especially when she learned that Molly was barely twenty, a full thirteen years younger than Kat. Yet when Molly came in and threw her arms around Kat as if they had been sisters for a lifetime, she felt the years between them drop away. She was safe with Molly. She knew that—had somehow felt it from the beginning.

When Molly arrived, Kat fixed pancakes for breakfast because that was her specialty. *They almost float off the plate*, David used to say. It was strange that David was so much on her mind that morning. They still hadn't spoken since she called him the morning after she left, but she knew she had to keep trying.

She shook off the thought and set the table while Molly chattered on about Jake's first few days on the job. He was starting with some simple stained-glass patterns, selecting the different colors of glass, cutting and foiling the pieces, and soldering them together. Molly said Rusty was impressed with how quickly Jake was picking up that part of it, but she wasn't surprised. She had seen his paintings at the art fair last spring and knew that he was a talented artist.

"Listen to me rattle on," she said. "I haven't let you get a word in edgewise. My mother would be scolding me about my manners."

"It's okay. I'm not much company today," Kat said, setting the pancakes on the table.

"It's not just today, is it, Kat? You've more or less been holed up in this room for two weeks. I haven't known you all that long, I know, but I think I can tell when something's bothering you."

"I'm not sure what you mean." Kat pushed a piece of pancake around on her plate, trying not to look at Molly.

"You keep to yourself most of the time, even when you have opportunities to go out. I invited you to dinner the other night and you just blew me off. Honestly, I might start taking offense if you keep doing that." She winked, obviously trying to lighten the mood, but when Kat only offered a weak smile in response, Molly reached across the table and grabbed Kat's free hand. "Seriously, Kat, is something wrong?"

Kat dropped her fork with a loud crash, louder than she expected, and pulled her hand free. She stared at Molly, searching her eyes for an echo of the other red-headed confidant who would have also asked the same question. She missed Beth more than ever.

"I don't know that I can talk about it, Beth. Not yet, anyway." Kat didn't realize she had said Beth's name instead of Molly's, and Molly didn't correct her.

Kat stood up and walked to the window. She had opened the curtains just before Molly arrived and now the sun was beginning to rise above the mountains that gave a backdrop to Rusty's house and shop. The sky was the color of the variegated roses in her yard back home—deep pink and pale orange tinged with a hint of yellow. She took a deep breath and spoke without turning back to Molly.

"I've done something awful. Something selfish. And I don't think I can make it right."

"It can't be that bad," Molly said, her voice sounding as if it whistled through a tunnel.

"It is," Kat said, her words sticking in her mouth.

"Okay, that's enough." Molly was behind Kat now, pulling her around to look her in the eye. "It's time to stop the self-pity. I don't know what you've done, and, honestly, I don't care. You may feel like whatever you've done has killed you inside, but it hasn't. I think it's time for you to get out of your head and find life again."

Kat shook her head, but Molly gently cupped her hand under Kat's chin to stop the movement.

"Don't resist it. I can be pretty damn persuasive. Just ask Jake." She laughed with a full-throated laughter that filled the room. Kat felt her shoulders relax and a tingle that moved down her arm to the tips of her fingers. "There, I see a smile," Molly said as she took a step back. "Now, Jake and I are going to a club tonight with Rusty and LuAnn, and you're going with us. And don't you say anything, because I refuse to hear another 'no' come out of your mouth. You hear me?"

Kat nodded as if she had a choice.

"Come on now," Molly said as she took Kat's hand. "Let's eat these pancakes before they get cold and soggy."

After Molly left, Kat sank onto the couch. It's not that she didn't desperately want to believe her new friend. She wanted to resurrect the life that had collapsed within her. She wanted to feel joy without its now constant companions of guilt and sorrow. But as she pressed her head into her hands, she doubted even Molly had that kind of power.

6

THE CLUB MOLLY MENTIONED turned out to be Smokey's, a bar out HWY 321. Kat hadn't been to many bars—her parents frowned on them when she was younger and David preferred to drink at social functions at work or home. It wasn't that Kat objected to bars; they just weren't part of her normal world.

Under the waning moon, Kat couldn't tell much about the building itself, but the big sign above the door was lit up. It spelled out Smokey's in bold black letters, with the *Y* in the shape of a martini glass and a cowboy hat perched on the top of the *S*. Neon signs glowed in the windows: Budweiser in fat white letters and Miller Lite in the middle of a blue circle.

It's probably one of those honky-tonk bars, Kat thought. She was surprised because Molly and Jake didn't seem like honky-tonk kind of people. It certainly fit Rusty and his wife, LuAnn, perfectly, though, and they were the ones who picked Smokey's for the evening out.

Inside, the room was large and open, but the dark oak paneling on the walls and ceiling gave it a cozier feel. The bar itself was along the back wall, a row of black leather stools on the front side and shelves of assorted liquors behind the bar. The rest of the room, except for a stage on one side, was a mix of tables and high tops. A gray-haired man was behind the bar, serving up drinks to a row of men in cowboy hats or ball caps. A few women were sitting at the bar, too, but they were turned to watch the young man on the stage.

Kat turned her head to watch him, too. He was strumming his guitar and singing "Blue Eyes Crying in the Rain." Kat couldn't take her eyes off him, the way he swayed his hips slowly in jeans that hugged every curve. His voice was sorrowful as he lifted his head and closed his eyes while he sang about leaving some woman, as if it was deeply personal. Then his eyes opened, and it seemed to Kat he was looking straight at her as he sang. She wanted to look away from him, but the pain conveyed through his eyes stirred the pain that lingered in her chest. She couldn't move.

"Looks like there's a table back there," Molly said as she tugged on Kat's arm. Kat turned to follow Molly and the others, but as soon as they were seated at the table, she focused again on the singer. He had set his guitar down and was singing another song, one she hadn't heard before. It was a faster tempo and he was strutting around the stage, clapping his free hand against his thigh while the band was playing behind him. His long brown hair flowed around his face as he moved, and Kat thought he was the prettiest man she'd ever seen.

"What'll you have?"

Kat looked toward the voice to find a tall, brunette woman in a plaid shirt, unbuttoned at the bottom and then tied at her waist. The woman smiled at Kat and asked again, "What'll you have, honey?"

"Oh," Kat said. She wasn't sure if she hadn't heard her friends order because of the noise level in the bar or because she'd been focusing so much on the singer. "Gin and tonic," she shouted over the music, hoping the others hadn't realized why she was distracted.

"Isn't this great?" Molly said as she leaned over and spoke into Kat's ear. "I'm so glad you came."

Kat nodded and smiled. It's not as if she had much of a choice. Molly practically dragged her to Rusty's car and shoved her onto the back seat next to Jake. Kat had taken in the scent of Jake's Brut, the hint of citrus and vanilla that was somehow both fresh and masculine. She hadn't seen Jake in several days, and the smell of a well-groomed man made her face flush. She was grateful it was dark so no one could see her.

Kat sipped on her drink, watching and listening to everything. The men at the bar flirting with the women. The women laughing, like they needed to show how interested they were. People dancing and clapping. Rusty and LuAnn leaning toward Jake and Molly, trying to talk over the music. The sounds overwhelmed her: drumbeats, glasses clinking, laughter, and meaningless chatter that formed a single intoxicating rhythm. A flutter vibrated through her chest awakening something deep in her, something she couldn't name.

"Are you okay, honey?" LuAnn touched Kat's arm to get her attention.

"I'm okay. Just daydreaming, I guess." Kat smiled, but she wanted more than anything to lose herself in that rhythmic cacophony again. It was the sound of ordinary life.

"I know just what she needs," Molly said as she hopped up from the table and headed to the bar. Kat watched her a moment, then she felt LuAnn tapping her arm again.

"Are you settling into the apartment?" LuAnn said. "We haven't seen much of you since you arrived. I hope the apartment is working out." LuAnn's Dolly Parton blond curls bounced as she spoke.

"Oh, it's very comfortable. I so appreciate you renting it to me on such short notice."

"It's nice having you there—makes me feel like Randy's still up there when I see the lights on."

Kat hadn't told anyone that she had children, so LuAnn had no way of knowing that the mention of her absent son peeled the scab off Kat's guilt over her own children.

"Here you go," Molly said as she produced two tall glasses filled with an orange and red concoction. "It's a tequila sunrise. Sure to make you forget all your troubles."

Kat stared at the drink. Normally she wouldn't have more than a single drink, but she found it hard to argue with Molly. Molly raised her glass in a mock toast before taking a big sip from the drink, and Kat did the same. The sweetness coated her mouth and the sharpness slid down her throat. She took another drink. A warmth began to spread through her body, and she felt her shoulders lose the tension they had been holding all night. Without even realizing it, her shoulders began to sway to the music.

When the electric guitar announced the beginning of "Ramblin' Man," Molly jumped up. "Oh, I love this song. Let's dance." She tried to pull Kat up to join her, but Kat shook her head. "Come on. I know you want to," Molly said, ignoring the headshake. Kat looked back at Jake for help, but he shrugged his shoulders as if to say 'I'm glad it's not me.' Kat had always been self-conscious about the way her body moved and would have never been seen on a dance floor back home, but somehow Molly managed to coax Kat to her feet.

Kat hung close to the safety of the table while she shifted from one foot to the other and clapped her hands to the beat. Molly danced her way to the center of the room, her hands clapping high above her, seemingly unaware of anything but the music—unaware even that Kat hadn't followed her. Molly's body moved like water flowing down a hillside, rippling as she arched her back and waved her arms above her head. Kat wondered if she would ever be uninhibited like Molly—not just doing something without caring what anyone else thought about it but being so lost in something that nothing else mattered.

As Kat watched the red ringlets of Molly's hair bounce a rhythmic dance of their own, she thought about the first time she saw Beth on the University of Kentucky campus. Kat was walking from the classroom building to the library when she noticed a crowd gathering near the administration building. She had never been someone who was drawn to a crowd, especially an unruly one, but the journalism class she had just come from had encouraged her to sharpen her curiosity.

As she approached, she heard the chant before she could see who was chanting. "One, two, three, four! We don't want your fucking war!"

Kat knew war protests had been popping up on campus—on many college campuses—but she hadn't seen one yet. She edged closer until she saw a group of seven or eight students, some of them holding signs: *Stop the War! Get Out of Vietnam!* Most of the protesters were men, but Kat's eyes locked onto the lanky woman standing in the middle of the group. A light breeze made wisps of red hair dance around her face and she pushed them back with the same charged energy she used to shout the chant.

Kat had never heard a woman use such language. Everything her strict Methodist parents had taught her told her that such language was immoral, especially coming from a woman. Kat watched this young woman's mouth and eyes scrunch with anger as she shouted right in the face of a man in uniform. Kat wanted to go up to her and slap her face for being so disrespectful. Instead, she turned in disgust and walked toward the library, the angry chants still swelling behind her.

"Maybe she should go to Vietnam," Kat whispered as she clutched her books to her chest. "Then she'd see what those brave soldiers are really doing over there."

The memory stopped Kat cold, her body suddenly thick and heavy. The electric guitar was wailing the Southern rock finale of the song, but all Kat could see was the mass of arms waving above bobbing heads. The air grew stifling and Kat felt her whole body flush, heat that pushed from her face down through her torso, spreading to her arms and legs like molasses oozing from a jar. The mix of heat with the buzz of alcohol made her feel like she was going to be sick. She forced her way past people until she found the door, stepped outside, and inched toward the parking lot. A rush of cold air swept over Kat's body. She heard her gasps echoing off the mountain rising out of the fog across the road. When the door opened behind her, Kat flinched. She realized the music had stopped. All she heard was a quick snatch of voices and clinking glasses before the door closed again, then the crunch of gravel as steps came closer to her.

"Are you alright?" LuAnn's arm slipped around Kat's shoulder. Kat wanted to turn around and throw her arms around LuAnn, to tell her everything—everything—that she had done. How she had left her children without saying a word. How she had somehow willed her sister-in-law to Vietnam, to her death, long before they became friends. How she yearned now for all of them. How she felt her heart breaking into a million pieces.

But LuAnn wouldn't understand. No one ever would.

"I just needed some air," she said, squeezing LuAnn's arm. "Go on back inside. Just give me a few minutes, and I'll be back in."

"You sure, honey? We can leave if you need to."

"No. I don't want to spoil everyone's night. Just a few minutes. That's all I need."

"Okay. You come get me if you need me, alright?" LuAnn patted Kat's shoulder before heading back inside.

A quiet settled on the parking lot. Kat listened to her breaths as they slowed. In the light filtering through Smokey's windows, she could see the wisps of air as they escaped her mouth, but she still didn't feel the cold. Somewhere from behind her, Kat could hear a creek rushing past. It was as if it was calling to her, as if it understood that water had always been a comfort to her. There was something sacred and purifying in it.

Kat walked behind Smokey's toward the sound. Down an embankment, the water was singing its ancient song as it tumbled over rocks. Even though she couldn't see the water, she felt its movement. Felt it pulsing like blood through veins. It was alive, and for a moment, she felt alive—felt her own blood pulsing. The crisp autumn night sharpened the sound of the water. Like an urgent longing for what awaited it downstream. Almost like a prayer.

She wanted it to be a prayer. It had been too long since she had prayed, really prayed. Not the rote prayers found in church or before meals. But to speak to God in the most intimate of ways. Surely by now, though, God was tired of waiting for her. More likely, he was finished with her all together after what she had done.

She was lost in the moment until she heard the gravel crunching behind her. Her first thought was it was probably LuAnn again or Molly coming to check on her. When she turned her head toward the sound, she saw the silhouette of a man, the red glow of a cigarette by his side. Kat tensed and wondered if anyone would hear her if she screamed. The man moved closer, until she sensed the warmth of his body behind her. Her breaths grew quicker, and she was grateful that the sound of the water was strong enough to obscure the deepening of her breaths.

Then the man began to hum before the words came soft and clear.

As I went down to the river to pray,
Studying about that good old way;
I will wear the starry crown,
Good Lord, show me the way.

She recognized the man's voice—the singer from the band. She recalled his face and the curve of his body and she felt her face flush hot. Kat wanted to lean back and melt into him, to feel his warmth against her. She steadied herself against a tree.

When he stopped singing, she glanced back. He was farther away than she realized. Did he even know she was there? He tossed his cigarette to the ground, covered it with his foot, and headed into the bar. She turned back to the water and listened to its yearning, its desperation. Its prayer. This time, she didn't hear the gravel crunching when Molly came to her.

"There you are. I was getting worried," Molly said.

"Sorry. I just needed to hear the water. I guess I lost track of time."

"Was that Wyatt out here with you?"

"Wyatt?"

"The lead singer for the band."

"Oh. I guess so." Kat was embarrassed, although she didn't know why.

"Way to go, girl. He's super cute." Molly gave her a playful nudge.

"It was nothing," Kat said. "He didn't even see me."

She wanted Molly to stop talking so she could listen to the water. More than anything she'd ever wanted, she wanted to hear the prayer as the creek moved past her.

7

KAT STARED AT THE HELP WANTED SIGN in the store window. The money she had brought with her was almost gone, so she needed a job. But she hadn't worked outside her home since she was newly married. How would anyone take her seriously? She was a hard worker, but with limited experience, no employment history in over ten years, and no transportation, it was going to be difficult convincing someone to take a risk on her.

The store was just up the road from her apartment, a short brisk walk away, which was exactly what she needed since town was almost three miles away. The store, a pottery shop, was quaint, and like so many buildings in the area, was almost certainly an old log house that had been converted into a store. Kat appreciated old houses—her own home back in Kentucky was nearly two hundred years old. She had fallen in love with that house as soon as she walked into it with the realtor. But as much as she loved the history of the old house, it was her family, especially the girls running up and down the stairs or between the kitchen and the den, that brought life into the house.

She took a deep breath before opening the door to the pottery shop. A bell chimed when she walked in, but no one was in sight. Rustic shelves, filled with pottery, lined the walls. A table in the middle of the room contained mostly vases and large bowls and, unlike the plainly glazed pottery on the shelves, these items were decorated with unique glazing techniques or hand-painted designs. Under different circumstances, Kat would have explored the table for a piece to add to her own pottery collection back home.

"May I help you?"

A man was standing in the doorway to a room at the back of the store. He was wiping his hands clean, but his arms and shirt were speckled with taupe-colored clay. Some of his wavy shoulder-length hair was almost as black as coal, but several bits of gray showed up here and there, especially in his beard and mustache.

"Yes. I've come about the job," Kat said. "I mean, I saw the help wanted sign out front."

The man cocked his head and pursed his lips, sizing her up, she imagined. "You ever work with pottery before?"

"Oh, are you needing somebody to make pottery?" Kat tried to mask her disappointment.

"No, but it helps if you've worked with it. Makes it easier to talk to the customers."

"Well, I don't generally have trouble talking to people. I've worked retail before, and I love pottery. I've been collecting it ever since my grandmother gave me a couple of Wedgwood pieces."

The man frowned. "We don't have any fancy pieces like that in this place."

"What you have here is fancy enough for me. Don't get me wrong. I love the Wedgwood, but mainly because it reminds me of my grand-mother. Most of my pieces are from local craftsmen, like what you have here. Did you make all of these?"

"Most of them are mine. I consign a few pieces every now and then."

"Is this one of yours?" He nodded when she picked up a tall mossy-green candleholder. The sides were painted with brown and yellow leaves that cascaded down from the top. "Fall is my favorite season. I'd have something like this out all year round."

He smiled. "I see what you're doing. Very smooth." He threw the towel he'd been holding over his shoulder and moved fully into the room. "I tell you what, if you can start first thing in the morning, the job is yours. It's nine to five Tuesday through Saturday and pays three dollars an hour." He reached out his hand to confirm the offer.

Kat hesitantly took his hand, afraid that it was some cruel joke. "You mean it? I can have the job?"

"You bet, Miss ..."

"Turner. My name is Kat Turner."

"Cat? Like Cat Stevens?"

Cat Stevens—that's who he reminded her of. She loved Cat Stevens's songs, especially "Where Do the Children Play?" and "Morning Has Broken."

"Not exactly," she said. "It's Kat with a K."

"Well, Kat with a K. I'm Robert, with an R." He flashed a playful grin. "But everyone just calls me Pony."

"Pony?"

"Apparently, when I was little I loved it when my grandpa would do 'Ride Little Pony.' I'd beg him to do it so often that he started calling me Pony. It just stuck." He shrugged.

Kat laughed. Working with Pony would at least be interesting. She thanked him before promising to be back before nine the next morning.

On the path from Pony's shop to the quilt store next door, Kat passed an older couple headed the other way. The couple nodded a friendly greeting, and she responded with a 'good afternoon' to them. For the first time in a long time, she knew she meant it. After they passed, she looked into the cobalt blue sky that stretched out in front of her, shading her eyes against the glare of the afternoon sun. A hawk, its wings spread in total surrender to the current, glided higher and higher. It teetered from side to side, like the girls did when they pretended a chalk line was a tightrope and they tried not to fall off. The hawk circled back and called out, like an invitation to come see the world from high above. An unexpected contentment welled in her, and that feeling floated with her all the way to Rusty's shop.

"I got a job," she said as she bounded into the office at the back of the shop.

Molly jumped at the sound of the door banging against the wall. "Good god, Kat. You scared the hell out of me."

"Sorry," Kat said, giggling like a schoolgirl. She plopped down on the seat across from Molly. "I'm just so excited."

"I can see that. But are you going to keep me in suspense all day, or am I supposed to guess?"

"Guess?" She looked puzzled. "Oh, you mean the job." Her head really did feel like she was touching the clouds with the hawk. "I start work tomorrow over at the pottery shop. The owner seems a bit of an odd duck, or should I say an odd pony?" She giggled again, though Molly clearly didn't understand the joke. "But I think it'll be okay."

"That's great, Kat. What will you be doing?"

Kat looked startled. She had forgotten to ask what the job entailed. She knew it was full time and she would be making enough to pay her rent and buy groceries. That was enough to know, wasn't it? She assumed it involved helping customers in the store, which she was comfortable doing. But what if he wanted her to do bookkeeping or manage the kiln while he was out? Would he fire her as quickly as he hired her when he found out how little experience she really had?

Too embarrassed to admit she didn't really know, she simply said that it would mainly be handling the customers. Molly pursed her lips and furrowed her brow, as if she was disappointed it wasn't something more exciting. But the frown disappeared as quickly as it had come. When she stood to give Kat a hug, the florescent light moved across her face. Kat saw a scar just above Molly's left eye that she'd never noticed before. It looked like a tiny pink river that flowed down into her eyebrow.

"You know what this means?" Molly said, her voice once again animated. "We have to celebrate tonight. How about we go out after supper?"

"Jake, too?"

"Maybe. But he's not much for going out. I guess that's something you two have in common—you'd much rather stay home."

"Well, not tonight," Kat said. She surprised herself by how bubbly she was. From the moment Kat left her home, she had buried herself in grief and guilt, as if it was somehow penance for what she had done. The only respite she had allowed herself was the trip to Smokey's the week before, and that was only because Molly had practically dragged her there. But the experience by the creek had awakened something in her—like the crocuses in her front yard that burst through the ground at the first hint of spring's warmth.

"How about going to Smokey's again?" Kat said.

"Smokey's? Now why would you want to go there?" The light in Molly's eyes intensified as she tapped her finger against her lips. "It wouldn't have anything to do with a certain singer, would it?"

"Oh, Molly, stop being ridiculous," Kat said. She knew her face was flushing pink, but she also knew that Molly was closer to the truth than Kat wanted to admit. She *did* want to see Wyatt again. Remembering Wyatt standing behind her above the creek bank felt like a dream. She needed to know if anything had really passed between them.

———————

That evening the music spilled into the parking lot when they opened the door at Smokey's. Kat rubbed her palm against her slacks, trying to dry the sweat. She didn't realize she'd be so nervous. It was foolish to make whatever happened at the creek into more than it really was, and she knew that. Wyatt probably didn't even know she existed. Yet when Kat stepped through the door and saw a woman with platinum blond hair on the stage instead of Wyatt, she felt the weight of disappointment deep in her chest.

Molly, who obviously didn't care that Wyatt wasn't singing, dragged Kat to a high-top table near the stage. She was already ordering a beer and swaying her shoulders to the music before Kat even sat down. At first,

Kat shook her head when the waitress asked if she wanted anything, but then changed her mind. This night wasn't about Wyatt anyway. She was there to celebrate her new job and that's exactly what she was going to do.

The bar was not as crowded as it had been on the weekend, but it was a Wednesday night and most people were likely in a church service somewhere—like she would have been back home. The woman on stage was singing "Jolene" and trying a little too much to act like Dolly Parton as she belted it out. But the song had Kat bouncing to the music anyway.

"You seem to be in a better mood than you have been for the past couple of weeks," Molly said when the song was finished.

"I think I'm finally coming out of a fog," Kat said. The band, which had finished with their set, started packing up their equipment, so the room had grown quieter. "I have to admit, it does feel good. I really don't know what I would have done without you, Molly. I hope Jake didn't mind me taking you away tonight."

"It wouldn't have mattered if he did." Molly took a drink. "He's been kind of pissy lately. Sometimes it's good just to stay out of his way."

"I hope everything's okay," Kat said. Molly and Jake seemed inseparable, so Kat was confused. She remembered, though, the tension in his voice during the trip to Gatlinburg—when they both thought she was asleep.

"Oh, he'll be alright in a day or two. He just gets moody sometimes. I guess it's that artistic temperament of his. Can you love and hate something at the same time?" Molly laughed, but Kat understood the familiar dissonance more than Molly knew. "I hope the music's not done for the night," Molly said, seemingly eager to change the subject. "I've been waiting all day to get my boogie on."

Kat laughed at the youthful expression coming from Molly.

"Me, too," Kat said.

"*You've* been waiting all day to see Wyatt." She fluttered her eyes and patted at her chest, like a heart flutter.

"You're too much, Molly." She slapped at Molly's arm. "Anyway, I am *definitely* not looking for a relationship right now."

"Sounds like you're still licking your wounds from an old one."

"Something like that." Kat hadn't been able to bring herself yet to tell Molly about David. Maybe it was time. But she had no idea where to start or how much of the story she was ready to tell, so she just ended up saying very little. "I just have some loose ends to tie up before I'm ready to move on."

The truth was, Kat was unsettled that she couldn't stop thinking about Wyatt. In her mind, her marriage was over, but she knew that legally—morally—it was not. Yet Wyatt's voice, soft and reverent behind her, and the water, urgent and revered in front of her, played in her memory. If she saw him again and realized that everything had all been in her head, maybe it would tamp down the feelings that had grown more intense than was appropriate for her, a married woman, even one whose marriage was already in jeopardy.

"Well, look who the K-a-t dragged in," Molly said as she nodded toward the door.

Kat turned and saw Wyatt, with his guitar case clutched in one hand. A tinge of jealousy bloomed in her chest when he smiled at some woman near the door, and Kat hated herself for it. There was no reason to feel jealous, and she knew it, but she wanted that smile only for her.

"Oh, he's coming this way." Molly nudged Kat.

He passed by Molly and Kat without even noticing them as he stepped up on the stage. Kat tried not to care, told herself that, of course, he wouldn't know her. She was nothing to him. He went about his business—setting the case on the floor, pulling the guitar out, and plugging it into the amp—as if nothing had happened. As other band members joined him on stage, he fingered a couple of chords to warm up. When he finally stepped to the microphone and counted down, the guitarist behind him let the twang of the electric guitar introduce the song. Then Wyatt leaned into the microphone and started the familiar opening to "Sweet Home Alabama."

"Oh, we've got to dance," Molly said, grabbing Kat's hand. This time Kat didn't resist. She might have imagined everything with Wyatt, but something had changed within her that night, and she wasn't going to resist it. She found an open space on the floor and began to tap her feet from side to side. When she closed her eyes, her body felt the rhythm. She had never allowed herself to be that free, to feel music in her body and not care what it looked like to anyone else. She wasn't even focused on Wyatt. When the song came to an end, she opened her eyes and saw Wyatt watching her. At one time it might have embarrassed her, might have caused her to look away. But she saw the hunger in his eyes, a hunger that kindled in her the longing she had tried to ignore.

By the time he got to "She Believes in Me," the final song before the band's break, she sensed he was speaking directly to her. When he finished the final notes, his hazel eyes fixed on Kat again. She stared back at him—unafraid of the consequences. When she and Molly sat back at their table, she took a sip from the drink she'd been nursing all night. She pushed back the voice that told her what she was feeling about Wyatt was immoral or that she didn't deserve to be happy.

Molly tapped Kat's shoulder and pointed at Wyatt coming toward them. Before Kat could say anything, Molly hopped up and headed to the bar.

Wyatt climbed onto the stool next to Kat. He pulled a pack of cigarettes from the jacket he'd laid in his lap and offered her one. When she shook her head, he pulled a cigarette out for himself and then retrieved the lighter from another pocket. He cupped his hand around the cigarette, then Kat saw a puff of smoke rise above his hand. He pulled an ashtray toward him before looking her full in the face.

"That final song was beautiful," she said, forcing herself not to turn away from him.

"It's not as beautiful as listening to the water, though, is it?" He took another drag on his cigarette.

She wondered what he would make of her startled expression. "The sound of the water is beautiful," she said.

"Yeah, I try to go down to that creek whenever I have a break. There's a river that runs behind my house, and so it always sounds like home."

Kat liked the thought of that.

"Do you always sing by the water?"

"You heard that, did you?" He tried to look embarrassed, but she could tell he was pleased. Her eyes followed the slow movement of his head as he turned to blow the smoke away from her. She noticed his smooth and firm jawline and the way his long hair moved across his shoulder.

"Some experiences are meant to be shared," she said.

"That's so true," he said. "Maybe next time we share an experience like that, I'll even know your name." His eyes reflected the light just above them as he waited for her to answer his unasked question.

"Kat," she said. "It's Kat Turner." She dropped her gaze, suddenly aware of the dangerous game she was playing. Yet her chest tightened when his hand brushed against hers as he stood.

"Then I hope to see you around soon, Kat," he whispered as leaned next to her ear—the scent of cigarette and aftershave lingering even after he joined the drummer and disappeared out the back door. Kat took a sip from her drink and closed her eyes.

8

PONY WAS ALREADY TURNING A PIECE OF POTTERY when Kat arrived for her first day on the job. If he knew she was standing in the doorway, he didn't acknowledge it. Instead, he kept his head bent low over the wet clay as it swelled or contracted under his gentle guidance. Kat was captivated by the hypnotic movement of the clay, as if it were a dancer rounding her back or stretching her torso to elongate her body.

"Good morning," Pony finally said without taking his eyes off the clay. "You're early."

"Am I?" She glanced at her watch and realized it was twenty minutes until she was supposed to be there. "I just didn't want to be late on my first day of work."

Pony looked up at her. "An eager beaver, huh? I like that." He focused again on the pottery. "Give me a couple of minutes to finish this vase and I'll show you the ropes."

"No hurry."

Kat leaned against the doorframe. Watching Pony work the clay—the precision of his hands and the concentration on his brow—reminded Kat of David bent over his blueprints. There had been times that she had watched David work while she washed dishes or baked bread after the girls had gone to bed. She watched him move the ruler around the large drawing pad—watched his brow furrow as he was working out a detail to make his vision come to life on the page. Sometimes she would slip up behind him, put her arm around his waist, and rest her head against his shoulder just to admire his work. He would smile down at her and she would squeeze her hand against his waist. Sometimes it was hard to remember that she hadn't always felt lost and alone.

"There," Pony said as he slid a taut wire under the vase to release it from the wheel. He shut the wheel off and gently lifted the vase and placed it on a shelf to dry.

"Do you always start making pottery so early?" Kat said while Pony washed his hands.

"Not always. Some mornings, though, when I can't sleep, I come here and throw some pottery. It clears my mind—or refocuses it, I guess."

"Maybe I need to learn how to do that," Kat said, letting a tiny laugh escape. "My mind needs all the refocusing it can get."

"Well, if things work out, maybe I'll teach you." He gave her a wink as he passed by her. She followed him into the store and to the counter by the front door. "We're not fancy around here. No cash register or anything. Just this receipt book and an adding machine."

"I think I can handle that," she said. She was relieved that she wouldn't need a refresher on working a register. "How busy does it get?"

"It's not usually super busy. Kind of a steady trickle throughout the day. That'll change, though, for the next few weeks—the closer we get to Christmas."

Christmas. Kat had tried not to think about the holidays. Thanksgiving was only a week away and Christmas was not that far behind. She wasn't sure how she was going to make it through the next few weeks.

Pony didn't seem to notice that Kat had become distracted. He was showing her how they wrapped the pottery for a customer and where they kept the business cards they placed in the boxes. Kat nodded, like she was paying attention, but she kept thinking about Thanksgiving. Even though David's parents had always hosted Thanksgiving dinner, Kat insisted on it being at her house after Beth died. Somehow, Beth's absence felt more raw in her in-laws' house. At the time, Kat believed she was doing it to spare Betty some enormous pain. But the truth was, Kat couldn't bear being in the Hunter's house with all the pictures of Beth, especially the one of her crouched behind a Vietnamese boy, her arms wrapped around him. Kat couldn't imagine how Betty could look at that picture every day and not break into a million pieces.

She wondered what they would do this year, with her not there. Betty almost certainly would have the dinner back to her house, like Kat suspected she had wanted to do for the past few years. Kat didn't have a chance to complete the thought. A couple of women entered the store and nodded in Kat and Pony's direction before heading to one of the shelves along the wall.

"Looks like the show is on," Pony said under his breath. "I hope you're ready. I'll be in the back if you need me."

He had barely gotten the words out before he was gone, a streak of khaki and blue from the counter to the back door. Kat was amused. It was as if Pony wasn't comfortable interacting with the customers, which struck her as odd since he seemed pleasant enough with her.

"Let me know if I can help you with anything," Kat said to the women, who were examining the platters and bowls on the shelf.

"Are these made here?" one of the women asked.

"Yes, they are," Kat said as she slipped around the counter. "Let me show you how you can tell the quality of the craftsmanship."

She picked up a large bowl and began to show them the clean lines and the evenness of the glaze. She surprised herself by how much she remembered from talking with potters as she collected her own pieces. The women nodded with interest, and Kat felt her body relax. Even though she still didn't know how long she would be away from home, for the first time since she'd left, she felt as if she had found a piece of herself again.

Thanksgiving morning was the kind of crisp morning that would have certainly warranted a fire in both the kitchen and living room fireplaces back home. Kat shivered as she forced herself to crawl out from under the covers. She turned up the thermostat and waited for the baseboard heaters to hiss before shuffling to the kitchen to start a pot of coffee. The refrigerator was nearly bare—a half-gallon of milk, a couple of eggs, butter, left over chicken, and a handful of condiments. Not much in the way of Thanksgiving dinner for later, but that was alright with her. She had politely declined LuAnn's offer to join their family's dinner. She knew she wouldn't be good company with her mind focused on what was happening back home.

Kat poured a cup of coffee and turned on the television. She snuggled under a blanket to watch the Macy's Thanksgiving Day Parade, just as she had done every year since she was a little girl. She set her coffee mug on the table and curled up on the couch to watch the familiar balloons fill the television screen. For the first time since Jenny was two, Kat was watching the parade alone, but she could imagine Kris cuddled up in her sister's lap, calling out Kermit the Frog's name as he floated high above the crowded streets and bobbed in the wind.

Kat felt like she herself was floating outside her own body, as if she were looking down on some other woman huddled in a tight ball on the couch. This woman looked as if she were watching the parade, but a tear dropped down her cheek. Was her mind seeing something else—something that she couldn't bear to watch? Her fingers moved across her cheek and down to her mouth, lingering there as they traced her lips. Then she lowered her head into her hands, letting her fingers push deep into her hair and clutch at her messy blond locks. Kat wanted to feel sorry for this strange woman, who looked familiar. Kat wanted to feel sorry for the pain registering in this woman's shoulders as they shook when her deep sobs finally came.

But she didn't feel sorry for this woman at all. It was a pain of her own making.

Kat hadn't cried in days. She had pushed the tears back but, like her pain, they hadn't gone away. Her tears had collected, like rain against a windowpane, sliding down and pooling against her chest. Now the weight of those repressed tears rose out of her like a relentless tidal wave in the midst of a storm. When the sobs relented, she lay immobile on the couch, unsure that she would ever get up again—unsure that she even wanted to. Finally, the heaviness gave way to a troubled sleep. She felt the wind rushing against her face and heard a high-pitched noise penetrating her ears as she fell to the earth. Only the ringing of the phone spared her from the crash at the end of her fall.

"Hello," she said, still shaking the sleep from her body.

"Mary Catherine? It's David."

"David? Why are you calling?" A panic rose in her throat. "Are the girls alright?"

"Everyone's okay. I need to talk to you—to see you."

"David, we've been through this. I can't—"

"I'm here, Mary Catherine. Here in Gatlinburg."

"You're what?" She nearly dropped the phone. "How did you find me?"

"Your mother told me. She gave me your number."

Kat wanted to be angry with her mother, with the betrayal, since her mother had promised not to tell anyone after she had forced the information from Kat. Yet Kat knew that a confrontation with David was inevitable.

"It's Thanksgiving Day," she said. "What on earth are you doing down here?" She paused, hopeful. "Are the girls with you?"

"I'm alone—and I need to see you. Can you meet me somewhere?"

Kat stood silent. She wondered if she was still dreaming. But David kept talking—kept pleading to meet with her. When she finally said yes, she heard his breath crackle against the mouthpiece, like he had just let out a long, exhausted exhale. Only then did Kat feel her chest burning as she realized that she, too, was still holding her breath, afraid what would happen if she let it go.

9

THE SUN, WHICH HAD JUST STARTED ITS DOWNWARD JOURNEY toward the west, was deceptive. It was cold, especially in the shade with a light wind stirring. Kat shoved her hands into her jacket pockets as she paced in front of the gas station. When she chose to walk the three quarters of a mile from her apartment, she didn't take into account that she hadn't brought a heavier coat with her. She hadn't intended to be away long enough for the late fall chill to set in. As she shivered in the cold, she wondered why she told David to pick her up there instead of at her apartment.

When David finally pulled into the gas station in her two-toned, wood-paneled station wagon, Kat thought it was a bit odd. The station wagon, which was perfect for hauling the girls to their various activities, was more her car than his. He much preferred driving around in his silver two-door Mustang Ghia, the one he'd bought after his promotion five years before. At the time, Kat had thought it was a foolish, impractical indulgence. But it was money *he* earned from his hard work, so what could she really say about it? He babied that car, and until now, she never realized how much she had resented him for it.

When the car stopped in front of her, she had to push down a lump that was forming in her throat. David didn't get out to greet her, but instead motioned for her to get in. She took a deep breath before coming around to the side of the car. Instinctively, she glanced in the back seat before opening the door. David had said the girls weren't with him, but the empty seat still disappointed her. She collapsed onto the passenger seat without saying anything to David or glancing in his direction. It felt strangely like an awkward blind date, where both people knew immediately that it was a mistake but it was too late to do anything but press forward.

David sighed, as if he had expected her to speak, then he backed out of the parking spot. He turned the car down HWY 321 toward town. Kat shivered, still chilled from waiting in the parking lot for almost twenty minutes. A blanket lay puddled at her feet, so she reached down and dragged it across her lap and up to her chest. Only when she caught the faint aroma of baby lotion did she realize that it was Kris's favorite blanket, the one Grandma Hunter had given to Jenny and had been passed down to Lizzie and now to Kris. Kat pulled the blanket to her face and let the scent revive the memory of a dripping wet girl fresh out of the bathtub. The girl was screaming, arms and legs flailing, as Kat tried to find a towel to clean the shampoo from the girl's eyes. Bath time was a battle with the strong-willed Kris, who constantly pushed away Kat's hands with 'I do it.' Kat had to hold Kris's arm tight, tight enough that red marks remained on the arm when Kat finally let go. Sometimes Kris would break free, running from the bathroom with her naked pink flesh glistening. A harsh scolding sounding too much like her own mother awaited Kris when Kat finally caught up with her, which sent Kris into screaming fits again. By the time pajamas were on the still-squirming girl and she was tucked into bed, they were both in tears.

Something about the memory now felt strangely tender.

Kat lifted the blanket to her cheek then lowered it to her lap. She watched as hillsides full of bare trees gradually gave way to paved parking lots nestling squat buildings full of souvenirs—gawdy T-shirts or stuffed black bears or kitchen magnets with some inspirational sayings on them—then to two or three-story motels or busy pancake houses. The main road through Gatlinburg was lined with tourists and locals strolling down the sidewalks. Most of them were families. When they passed a mother and father walking with their two small girls, Kat dropped the blanket to the floor without looking at it, then wiped a tear from the corner of her eye.

"Where are we going?" she finally said.

"The entrance to the National Park is on the other end of town. I thought we'd stop somewhere in the park to talk."

Kat didn't respond. What was she going to say? It all seemed so surreal to her anyway—David sitting beside her in the car, as if nothing had happened between them. Yet she hoped he was there to work out when she could see the girls again, or at least let her talk to them on the phone.

The end of the town's main street gave way to thick forest, with trees standing like stark, brown soldiers, as if guarding something sacred. Kat thought about how the pond in the back of her yard, something that had always been sacred to her, had been protected by the trees that surrounded it. She felt safe among the trees, even now. Even without knowing what was coming next.

David pulled into the Sugarlands Visitor Center and found a spot at the far end of the parking lot. He shut off the motor then rested his head against the steering wheel. For the first time since she had gotten in the car, Kat looked over at him. His tall frame curved like a *C* as he slumped against the wheel. The sun, reflecting off the rearview mirror, made his blond hair almost glow. Yet his shoulders pressed down, as if weights were pulling them to the floorboard.

She couldn't bear to look at his anguish any longer and turned away.

She stared at a couple of pine trees in front of the car. Among the bright green needles on one of the trees were hints of brown—needles that were dying or were already dead. She had seen this happen to a tree in their front yard. The extension agent told them that certain insects in their larva stage love to bore into pines but by the time the signs of damage became evident it was too late to use any corrective measures. The only solution was to cut the tree down to protect the other trees around it. Out here in the forest, though, nature decided how long it would take for the tree to die or whether other trees would suffer the same fate.

Just like cutting down a diseased tree, Kat had tried to protect her family by leaving them. That's what she had been telling herself anyway. She was damaged. How many times had she snapped at one the girls, had pressed her eyebrows together and tightened her lips, just as her mother had done? How many times did she immediately regret it and scoop the girl into her arms, squeezing her tight—or worse yet, collapse onto the floor in a puddle of tears. Lizzie would be the one to comfort her, but Kat could see that each time something like that happened, Jenny grew more distant. This scene had been repeating far too often for Kat not to know she had to do something. She couldn't become her mother, so if she didn't leave—didn't figure out what was wrong with her—her disease would eventually infect all of them.

"I've made a mess of things, haven't I, David?" she whispered. She looked over at him again and waited for him to respond.

He was quiet for a moment.

"I loved you," he finally said as he straightened up and turned toward her. His eyes were wet and a wet trail glistened on his cheek. Kat couldn't ever remember him crying before, not even at Beth's funeral.

"I know," she said. She should have reached over to comfort him, but she didn't. "For what it's worth, I loved you, too."

"I can't say that it's worth a whole lot."

She stared at him for a while, not really knowing what to say.

"Why did you come here, David?" she finally said.

"You even have to ask?" He kept staring straight ahead. "You left, Mary Catherine. You left everything that ever meant something to you— or that I thought meant something to you. I needed to know why."

"It's complicated," she said. Her voice quivered more than she wanted it to. "I'm not even sure I understand it myself. All I do know for sure is that something changed after Beth died."

"She's been gone for six years. Isn't it time to get over it? You can't grieve forever."

"I can't choose when grief is finished, David. Beth was important to me. Even when she was thousands of miles away, she kept me grounded."

"She was important to me, too, Mary Catherine. For God's sake, she was my sister."

"I know that—and I'm not saying she wasn't important to you, or to your parents. But after she died, I lost my way. I lost myself."

"That sounds like some kind of New Age crap."

"It's not anything like that. I'm just trying to be honest with you."

"There's nothing honest about any of this." Any tender emotion that had registered on his face moments before was gone. The lines between his brows revealed the anger that bubbled underneath. "I thought I could do this, Mary Catherine. I thought I could talk to you, but I can't. I can't stand to look at you right now."

He pushed the car door open and climbed out, letting the door slam behind him. Kat watched as he slumped down on a nearby picnic table, his back to her and his feet resting on the wooden bench seat. He picked up a pinecone that had fallen on the table and threw it as far as he could into the tree line. She let him sit for a time before she got out of the car and sat down beside him.

"I'm sorry, David. I don't know what else I can say."

"Nothing. Just stop talking."

They sat in silence for a good long while. Behind them somewhere, children were shrieking and laughing. A young couple passed by with loaded backpacks on their way to some trailhead. Kat watched them until they disappeared down the road. She shivered as a wind whispered through the trees.

Finally, David climbed down off the picnic table and stood to face her.

"I'm going to file for divorce." The words didn't come out as a threat or even angry—just a statement of fact. Kat thought the words would have hurt more than they did. She should have felt something. After nearly twelve years, she should have felt something about the end of her marriage. Maybe she did. But it wasn't what she expected to feel.

"It didn't have to come to this," David continued. His voice cracked with emotion. "If you had just talked to me, we could have worked it out." It was his answer to everything, yet it never really answered anything.

"Maybe," Kat said, but she was convinced it wouldn't have made a difference.

David's face darkened. "I want custody of the girls. Full custody and no visitation."

"No custody and no visitation? You can't believe I'm going to agree to that."

"When you left, you gave up any right to be with them or to even see them."

"That's ridiculous." She wanted to slap him. "I was planning on going back. I *am* going back. I just need some time to sort things out." Her eyes narrowed as she stared at him. "Listen, I love my girls and you can't keep me away from them."

"I won't have you hurting the children again. I've been talking to a lawyer. You can be charged with child abandonment and you can be arrested."

Kat studied his face. He was a stranger to her now. Any feelings for him that may have been lingering evaporated with those words.

"You'd have me arrested?"

"I don't want to have to do it, but I will if you make me. You destroyed us, Mary Catherine—all of us. I want you out of our lives for good."

"I can't believe you'd be that cruel."

"Frankly, I don't care anymore what you believe, or what you want. Those are my terms. Let me know what I should tell my lawyer."

"You want me to decide right now?"

"I need to get back to my family. They're holding Thanksgiving dinner for me, and I don't want to disappoint the girls." He no longer pretended to hide his contempt.

He was rooted in front of her, as if he had become part of the forest. The trees had betrayed her, had turned against her. It was clear that he was one of them and that she was alone, stripped naked in front of them.

"Fine," she whispered. She had no energy to fight him. "Go ahead and pretend I'm dead. Mary Catherine Hunter will disappear forever." She slid from the table and headed for the car. "But I will never stop loving my girls. Never."

They drove back to the gas station near her apartment in silence. When David stopped the car, Kat reached for the door handle, but turned and looked at him.

"What you said earlier was a lie, wasn't it?" she said. "You could never have loved me if you would do this to me."

"It wasn't a lie—anymore than you saying you loved me and doing this to me. I really did come here today hoping that we could make it work." The emotion cracked in his voice again, and he paused to keep it from coming. "I don't understand what happened to you—to us—and I don't think I ever will."

Despite her anger, she felt pity for him, for what she had done to him. She climbed out of the car and closed the door behind her without looking back. Her girls were at Betty's house, and she had just agreed never to see them again. Tears burned on her face as she headed down the road to her apartment, and she let them burn.

10

Dear Kat,

Sorry I haven't had the chance to write until now. Tending to the various refugee camps keeps us busy. Not that I'm complaining about that, since that's why I came over here.

Most of the refugee camps are fairly close to the clinic, but yesterday morning, Dr. Michaels and I drove to a small village about sixty miles northeast of here. I was glad to be with Dr. Michaels, because he is so much kinder than Dr. Winslow. (Poor Carrie got stuck with him today.) The clinic insists on having an armed guard go with us to the camps. I get it. The Viet Cong are everywhere, which means no one is safe, even doctors and nurses. But I hate having the guard with us. Makes me feel like I'm a party to this fucking war.

The drive to the village was through some dense jungle. I have to confess that I was glad Lahn was standing in the back of the truck, with his gun perched across his chest. The trees and brush were so thick that you couldn't see beyond a few feet on either side of the road. You know me, I don't freak out often, but I swear I saw movement behind every tree. I was so relieved when the truck cleared the trees and I saw the thatched roofs of the village.

The people were going about their business. Women in those cone-shaped straw hats—you've probably seen them on news reports back home—were carrying pots and children were playing some kind of stacking game with sticks, at least that's what it looked like to me. Many of the huts were on pylons so they were elevated off the ground, and I saw a boy making a ladder for one of the huts, using an axe to chop notches into a log. Near the edge of the village were two burned-out buildings. I was told later that an American unit had come through a couple of years ago and tried to burn out the village. They either got bored or got distracted, because they moved on before they set fire to any of the other huts or hurt any of the villagers. It could have been so much worse.

So, more than most of the places I've been, these people were less than happy to see American faces, even if we were there with medicines and not weapons. We did the best we could to tend to the people who would let us examine them—some wound care, a few tetanus shots, and some general wellness checks. I was more distressed leaving there than I've been with any other village we've been to. You and I have had many arguments over the war—and I know that you've said that regardless of whether the U.S. presence in the war is justified, we have to support the soldiers—but knowing what could have happened in that village was unsettling. I'll tell you, Kat, it's one thing to bitch about the goddamn war in one's living room and a whole different thing to see the effects firsthand.

I guess I had that on my mind when we traveled back to the clinic, because it felt like the jungle had grown thicker. I found myself scanning the sides of the road more than I had on the way to the village, especially when I heard gunfire somewhere in the distance. I looked back and saw Lahn push Dr. Michaels and the interpreter down so that their heads were below the sides of the truck bed. The driver slowed down and motioned for me to scoot down, which is what I was trying to do when a soldier came stumbling out of the trees just in front of us. I recognized the American uniform before the soldier dropped to the ground, and without thinking, I pushed my door open and leapt out of the truck. The breaks squealed as the driver came to a stop. Lahn was yelling something at me but I didn't know what it was.

I was at the soldier's side, pulling his helmet off, by the time Lahn and Dr. Michaels got to me. "Are you insane?" Dr. Michaels was yelling. I hadn't seen him that angry before. "You could get yourself killed—and us, too, while you're at it." His hands were shaking, but I don't believe he was scared for himself. "He's injured," I told him. "I couldn't leave him lying there." He knew I was right, and I knew that if he had been the first one to see the young man, he would have done the same thing.

The soldier's face was pale and his shirt was covered in blood. When we pulled it loose, we saw that he had a belly wound. It was so bad that I was surprised he'd been able to walk at all. He tried to talk to us, coughing out bits of information. He'd gotten lost from his unit, which was on patrol. He found this road but was hit by gunfire. He ducked into the jungle then saw our truck and took a chance. At least this was what we pieced together from his ramblings.

Since I've been in-country, I've treated several South Vietnamese soldiers, but today was the first time I worked on one of ours. We usually don't see them since they have their own medical units. Anyway, most of the American fighting is in North Vietnam now, and mostly from the air.

After examining the soldier, it was clear he'd never survive a trip out of the jungle. But it was also clear that he was unlikely to survive at all. Out in the jungle, Dr. Michaels didn't have a chance of saving him, but he did what he could. I rested the boy's head in my lap—and that's what he was, a boy, probably no more than nineteen—while Dr. Michaels worked on him. As I smoothed his hair, trying my best to comfort him, I wondered if he would have burned the huts of Vietnamese villagers if he had a chance. Maybe he already had done some things like that. War does some fucking things to your mind. I wanted to hate him, for everything he stood for, but as I studied his face, I knew that it wasn't him I hated. Goddamn this fucking war.

I held him for what seemed like an hour, though it was probably only minutes, until his final gasp for air. I don't know how long I held him after that before Dr. Michaels touched my arm and said we needed to go. Whoever shot this young man could still be out there. Before we lifted the boy's body onto the truck—we weren't going to leave him in that goddamn jungle—I reached down and found his dog tag. Timothy J. Sullivan. It's a name I'll never forget.

When I get back home, I'll probably still be spouting off about this fucking war, but if I start mouthing off about the soldiers who fought it, I want you to say the name Timothy J. Sullivan then tell me to fuck off. I'm counting on you to say those exact words, because if I ever forget that the war was full of Pvt. Sullivans, who died for no reason, I'll deserve every word of it.

How many days now, my dear Kat?

With much love,
Beth

11

KAT WAS BARELY OFF THE PHONE with Molly when Molly knocked on the door. Kat, still in her nightgown and robe, only had time to pull the bedcovers into a wad at the end of the daybed, but since it was just Molly, Kat really didn't care. She ran her fingers through her hair and opened the door.

"I'm so glad you're awake," Molly said as she burst in. "I couldn't wait to tell you." She brushed past Kat and threw her coat on the couch on the way to the kitchen. The bead curtain clinked as she parted it, then she pulled a Coke from the refrigerator and popped off the lid. Kat had never seen anyone drink cola in the morning the way Molly did.

"Must be something big," Kat said, trying to suppress a yawn.

"So big that I got up this early on a Sunday morning, especially since we didn't get in until late last night." Molly sat on the couch and took a long gulp from the Coke bottle. The lamp behind her made the curls glow, so that she looked like the Madonna in a medieval painting.

"I didn't think you and Jake were coming back until tomorrow."

"That was the plan." Molly took another sip, her movement slow and deliberate this time. Kat thought it was odd that Molly seemed to be moving in slow motion just to take a drink. Molly lowered the drink and continued. "Thanksgiving dinner started out okay. No drama, but I braced for it. I told you how Dad is. Sure enough, just as Mom was dishing out the pumpkin pie, Dad started. He tried to act coy, by asking about Gatlinburg, then he started asking Jake when he was going to get a real job and when he was going to make an honest woman of me. Jake was getting mad—I could tell. He finally had enough and went out for a smoke."

Molly leaned back. Her mouth pulled sideways in her familiar smirk as she stared at the ceiling. Kat had been watching her, trying to interpret the meaning of every expression, every movement to figure out why Molly was here this early in the morning. Nothing was matching the giddiness of her earlier phone call.

"I was so upset," Molly said, looking back at Kat. "I told Dad that he was being a jerk and I slammed my fist on the table. Scared the hell out of him and Mom. 'We're leaving,' I said and I marched upstairs, packed our bag, and got ready to leave. By this time, Dad was engrossed in the Cowboys' game, like he didn't believe me when I said we were leaving. That pissed me off even more. Mom, who was washing the dishes when I came back down, begged us to stay, but I told her I couldn't stand another minute there." Molly sat the cola on the coffee table, again her hand moving in slow motion. She leaned forward, like she was expecting Kat to speak. But Kat simply stared, unsure how she was supposed to respond.

"No wonder you got home early," Kat finally said.

"I swear, Kat, you can be so dense at times." She threw her head back and laughed. Any other time, Kat would have laughed, too, but this morning she couldn't find the humor.

Molly stopped laughing. "Oh, honey, I didn't mean anything by that. It's just that I've been trying to get you to notice ever since I walked in the door."

"Notice what?"

When Molly raised her left hand, Kat saw the thin gold band.

"You're married?"

"I can't believe it myself. There we were, driving home and making fun of my dad. When we got close to Jellico, Jake says, 'Let's get married.' Like all of a sudden, out of the blue. At first, I thought he was joking. I mean, we've talked about marriage before, but neither of us have thought a piece of paper was all that important to signify our love. But by God, he was serious."

Her hands moved as she talked, and now Kat couldn't see anything else but the glint of the gold band every time it was hit by the light.

"I was afraid it would just prove Dad right—you know, Jake making an honest woman of me and all. I said as much to Jake, and he actually got pissed with me. You know how he is—'he's his own man.'" She puffed out her chest for emphasis.

Kat watched Molly. Watched as red blotches appeared on her friend's neck. Watched as she pulled a strand of hair straight and then twirled it around her finger. Watched her lower her eyes like a demure schoolgirl while she described the wedding dress she found on sale, the one with the capped sleeves and flowing skirt. Watched as she threw her head back and cackled about the justice of the peace that moved like Tim Conway's old man. By this time, Kat was laughing, too.

"Sounds like you had quite the adventure—just like you like it, Mrs. Malloy," Kat said.

"Oh, it's still Fisher," Molly said, no longer laughing. "I told Jake that I'd spent my whole life as Molly Fisher and I wasn't going to change that. Besides, can you imagine Molly Malloy? It sounds like the start of an Irish limerick."

"And Jake doesn't have a problem with that?"

"He's a liberated man. He doesn't buy in to all that patriarchy nonsense and neither do I. I mean, don't you feel that Kat Turner is as much a part of your identity as your blond hair and blue eyes?"

"I guess." Kat gave a momentary thought to telling Molly that she had been married, or rather, that she *was* married. But telling Molly now would only raise questions that Kat wasn't prepared to answer.

"It's just that not many women are brave enough to keep their maiden name," she said.

"Maiden name." Molly sighed. "Still bound to the patriarchy, aren't we?"

The words could have just as easily come from Beth's mouth, and it startled Kat.

"Did I stick my foot in my mouth again?" Molly said.

"What?" Kat realized that she had grown silent. "No, not at all."

When Molly left, Kat slid back the curtain to watch her cross the gravel drive to her apartment. After Molly disappeared from sight, Kat let the curtain drop and turned back to the room. She reached behind her and switched off the ceiling light then pressed her body against the wall. As the light around the edges of the curtains filtered in, the dark room took on a hazy yellow glow. She had followed Molly to Gatlinburg because her red curls breathed life into a memory. She had no idea who Molly was back then on the bus, and Kat still didn't know much about her, but they had forged a friendship. Kat wondered, though, if that friendship would be tested if Molly knew the truth.

She finally plopped on the couch, then fell backward with a sigh. She stared upward, at the shadows that moved across the ceiling. She watched the shadows until her eyelids felt heavy and the room went dark.

———————

In her dream, Kat heard the cicadas. The sound was so vivid she could feel the sticky night air cling to the nape of her neck. Even with a starless sky, she knew Grandma Turner's prize-winning salmon-colored roses were in full bloom just beyond the porch. Kat squinted to see them, but even the light from the living room window couldn't penetrate the black night. She rested her chin on the railing, as if she was a little girl again, and breathed in the smell of the freshly mown grass. Her breath rose and fell like the hum of the cicadas as she waited for the fireflies to twinkle like stars across the yard. When the screen door creaked, she didn't need to turn around. She knew who it was. Who it should have been.

"There's fresh cookies in the kitchen, if you want one."

The voice was familiar. Comforting.

She waited for a moment, letting the image of Grandma Turner gather from fragments of memory. When she finally turned toward the voice, expecting to see the familiar red gingham apron, she was startled instead to see Betty and a small girl standing in the doorway. Seeing David's mother there was jarring, but the red-headed girl standing next to her nearly dropped Kat to her knees. Neither of them belonged to that time or to that place, so she had to know why they were there. Yet when she tried to move toward the them, her feet were heavy with mud. She had no idea where the mud had come from, but it oozed across the porch like blackstrap molasses.

Betty tried to speak.

"I can't hear you," Kat shouted above the cicadas, whose buzz had grown so loud that she had to clutch her ears. She called again to Betty. "Please. Please help me."

Kat reached toward the door, straining against the pull of the sticky mud. Betty didn't move, except to pick up the child. The girl squirmed against Betty's tight grip. Only then did Kat realize the girl was now Kris, who was stretching out her arms toward Kat and crying 'Mama.' Kat tried harder to free her feet from the mud, but she only sank deeper. When she looked at the door again, Betty, with the child safe in her arms, shook her head, turned, and disappeared into the house.

The light from the living room faded into darkness. In the eerie blackness, Kat's heart thumped against her chest as the cicadas' vibrating timbals grew louder and louder.

———

The dream stayed with Kat for days. Even as the winter chill was settling into the frost-covered valley outside her apartment, she suffocated from the remembrance of the sticky summer air. The song of the cicadas. The spicy sweetness of the roses. The stickiness of the thick mud around her ankles. The salty bitterness of tears escaping down her daughter's flushed cheeks.

The dream was a sign. Kat knew it. She wasn't given to superstition or omens, but she couldn't shake the panic that filled her. The dream confirmed that she had made a mistake agreeing to David's terms. She had to take it back. She tried to imagine saying that to David, but she had seen his eyes when they spoke in the park—not just the hurt and the hate, but the determination to punish her. He wouldn't listen to her. She knew that now. But maybe he would listen to his mother. She felt certain that if she could just talk to Betty, Betty would understand.

The last conversation she had with Betty was two weeks before Kat left. Kat had come back from the library, the copy of *The Feminine Mystique* safely tucked away before Betty arrived to can tomato juice. Kris was already down for a nap, Jenny and Lizzie were next door with their friends, and the canning jars were washed and ready.

"How was the library this morning?" Betty said as the washed and stemmed the tomatoes.

"The girls enjoyed it. A nurse was there with books about doctors and nurses. The girls were excited, because she even brought a real stethoscope," Kat said as she took the tomatoes from Betty and cut them into chunks. "She reminded me of Beth."

Betty stared out the kitchen window, mindlessly washing the tomatoes. Kat was sure she had upset her mother-in-law. It's not that Betty didn't talk about Beth, but it was rare for Kat to open the topic. As much as Kat needed to talk about Beth, she knew it brought fresh pain to Betty.

"I could see Beth doing something like that," Betty finally said. "She loved children. I always thought that she'd be a good mother someday."

"Me, too," Kat said, trying to steady her trembling hand.

Betty continued to look out the window. "I think in some ways she was envious of your family." She looked at Kat. "Of course, that's not to say she wasn't happy with the choices she made."

Kat slid the cut tomatoes into the pot and asked Betty how many quarts of juice she thought they'd be able to get. She was glad to change the subject, but the word 'envious' remained fixed in her mind.

It was the word that persisted after her dream.

Kat stared at the phone before picking up the handset a dozen times—only to lose her nerve. Finally, she dialed, watching the rotary turn and fall back into place after each number. Her stomach tightened with the first ring. After the fifth ring, she almost hung up, but then someone answered.

"Hello," the voice said, a bit out of breath. "Hello. Is anyone there?"

The voice—the one Kat had been waiting to hear—stopped her cold. It sounded so much like Beth's voice.

"Mrs. Hunter? It's Mary Catherine."

"Mary Catherine? What are you doing calling here?" She paused. "David's not here."

"I'm not calling to talk to David."

"The girls aren't here, either."

Kat's hand pressed hard against the receiver. "As much as I would love to talk to the girls, I called to talk to you."

"To me? What could you possibly want with me?"

"I've always been able to talk to you, more than even my own mother. Actually, I *needed* to talk to you. You know David is filing for divorce."

"Of course, I do."

"He wants to keep me from the girls," Kat said.

"I was against it. I told David it was a mistake to even suggest such a thing to you." Her voice quivered. "But then you agreed to it. You *agreed* to it."

"I didn't. Not really. I mean, I didn't sign anything."

"You might as well have, because you told him you'd agree to it. You gave up your children. Just like that, without a fight, you gave them up." She paused and caught her breath. "I used to think you were a good mother, but a good mother would never do this."

Kat realized it was hubris to want something from Betty. What mother wouldn't stand with her son against a woman who had abandoned her own children? But she couldn't give up, not just yet.

"I want to fight this, Mrs. Hunter. But my head's all messed up right now. I can't stop thinking about Beth."

"Don't you dare bring Beth into this. She would be horrified by what you've done. She sacrificed everything to protect children. She loved children."

Kat blinked back tears. "I made a mistake, Mrs. Hunter. Can you talk to David—explain it to him?"

"I don't know why you would want me to do that, Mary Catherine— why you'd even expect me to do it—but I don't want to be in the middle of this, and I won't betray my son by speaking to you anymore. Please, don't call me again."

The phone went dead.

Kat placed the receiver back on the cradle and pulled her knees to her chest. She watched the wax in the lava lamp reach upward like a hand lifting in prayer. Yet no matter how close to the top it came, it couldn't maintain the heat that sent it rising, causing it to slowly collapse in a puddle at the bottom of the lamp. The wax was at the mercy of the tug between hot and cold, being pulled in both directions.

12

SNOW HAD BEEN FALLING SINCE EARLY MORNING, covering everything like a white apron. A calmness came with seeing the brown dullness of winter hidden beneath an alabaster glow. Kat watched the mounting snow and wished her life could be covered over so easily. She let the curtain drop back into place and turned to face the Christmas tree, all lit up, in the corner of LuAnn's den. Kat would have avoided Christmas if she could have, but it was all around her, especially at the pottery store. Christmas music played on a constant loop while customers came and went all day, and she was obliged to say Merry Christmas after each purchase. She sank onto the couch with a sigh and quickly wiped the tear away when she heard LuAnn's footsteps.

"Sorry, honey," LuAnn said as she rushed back into the room and plopped on the recliner near Kat. "That was Randy on the phone. He just wanted to let me know he's staying at his girlfriend's house until the snow stops." She glanced at her watch. "I do hope he'll make it home before the Christmas Eve service tonight. Lord knows, he wears me out sometimes." Her laughter rumbled from her throat as she slapped her knee.

"I bet you're glad to have him home for the holidays, though," Kat said. It was what she was supposed to say, what a polite friend would say. Yet the words carried a trace of envy that she couldn't hide. If LuAnn noticed, she didn't show it.

"Lord, honey, I joke about it all the time, but I wouldn't have it any other way," LuAnn said. "I know it's natural for children to grow up and move on, but he's our only child, and we honestly didn't think we'd ever be able to have any. Then he come along and surprised us, my little miracle. Of course, he hates for me to make a fuss over him now that he's grown. Says I'm too protective. But I just tell him that's too bad. He's my baby and always will be." She shook her head and laughed.

Kat tried to smile, but she felt the lump forming again in her throat and for a moment, she wasn't sure if she had stopped breathing. She looked up at the ceiling as she blinked back tears.

"Honey, what's wrong?" LuAnn moved next to Kat on the couch. "Now don't you mind me. I'm just a silly old mama bear." LuAnn truly was a den mother—fiercely protective of everyone she loved. She had brought Kat into that circle of people, and when she looked at Kat, her eyes were soft and disarming—everything Kat had wanted her own mother to be.

"I'm sorry," Kat said when she finally had gathered herself. "It's just that this Christmas has been horrible for me. You see, I have three girls, and I miss them terribly."

LuAnn cocked her head and a furrow formed between her eyebrows. It was as if the words had been tossed in the air and then settled into unrecognizable heaps in her mind. As LuAnn was pulling the heaps of words together to make sense of them, Kat focused on the twinkling lights just over LuAnn's shoulder.

"You look too young to have three grown children," LuAnn finally said.

"No, they're not grown," Kat said slowly. "They're with my husband."

"Husband?" LuAnn glanced at Kat's bare hand.

"Well, soon to be ex-husband," Kat said, folding her hands together to conceal her left hand. "He's filing for divorce."

LuAnn was still staring at Kat, still trying to make sense of what Kat was saying. "Oh, honey, that's awful. But I don't understand. Why are your children with him and not with you?"

Kat knew in that moment that LuAnn would never understand. This woman had just spoken of her heartache when her grown son was simply away at university. How could she empathize with someone who had chosen to walk away from her children? How could she understand a mother unwilling to fight for them? LuAnn's bewilderment at such an unusual circumstance confirmed everything Kat had feared might happen if people knew the truth.

"He's a powerful man," Kat said as she looked away. She had not yet become so accustomed to lying that she could bear to look at LuAnn while the lie was spilling out. "He told me I would never see my girls again."

It wasn't a complete lie, she told herself.

"He can't keep your children from you, can he?"

"I'm afraid he can, and he will. I'm certain of that."

"You can fight him in court. Surely a judge wouldn't let this happen to a mother and her children."

Kat stood up and walked to the window. She wished LuAnn would stop making this so much harder.

"He knows people," Kat finally said. The snow had stopped except for an occasional flake that fluttered by the window. The barren maple tree between LuAnn's house and Kat's apartment cast a heavy gray shadow across the snow. She took a deep breath and faced LuAnn. "He said if I take him to court, he'll tell them things about me, things I've done," she continued. "None of it's true, but I can't prove it."

There it was—a lie that would now have to be her truth. Kat had now heightened her level of deception, perhaps an unforgiveable one. The man she had once loved—the man who was only lashing out because of the pain she had caused—would now be the villain in her story.

LuAnn enveloped Kat with her big, soft arms. "It'll be okay, sweetie. It'll be okay," she said as she patted Kat.

Kat buried her face in LuAnn's shoulder, taking in the faint scent of Cachet on LuAnn's sweater. Kat needed that hug more than she realized, but she had not earned it. Her secret would now have to remain in the shadows.

"It'll be okay," LuAnn kept repeating, like a gentle lullaby.

After that, LuAnn insisted that Kat join the family for the Christmas Eve services at the Baptist church. If she could have said no, Kat would have. She hadn't stepped foot in a church since she left home, so it seemed hypocritical for her first time to be celebrating the birth of a baby—the Savior. Kat worried about not having the appropriate clothes for church. She hadn't brought any dresses with her because she hadn't expected to be away from home for weeks. LuAnn assured her that her slacks would be fine since the service was at night.

As Kat trudged through the snow back to her apartment, she was glad Molly had taken her to a thrift store for a winter coat, hat, gloves, and especially boots. The stairs were slick with snow, so she made her way up carefully, occasionally looking back at LuAnn's door. Pieces of her story now drifted with the snowflakes. She feared it was only a matter of time before the rest of her story would create a blizzard she couldn't control.

"They're usually very friendly," LuAnn said as they were about to enter the River of Life Baptist Church. "The Christmas Eve service is a little different, though. We enter quietly and go straight to our seats. We'll leave just as quietly. It makes for such a beautiful service." She squeezed Kat's hand to reassure her.

The lights inside the church were dim, but not dark. It was a small country church, very similar to one of her father's early churches. The beautiful black walnut pews were still pristine—not yet covered in padded fabric like a vast number of churches were doing. The windows were clear glass, without the ornate stained glass that was familiar in dozens of the churches she'd grown up in. The solid white oak podium was off to the side and the platform in front of the church was lined with poinsettias. An empty manger, filled with hay and positioned under a roughly crafted stable, was on one side of the stage.

Each windowsill cradled a single lit red candle nestled among holiday greenery— a mixture of fresh cedar, pine, boxwood, juniper, magnolia, and holly. As Kat watched the amber flicker of light in the window at the end of her row, she remembered the white candles at her Christmas Eve wedding twelve years before. It was a dim gray winter afternoon, so the candlelight gave a dream-like quality to the church. It all felt like a distant dream now. She was carrying her bridal bouquet of white roses and pale pink lilies, but also an *unspeakable secret* according to her mother—a baby conceived before the marriage. Her father wouldn't look at her as he left her at the altar with David. When David slipped the ring on her finger, her hand trembled, although now she wasn't sure why. She could barely recall the young woman who, despite her nerves, thought she knew exactly who she was—who she wanted to be.

Kat looked down at the Christmas program in her hand. She scanned the names, even though she figured she wouldn't know anyone unless they lived in the artist community. She noticed that Kitty Nelson's son was playing a shepherd. Then she saw Wyatt Jenkins's name beside "O Holy Night." Without meaning to, she raised her head and began scanning the room. He was sitting in the front pew, the curve of his nose and his long brown hair visible from the bright lights above the stage.

She turned her head away and watched the reflection of the candle against the glass. Even as the piano began "It Came Upon a Midnight Clear," she stared at the flame. Then she heard the sweet voice of a child reciting the beginning of the Christmas story. When she turned her attention to the stage, a boy, maybe eight or nine, in what looked like his bathrobe was just in front of Wyatt. Several children were gathered at the edge of the stage, waiting for their part in the program. The angel, a petite girl with dark brown hair, was tugging at the front of her dress, then reaching back to feel the fur that trimmed the netting of her wings. One of the shepherds was waving to what was surely his parents. Soft laughter skittered across the room.

Mary and Joseph walked across the stage and knelt by the manger as the boy continued to narrate. Joseph, apparently a bit bored, took his staff and began waving it like a sword. More laughter skimmed the room. Mary took a baby doll from behind the manger, wrapped it in a blanket, and placed it in the manager. Kat followed the movements of the girl. Lizzie had been Mary in the Christmas pageant the year before, and it was hard not to see the curve of Lizzie's cheek in this Mary.

The piano began the introduction to "O Holy Night," and Kat moved her eyes to Wyatt, who was now standing in front of the stage. He looked up at the ceiling before letting his smooth baritone drift through the room. Kat wanted to watch Wyatt, but her gaze was drawn back to Mary, who lovingly peered into the manger at her make-believe baby. Kat remembered that the real Mary had treasured everything that had happened to her—every wonderful and fearful thing—and pondered it in her heart. Of everyone in the Christmas story, Mary alone knew that her heart held both adoration and foreboding. Kat's eyes didn't move from the girl, even when Wyatt's voice reverberated throughout the room during the song's chorus. *Fall on your knees. O hear the angel voices.*

"I need to get some air," she whispered as she leaned over to LuAnn. "Don't worry, I'm okay. Really." She squeezed LuAnn's arm, then grabbed her purse and slipped out of the pew. In the vestibule, as she found her coat, she heard the reverence in Wyatt's voice as the song finished. She put on her coat and stepped out into the cold.

The frigid air took her breath for a moment. It burned down into her lungs until she put her gloved hands over her mouth and nose and exhaled a pocket of warm air. The sky was almost black from heavy clouds, with only a sliver of moonlight. Still, the snow shimmered under the white light of a lamppost. Wind crackled through the icy tree limbs and for a moment, the rest of the world made no sound. Kat let her hands drop to her side as a peace tried to settle into her body.

"There you are." She looked over to see Wyatt coming toward her. He stopped a few feet away, his face still in shadows.

"Shouldn't you be in there?" She nodded toward the church.

"I slipped out after I finished the song. I'm not in the rest of the program anyway." He stepped closer, and she saw his cheeks bloomed with red. He hadn't bothered to put his overcoat on. "I saw you go out but I didn't see you come back in. Is everything okay?"

"Just needed some air," she said.

"Well, this is some air alright. You really ought to go back inside. It's probably in the twenties—or less—out here." He stamped his feet, the way people do when they're trying to get warm.

"I can't go back in there," Kat said. Her voice had a strange tone and she wondered if it was just the cold.

"Then at least let me take you home."

"I can't worry LuAnn and Randy. They'd wonder what happened to me. I'll be okay." Her breath became a cloud that hung between them.

"Well, I won't let you stand out here. If you won't go inside, and you won't let me take you home, at least let's go sit in my car. We can turn the heat on in there and warm up."

She nodded. He took her arm and led her to his car. They were quiet while the car warmed up. The church building slowly disappeared as the car windows fogged over. Kat didn't realize how cold she had become until the warm air stung her cheeks and hands. As the motor hummed, she grew sleepy, but she forced herself to stay awake. A long time ago, she would have fallen asleep and not been afraid of her dreams.

"You know, I'm going to start taking offense," Wyatt finally said. "That's the second time you've walked out on me while I was singing." He was clearly teasing her.

"Pure coincidence," she said. She hoped he could see her smile in the blue glow from the dashboard lights. "I didn't take you for a church man, though."

"Because I sing in a bar?"

"Something like that. I grew up thinking that bars were places sinners hung out. But, then, I was taught to be wary of all kinds of places, except church. My father is a pastor."

"Well, that explains a lot." He turned toward her. "The first time I saw you at Smokey's, you looked like a salmon swimming downstream. So, are your visits to Smokey's your way of rebelling?"

"Oh, I'm too old for rebellion," she said. She knew it wasn't the truth. Hadn't she renounced everything she had been before? "I mean, I really don't intend to be a rebel."

"Well, look at that. Kat Turner is a woman of mystery," Wyatt said as he let out a whistle.

"Is that bad?"

"Not for me. I like mysteries. It just means that I'll need to spend more time with you to figure it out."

In that moment, Kat wanted Wyatt, more than she had ever wanted any man. Yet she was terrified that if he ever learned what made her so mysterious, he would despise her.

"My life is very complicated right now."

"We can take it slow," he said. He put his hand over top of hers. "But I would like to kiss you right now, if that's okay."

She turned her hand over to fully grasp his, as her way of saying yes. When he leaned toward her, she caught the faint scent of tobacco smoke on his jacket.

His lips were warm and tender.

13

KAT DECLINED LUANN'S INVITATION to spend the night in the house, to become part of their family for Christmas morning. It wasn't her family, and she couldn't bear watching them celebrate knowing that her girls wouldn't be opening the gifts she'd sent them. David called just to let her know he had donated the gifts to a local charity. He didn't even give Kat a chance to say anything before he hung up.

So, Kat stood at the bottom of the stairs to her apartment knowing that only an empty room, with no holiday decorations, awaited her at the top. She stood, letting her breath curl in wisps into the frigid air. She wondered what it would be like to stay there all night, staring up into the light above her door, watching tiny snowflakes drift down to her until she was no longer able to feel anything.

In the stillness, Kat heard the twitter of a bird gathering nourishment at LuAnn's feeder. It was strange for a bird to be there at that time of night. She walked toward the sound, but the crunch of the snow startled the bird and it flew away. Kat kept walking. Walking down the path, which was lost under the snow, past Rusty's glass shop, past the quilt store, until she was standing in front of the pottery shop. This place had come to embody her longing to make sense of the world—by learning how, in the artist's hands, earth and water could be formed into an invocation.

Kat walked to the back of the building and saw the light through the window. She opened the door to find Pony at the kiln.

"What are you doing here on Christmas Eve?" she said as she removed her coat and gloves. She stamped her feet to free the snow from her boots and pant legs.

"I could ask you the same question," he said, picking a mug from the kiln and laying it on the nearby table.

"It's been a hard Christmas. A hard holiday season, really," she said. She sat on a stool at the table where Pony was putting the pieces he'd pulled from the kiln.

"You *have* been kind of quiet lately." Pony pulled another mug from the kiln. He turned the mug sideways, inspecting the blue-gray glaze that dripped down into the sandstone below it. Though Kat had only been working with Pony a short time, she'd seen that look. "Still doesn't explain why you're here."

"Can't get anything over on you, can I?" She smiled and rubbed her finger over the rim of a mug. "I just couldn't face my empty apartment, so I thought maybe I'd practice getting the clay centered." Pony had started teaching her to throw pottery, and she was still trying to master getting the clay centered on the wheel. "You said I could come any time after hours to practice."

"Of course. Centering is important in all parts of our lives." He inspected another mug, but rather than placing it with the other mugs, he dropped it in a box beside the table. The sound of the pottery breaking startled Kat. Pony looked at her and smiled. "It's also good to be able to let go. Sometimes we need to start over, and that's okay."

Kat stared down at the broken pieces of pottery. Pony handed her a mug and waited. She scanned it, turning it over. The glaze had fired unevenly, but only a potter would recognize the flaw.

"It's not that bad," she said. She handed him the mug. "We could sell that easily. No one would really know."

"I would." He gave her back the mug. He motioned for her to throw it into the box. She hesitated, but he motioned again for her to drop it. She held the mug over the box for a moment, then she let it fall. The mug clinked, almost like chimes, as it shattered. She stared again at the pottery sherds.

Pony went back to the kiln and Kat followed him. They worked in silence as they pulled the rest of the pieces from the kiln. If one of them came across a flawed piece, they took turns throwing it into the box.

"I don't know about you," Pony said when they finished, "but I'm ready to head home." Kat nodded.

"If you'd like, we can meet tomorrow afternoon and work on that centering."

"I'd like that," she said. She put on her coat and opened the door, stepping back into the cold air.

"Are you going to be okay tonight?" Pony said. He looked at her the way David sometimes had, only with understanding in his eyes.

"I'll be okay."

She closed the door behind her and began the walk back to the apartment. Her home. The snow crunched under her feet and echoed through the trees across the road. She stopped to consider the trees, their bare branches capped white. Perhaps they hadn't abandoned her after all. Perhaps they were still protecting her. Maybe they were whispering to her to move on with her life.

She had no choice but to move on, but she knew that as long as she was separated from her daughters, grief would live in the hollowed-out place in her chest—and even the strongest trees couldn't protect her from that.

TWO

14

THE LONG, GREEN LEAVES OF THE CORN STALKS quivered above the brown pickets that framed the garden. The nearby tomatoes, just turning red, were nestled in their cages in a neat row. Green beans rose high on a trellis, like a leafy tower. From the porch, Kat could see it all, and she could hear the river just beyond the garden. She sipped her lemonade and reached down to pet Luna, Wyatt's golden retriever. Kat closed her eyes, her hand still stroking Luna's fur, and listened to the water. She would have made time stop, if she could have, and just breathe in the peace that, too often, felt elusive.

But she had more chores to do before Wyatt came home.

Nearly three years had passed since Wyatt first kissed her. He had wanted to marry her the year before, but she told him she wasn't ready yet. So, when he asked her to come live with him instead, she surprised herself by saying yes. Even with her divorce papers long since signed and delivered, Kat sometimes felt like an adulteress living with Wyatt. Kat was sure she heard her parents' whispered disapproval the first time she walked into Wyatt's house with her suitcases in hand. Yet, every time Wyatt gathered her into his arms and she pressed her cheek against his chest, she brushed away everything but contentment. It was that same contentment she felt when she listened to the river, which gurgled and rippled over the rocks.

With her eyes closed, she could see the boulder in the middle of the river, just past their house. She could see the greenish-gray water meet the rock with enough force to foam white before it slid around the sides of the boulder and traveled on. How strange it was for such peace to emanate from such a forceful confrontation.

"What is it, girl?" Kat said, leaning forward in the rocking chair as Luna stood and thrust her nose between the balusters, her ears pricked.

"It's okay, Luna. It's just me," Molly called as she rounded the corner of the house. She waved at Kat. "I saw the car out front, so I figured you were home. Hope you don't mind me just popping in."

"Mind?" Kat said as she threw her arms around Molly. "You're always a welcome sight. Do you have time to sit for a spell?" Molly had on her name badge from the cabin rental company.

"A minute or two," Molly said.

"Good. Let me get you some lemonade. It's too hot without something cold to drink." Before Molly could say anything, the screen door was already creaking shut behind Kat. It took a moment for Kat's eyes to adjust to the dimmer light in the kitchen. The pitcher of lemonade was still on the counter, condensation sweating down its sides. Kat reached for a glass from the cabinet beside the back door. She caught sight of Molly, who had settled into a rocking chair, staring out into the yard. Ever since she had married Jake, Molly had seemed preoccupied somehow, as if she was trying to remember something important.

"Here you are," Kat said, handing the glass to Molly.

She took a long drink, and then looked out into the yard again. "You sure have a beautiful place here."

"Yeah, it is. Wyatt said his parents knew the minute they saw this land it was where they wanted to raise a family. He loved growing up here, always playing in those trees and in the river. I can see why." Wyatt had told her that when his parents were killed in the car wreck, after he'd moved to Knoxville, moving back here was the only thing that kept him going. At the thought of her own separation from her parents, she grew quiet, the low creak of the rocking chair against the porch filling the brief silence. "Sometimes I just sit out here and listen to the river where I can forget—" She let her voice trail off.

"I'm sure being here with Wyatt helps," Molly said. She was tracing lines through the condensation on her glass. "I'm really glad things are working out for you and Wyatt. Honestly, I wasn't sure they would."

"Well, that's a horrible thing to say." Kat stopped rocking and looked at Molly. When she saw Molly's grin, she flopped back against the chair and started rocking again. "I swear, Molly Fisher, I never know how to take you."

"Come on," she said, her hand swatting the air. "You know how much I adore you two—and you're *perfect* for each other." She sipped her lemonade. "Seriously, though, I wasn't sure I'd ever see you this happy, after those first few months here in the mountains."

"I *was* in a much darker place back then, that's for sure. But I'm getting better." She should have added an "I think" to the end, but she knew it wasn't the right thing to say.

Luna jumped to her feet again and barked at something far out in the yard, causing Kat to slosh lemonade onto her shirt. She reached for one of the napkins on the table and began dabbing at the wet spot. "What about you and Jake?" she said. "How are the newlyweds doing?"

Molly laughed, the deep belly laugh that Kat loved. "Once we passed the two-year mark, I think we're just considered an old married couple." But Kat saw something different in her eyes. Kat hadn't seen Jake in months. Molly was always making excuses for his absence. He was busy, she said, opening his own studio so he could concentrate on painting. That wasn't the whole story, though, according to LuAnn. She told Kat that Jake was always arguing with Rusty about how to run the glass studio, so Rusty finally told him if he wanted to run a business so much then he was welcome to go try. Jake was what her Grandma Turner would have called an odd bird, though Molly just called it an artistic temperament. Whatever it was, Kat preferred to spend time with Molly when Jake wasn't around.

"Things are okay with Jake and me," Molly said. "I mean, Jake's spending a lot of time getting his studio set up. Leaving Rusty's has been harder than he imagined, so he's moping around the house all the time." She stopped her chair and leaned over the arm rest toward Kat. "So, I came up with a brilliant idea. He's turning the big 3-0 on Thursday, so I'm throwing a birthday party at Smokey's on Saturday."

"Saturday?"

"Yeah, sorry for the short notice, but I had to talk him into it. He's stubborn like that."

"Well, I'll definitely be there," Kat said. "But Wyatt's got a gig in Knoxville on Saturday."

"In Knoxville? You're not going with him?" Kat shook her head. "Well, I'm not sure how comfortable I'd be sending my man alone into those clubs with all those drunk women."

"Hey, I trust Wyatt. Anyway, as much as I love to hear him sing, I can't go to *every* gig. He understands that." Suddenly, though, Kat questioned whether that was true.

Molly glanced at her watch. "Oops, I'd better run. They'll think I'm playing hooky this afternoon." Kat gave her another hug, then smiled as she watched her disappear down the driveway. Molly was so much like Beth in that way, like a bolt of lightning that drops from the sky and then is gone.

When the car pulled away, Kat grabbed a pail and hat before heading to the garden. The blistering heat should have deterred her. Instead, it gave her strength, as if she were a delicate clay pot being fired in the kiln. To be working the earth again resurrected a part of herself that she was afraid had died. Kat looked down at Luna, who had dutifully followed her to the garden and was now nestled in the dirt at her feet.

The dog's panting chugged like a small motor. "It's okay, girl. We'll be inside soon," she said as she pulled a couple of green tomatoes off the vine. She gathered green beans and a few yellow squash.

"Fried green tomatoes and a squash casserole for supper tonight," she said to Luna as she closed the garden gate behind them. On the way to the house, she paused at the garage, which Wyatt had converted into a pottery studio for her. She still worked for Pony, part-time now, but she was also making her own pots to sell in the store. Her studio was like a church to her—sacred. Any time spent there was respite, and she considered taking just a few minutes right then to turn something simple—a small bowl or a simple vase. Yet she knew the few minutes that she would intend to spend would somehow become a whole afternoon.

Back in the kitchen, Luna lapped up a fresh bowl of water while Kat washed the vegetables. She laid the squash and tomatoes on the counter. The white half runners, she took to the kitchen table to string and snap. When she was finished, she pulled sheets off the clothesline and carried them to the bare bed in their room. The movement of her hand as she smoothed the sheet over the mattress was memory. Her hands moved effortlessly, just as they had done countless times before, to turn down the top of the sheet and tuck the bottom corners and sides. That her movements were echoes of the ones that sowed doubt in her mind three years earlier—enough to compel her to give up everything—brought renewed pain. As she pulled the comforter over the pillows, Kat stopped long enough to draw a deep breath to push the pain back into its hiding place.

When it was almost time for Wyatt to be home, Kat put the green beans on the stove, with bits of bacon for seasoning. She put the squash casserole in the oven and stirred the cornmeal and breadcrumbs together for the tomatoes. As soon as she heard Wyatt's van pull into the driveway, she slid the pork chops into the skillet. He whistled as he came up the steps to the porch, then stomped his feet just outside the door. Luna stood at the door, her tail wagging, ready for him to come in.

"Hey, girl," Wyatt said, ruffling Luna's fur when she put her front paws on his thighs. He was covered in white dust. Even his hair, which was shorter than when they met, looked like a flocked Christmas tree.

"Don't get her dirty," Kat said as she glanced up from the skillet. "You're filthy."

"I was doing drywall today for a restaurant in Pigeon Forge. Do I have time for a shower?"

"You'd better." She laughed. This was their frequent banter when he came home from his construction jobs. As usual, Wyatt pulled off his T-shirt and jeans and dropped them on the floor, a small cloud of dust billowing from them. Kat let out a whistle, leading Wyatt to take a deep bow. She watched as he strutted, nearly naked, out of the kitchen. Never had she felt this way about David. She thought she had loved David. Her parents had drilled into her that marriage was the goal, and David was a good man—a good provider. Yet all she had ever heard about marriage was about submission, not love. Obligation, more likely. David had never intentionally made her feel this way, but she felt it anyway.

Wyatt came up behind her, fresh from the shower, and wrapped his arms around her waist while she set the pork chops and tomatoes on the table. She breathed in the woodsy scent of Stetson. "How was your day?" he said as he kissed her neck.

"Molly stopped by today," Kat said as they sat down for dinner. "She's having a birthday party for Jake on Saturday."

Wyatt helped himself to tomatoes and squash. "I'm sorry I'll miss it. You going?"

"I told her I would." She cut a piece of pork, pausing before putting it in her mouth. She looked across at Wyatt. "Does it bother you that I don't go with you to all of your gigs?"

He glanced up from his plate as he cut his tomato. "Of course not. Why would you think that?"

"I don't know." She hesitated. "I just don't want you to ever think I'm not proud of you—or that I don't want to spend time with you."

Wyatt looked at her fully now. "My love for you doesn't depend on what you do or don't do for me. I'm not David."

"I know that," Kat said, looking past Wyatt. Any time David's name came up, she couldn't look at him. Like everyone else in their small community, she had let him believe David was a monster, responsible for ripping Kat's children from her and for continuing to keep them apart. The lie had hung between Kat and Wyatt for almost three years, always chafing against the contentment she felt she didn't deserve.

"Why don't we go out to the river tonight," he said. "I've been aching all day to listen to her."

Kat nodded. The river was always a place of peace for them both.

———————

An hour before sunset, Kat picked up the quilt tucked away under the table by the back door. She stepped out onto the back porch and sprayed insect repellant on her legs and arms, then waited for Wyatt. He was carrying his guitar case when he came out, with Luna trailing close behind. Luna had accepted Kat coming into the home, had even been a constant companion when Wyatt was away, but there was little doubt that the bond between Luna and Wyatt was not to be usurped.

As they walked past the garden, the sound of the river grew louder. At the back of the yard, they followed a path through a grove of trees to a small grassy outcrop perched just above the water. The sun, not yet behind the mountain, cast a shadow over the river, but a patch of water caught sunlight and sparkled like sequins. Kat spread the blanket as she sat down, feeling the prickly grass beneath it. Wyatt sat across from Kat and pulled the guitar out of the case. He tuned a couple of strings. Kat watched the water tumble against rocks as Wyatt finally began to sing. It was a familiar hymn to her: "All Creatures of Our God and King." Kat closed her eyes. The sound of rushing water made her feel weightless, as if she was floating above the earth, hearing it move below yet also aware of the stillness in the air around her. Without being aware of it, she was singing along with Wyatt. Her voice played harmony with his. When the music stopped, she didn't move.

"Now that was church," Wyatt said.

Kat fell backward onto the quilt, the rush of the river still in her ears. "Does it bother you that we don't go to church?" she said, staring into the yellowing twilight.

Wyatt put his guitar in the case and lay down beside her. "You fret more than any person I've ever known," he said, staring up into the same sky.

"You didn't answer the question," she said.

He rolled over to face her. "No. No, it doesn't bother me." He stroked her hair then let his finger move down her shoulder and trace her breast. He leaned down and kissed her. "If there are people who want to wag their tongues about us living together, then I'm perfectly fine with meeting God out here by the river."

Kat laced her fingers through Wyatt's. "But I'm the reason they're talking—the reason we're not married."

"You're Delilah, aren't you?" He poked her in her rib. "I mean, you *are* the one that tricked me into cutting my hair. Now I have no willpower when it comes to you."

"I'm such a bad influence on you, Mr. Jenkins," she said. She reached up and kissed him.

"Yes, ma'am, you are." He gave her another quick kiss then sat up. He snatched the guitar again and began playing. Kat knew the song as soon as he started singing. "The River is Wide" was one of his favorites. She had never been able to decide if the song was a tribute to great love or a lament about the fleeting nature of love. Behind her, the river endured. Above her, the trees were black against the darkening sky, the leaves silhouetted against the blue-gray clouds.

Kat looked over at Wyatt, who was starting to disappear among the shadows. They would soon gather the quilt and stumble their way in the dusky twilight toward the single light shining on their back porch. They would settle into bed, Kat staying awake until Wyatt's breathing transformed into a raspy snore. She would drift off to sleep understanding the fragility of love.

Yet in that moment, with a blush of red beginning to outline the clouds above her, Kat listened to the song drift over her like a prayer.

15

KAT PLUNGED HER FINGERS INTO THE BUCKET, then splashed the cool water over her hands. The sand-colored clay stubbornly clung to her hands, but as she gently rubbed her palms and the back of her hands, the clay began to dissolve into the water below. She rubbed her fingertips together to dislodge clay from her nails, then lifted her hands high to let the water cascade back into the bucket. The sound of the water echoing in the garage was as soothing as the rhythmic whir of the kick wheel had been when she turned the bowls, which were now beginning to dry on the shelf.

She wiped her hands on her apron before hanging it on the peg by the door. She wished she could turn just one more bowl, but the hour was later than she intended, which meant she was going to be late for Jake's birthday party. Maybe she'd have a chance to turn another bowl after the party. She showered and then put on her pastel blue capris and the matching camp shirt she'd laid out on the bed, even though she knew she'd be out of place in the sea of denim and cowboy hats. She grabbed Jake's gift, a VHS documentary of the Beatles, off the kitchen table and was almost out the door when the phone rang. She hesitated, but then picked up the receiver from the wall-mounted phone by the door.

"Hello," Kat said, exasperation in her voice as she juggled Jake's present, her purse, and her keys.

"You really should use better phone manners, Mary Catherine."

Hearing that it was her mother's voice on the other end of the phone added to Kat's irritation. She never knew when to expect the call, but it seemed to always come at an inopportune time. Kat had given her mother the phone number after she moved in with Wyatt, hoping her mother might eventually relent—might be willing to convince David to change his mind about letting Kat talk to the girls. But her mother was as stubborn as she was self-righteous, always ready to point out the consequences of sin. Kat wished now she had never given her mother the phone number.

"Sorry, Mom. I was just heading out the door." She tried to soften her voice as she eyed the clock.

"I certainly don't want to interrupt your activities." Her mother's tone was icy—that haughty, sanctimonious tone that Kat hated. Kat held back a sigh but wasn't able to cover her irritation.

"I answered the phone, didn't I?" she said. "What do you want?"

"Honestly, after everything *you've* done, I have no idea why you're so hostile to *me*."

"I don't mean to be." Years of practice taught Kat that pushing back against her mother's words never resulted in making Kat feel better. She laid the present and her purse on the table and stuffed the keys in her pocket. "I simply meant that you must have a reason for calling."

"I do." She paused, for dramatic effect, Kat figured. "I saw Jenny at the mall today." Kat sank onto a chair but said nothing. "Are you still there, Mary Catherine?"

"Yes. Yes, I'm still here." She picked at the fringe on the edge of the woven placemat in front of her. "You saw Jenny?"

"She was with some friends, but I was able to speak with her alone for a couple of minutes. You know that David doesn't let us see the girls much anymore."

Kat ignored the final comment. "Did Jenny look okay?"

"She seemed happy enough. Talking about school starting soon and David's new girlfriend." Kat waited for more, but, again, the hesitation seemed calculated. "She's someone from work—the girlfriend, I mean."

Kat really wanted to hear more about Jenny, but previous phone calls had made it clear that withholding details about the girls was her mother's way of punishing Kat.

"And Jenny seems okay with David's girlfriend?" Kat traced the yellow lines in the placemat.

"She said she was pretty."

Kat balled up the placemat under her palm. "That's good," she said. "I'm glad David's dating." The odd sense of relief startled her, not just about David but about the girls. "They're better off without me," she said, forgetting that her mother was still on the phone.

"They're not, Mary Catherine. They're not." Her mother's voice was surprisingly tender. Kat stood and moved to the window, the phone cord stretching behind her back. The summer sun, still visible above the mountain, was glinting off the tin roof of the garage.

"My girls deserve better than an emotional wreck. David has always been the stable one," she said. She squinted her eyes against the sun. "It's too late anyway. The girls would never forgive me now—not after all this time."

"For the life of me, I don't understand you." The stiffness in her mother's voice returned. "You ran away and then gave up. You've just surrendered—and you don't care what that's done to any of the rest of us. I don't even know why I bother to talk to you."

"Then don't bother." Kat regretted the words as soon as they were uttered—not because they weren't true, but because she knew she'd pay a price for them.

"It seems you're right, then. Everyone is better off without you."

"I'm sorry," she whispered before she hung up. Her feet pressed hard against the floor, trying futilely to stop the tremors in her legs. She leaned against the window frame as she stared at the garage door, her fingers, as always, longing to feel the cool clay beneath them. Yet it was Jenny's face that filled her mind. People had always said Jenny was the spitting image of Kat. She wondered if her daughter's blond hair was now curling past the shoulders, just as she had let her own hair grow. Or if Jenny, at almost thirteen, was starting to change into a woman, starting to notice boys and be noticed by them. Or if Jenny had asked about Kat when she had the chance at the mall.

Kat wished Wyatt wasn't in Knoxville. She wanted him to walk up behind her and fold her into his arms. It scared her that she depended on him so much.

Kat heard the tap of Luna's toenails on the linoleum before she felt the cold nose nudge her hand. She knelt and patted the dog's head. "Aw, girl, you always know, don't you?" she said. Luna licked Kat's cheek. "You know that I'm hurting, but you have no idea what I've done. I bet you'd never abandon your babies, would you, girl?" Luna lifted her paw for a handshake. Kat smiled and took the paw. "If only it were that easy." She stood, picking up Jake's gift and her purse. "Nothing left to do but go to the party, huh?" She gave Luna one final pat before heading out the door.

———

Jake and a dark-haired woman were outside when Kat pulled into Smokey's. She didn't recognize the woman, but they were laughing as the cigarette smoke curled between them. "Hey, Jake," Kat said, as she passed by them on the way to the door. Jake gave a quick nod but went back to his conversation. Kat glanced back at him before going inside.

The room was quieter than usual because the live music was still an hour away from starting. Some country music was playing through the speakers, and four men were chatting over their drinks at the bar. Molly, in her straight-legged jeans and plaid shirt, was with a small group of people, mostly women, near the bar. She excused herself and came rushing toward Kat. "Where have you been? I was starting to think you weren't coming."

"Just got a little behind schedule. I'm here now, though," Kat said as she laid the present on a nearby table.

"Well, I'm glad you finally made it." The light in Molly's eyes eased the weight in Kat's chest. "Did you see Jake when you came in? The birthday boy seems to have disappeared."

Kat hesitated. "He was out front smoking."

"Oh, that man. Anything to avoid being in here," Molly said with a wave of her hand. She was out the door before Kat could say anything to stop her. Kat watched the door and wondered if she should follow her friend.

"I haven't seen you in forever." Kat turned to find LuAnn standing next to her. "Are you that surprised to see me?"

Kat realized she must have looked startled. "I guess I am a little surprised because—"

"Because of what happened with Jake and Rusty?" LuAnn smiled her warm den-mother smile. "If it was just for Jake, I probably wouldn't have come. The truth is, I can't seem to refuse Molly anything."

"I know what you mean," Kat said as she looked again at the door. She was about to excuse herself and head outside, but Molly and Jake came in. The dark-haired woman wasn't with them.

"I found the birthday boy," Molly shouted. "We can get the party started."

Jake followed Molly to a table topped with presents. His mouth didn't hold any slack, didn't carry any emotion. His eyes were fixed straight ahead, refusing to engage with the people gathered around the table. Molly seemed oblivious to Jake's mood and brought out a cake, topped with thirty candles, and set it in front of him. The only time Jake looked at her, a quick fiery glare, was when she lit the candles.

"Oh my, I almost forgot," she said just as everyone took a breath to sing. She pulled a cone-shaped party hat out of a nearby bag. When she placed the glittery hat with metallic fringe on Jake's head, everyone laughed. But Kat thought she saw his lips tighten as they began to sing. She was certain she saw the rage build in his eyes just before he slammed his fist on the table. Everyone around the table jumped and stopped singing. Even the men at the bar grew quiet. The room's focus was on Jake, which seemed to anger him even more. He stood, the screech of the chair against the concrete floor echoing in the room. In one swift motion, he ripped the birthday hat off his head, flung it to the table, and flipped the cake onto the concrete floor, narrowly missing Molly, who flinched back a step. He stormed past Molly and out the door. LuAnn stooped and snuffed a couple of the candles that had not been crushed by the cake. She gave Kat a knowing look when she stood up. Kat moved toward Molly, but Molly waved her off and ran out the door after Jake.

When the door closed, the room was still quiet. No one seemed to know what to do. Finally, the bartender motioned to one of the waitresses, who then disappeared into a back room and returned with a trash can and a mop. The men at the bar returned to their drinks. Even the other party guests moved off to another table and ordered drinks. The waitress mopped. Glasses clinked. Idle chatter and loud laughter filled the space around Kat. Yet she was suspended in the moment she had just witnessed.

"I've never seen Jake like that," Kat said to LuAnn, who was still standing beside her. "Have you?"

"Not quite like that, but after how he treated Rusty, I'm not surprised."

"I can't leave her out there alone. Not with him acting like that." She started to leave, but LuAnn grabbed her arm.

"You stay. I'll go see to her."

Kat pulled her arm free. "*I'm* going." LuAnn looked hurt, but she turned and went to a nearby table.

When Kat got out the door, she couldn't see anything as she had to shade her eyes against the low-hanging sun, but she heard the voices. She turned her head toward the voices and saw the silhouette of Jake standing behind his car door, one hand gripping the roof of the car, the other the top of the car door. Molly, who was turned away from Kat, was clutching Jake's arm.

"Please don't go," Molly pleaded. Her voice carried a tremor Kat had never heard in it before. "I said that I'm sorry."

"I told you from the start that I didn't want this asinine party, but you didn't listen, did you? Today was all about you—it's always about you." Jake's voice exploded across the parking lot. Kat started to move toward them but froze for a second at the sound in his voice.

"Please stay," Molly pleaded. "We don't have to continue the party. We can just have drinks with our friends."

"They're your friends, not mine. Now get out of my way." He shoved Molly hard. She stumbled back against another parked car before slumping to the ground.

"Oh my God," Kat called out. "Molly!" She could see Jake fully now, and he glared at her before he slammed his door and screeched out of the parking lot.

"Are you alright?" Kat said as she knelt beside Molly, gravel digging into her knees. Molly looked up at Kat, her eyes vacant. Kat wrapped her arms around Molly's shoulders. For a moment, she breathed in the sweet, floral scent of Molly's hair. Yet something about the way it made her feel caused her to pull away and stand up. Maybe it was seeing Molly crumpled in a heap, needing help for the first time since Kat had known her. Maybe it was something deeper. Whatever it was, it frightened Kat.

She reached a hand down to Molly. "Come on, let's get you inside," she said.

Molly looked at Kat again, terror now in her eyes. "No, I can't—I can't go back in there."

"Okay. Okay," Kat said. "You don't have to. I'll take you someplace else, if you want me to."

"Home is fine," Molly said as she took Kat's hand. "He'll be cooled down by the time I get there."

"Are you sure that's a good idea?"

"I want to go home," she said firmly.

"Okay, I'll take you home."

They walked to Kat's car at the other end of the lot, and Kat could feel the tremble in the small of Molly's back. She helped Molly into the car and was shutting the door when Molly cried out. "My purse. My things," she said. "They're inside."

"I'll get them," Kat said, giving a reassuring touch to Molly's shoulder. She shut the car door and took a deep breath. She didn't want to go back into the bar any more than Molly did, but her purse was in there as well.

The party guests eyed her when she came in. One raised a glass to her, and Kat wondered how anyone could be so cold hearted. LuAnn, sitting by herself at another table drinking a Coke, had gathered the presents and Molly's belongings. She motioned Kat over, her eyes full of questions.

"It's not good," Kat said.

"She okay?"

Kat shook her head. "I think she will be, though. I hope so, anyway." She picked up Molly's purse and the bag of presents. "I'm taking her home."

"Won't Jake be there? I could take her to my house. Let her stay the night." LuAnn's voice couldn't help but carry the honeyed tones of a doting mother. Sometimes Kat hated LuAnn for it. Something about it carried condescension, and Kat was beginning to wonder if that's what was behind much of LuAnn's apparent concern.

"She wants to go to her own home." Kat knew she let her irritation show too much, because LuAnn was biting her lower lip. Kat softened her voice. "Thanks for the offer, though. I'm sure she'll appreciate it." She grabbed her purse with her free hand. "I'll call her in the morning to check on her."

"Me, too," LuAnn called after her.

Molly was quiet when Kat loaded the purses and presents into the back seat.

"You still want to go home?" Kat asked when she sat in the driver's seat. Molly nodded. The sun was finally beginning to fall behind the mountains, casting a dull, gray heft over the valley. They drove for a few minutes in a silence that cut a canyon between them before Kat finally spoke again. "Is he like that often?"

"No," Molly said. Kat wondered if that was all she was going to get from Molly, but then Molly continued. "He loses his temper sometimes, like tonight. You know, that moody artist temperament." In the twilight, Kat could see the shadow of Molly's hands moving, pulling against each other. "He's never hit me."

"He did tonight."

"He just wanted me out of the way so he could leave."

They were almost at Molly's house, but Kat pulled into a parking lot of a nearby store. With the motor still running, she turned in her seat to look at Molly. "You don't have to put up with this."

"He's not really that bad. I just pushed him too far tonight." She paused and looked at Kat. "You may have been able to leave your husband, Kat, but I love Jake. I can't leave him."

The words stung, but Kat stayed focused. They didn't often talk about Kat's past. "I didn't mean you had to leave him. Just don't let him get away with treating you like that."

Molly didn't say anything, and Kat allowed her the silence.

"I'm pregnant," Molly finally said.

Kat took a moment to process the news. She was concerned the timing of the pregnancy could make Molly and Jake's relationship more tense, but she was more concerned the pregnancy would affect her friendship with Molly. She wasn't sure if she was ready to be around a pregnant woman, watching her go through all of the changes and preparations for a baby.

"I'm about ten weeks along." Molly's face was now cloaked in the dusk that separated them. "I was going to tell him tonight—at the party. A sort of birthday present." Her voice gathered the strength that had always been hers. "And you know what? I *will* tell him tonight. He'll be happy then, and everything will be alright for sure."

"Molly, I—"

"Everything will be alright, Kat. Now, take me on home. I need to tell Jake."

Kat wanted to object—wanted to convince Molly to come home with her—but Molly was stubborn. Anyway, who was Kat to tell anyone how to live her life? She pulled out of the parking lot then stopped the car in Molly's driveway behind Jake's car. She gave Molly's hand a squeeze before Molly got out of the car. Molly grabbed her bag and purse from the back seat, said a quick thank you, and rushed up the steps of the small, brick house. When the living room light came on, Molly was still standing inside the screen door, with her long curls almost touching the waist of her jeans. A shadow approached her, then Jake appeared.

Kat backed out, the headlights scanning the row of trees on the edge of the gravel driveway. The night was black, and the headlights reached out into the darkness to guide Kat down the familiar road to home. She was weary when she pulled into her own driveway. Even the arc of light from the floodlamp over the garage door, which tried to beckon her back to the potter's wheel, couldn't compel her spirits to lift. Instead, she turned toward the house.

Luna waited, tail wagging, as Kat opened the back door. Kat dropped her purse and keys on the kitchen table. She gave a quick rub to Luna's head and tapped her leg for the dog to follow. Luna jumped onto the bed and settled in her accustomed place at the bottom edge. Whatever weariness weighted Kat down, Luna seemed ready, with a lazy wag of her tail, to provide comfort.

Kat pulled off her clothes and threw them in the hamper. She slipped the white cotton gown over her head, let it drop over her hips and swing out just below her knees. She sank onto the bed, releasing some tension through a puff of air. Yet she was still plagued with a fretfulness as she replayed the incident with Jake and Molly. Her head settled on the pillow, and she listened to the night through the open window. Crickets chirped, perhaps in a futile attempt to attract a mate. In the distance, the river roared, but its movement was too fast to touch a rock or dangling branch for more than a fleeting moment. The sounds that usually gave her relief were instead wistful. Even so, she fell into a restless sleep.

16

THE AROMA OF FRYING BACON and freshly brewed coffee filled the house, rousing Kat from her sleep. She rolled over and looked at the clock. Nine o'clock. As a girl, she would have never slept that late on a Sunday morning, because Sunday mornings were frenetic—rushing to bathe and put on the proper attire so her family would be the first to arrive at the church. The preacher's family had to set the example. Kat wished she could have lingered in bed and slept the morning away, but she knew better than to ask her mother for even a minute more. Even after Kat married, the pressure to be a model parishioner remained, which was made all the more stressful trying to corral three children who themselves begged for a few more minutes of sleep. Back then, to sleep until seven felt sinful.

But now, Kat was able to take her time—to sit up and stretch like her old tom cat used to do when he was getting up from the sun-soaked spot in front of the living room window. It had taken some time for Kat to enjoy the new Sunday morning routine—to not wallow in guilt when Wyatt let her sleep while he fixed breakfast. Even after coming home at one or two in the morning after a gig, he was still up before her to cook breakfast. She had tried to tell him he didn't have to. "You spoil me too much already," she had insisted. "I don't spoil you enough," he said, stroking her hair. His tenderness had a way of making her feel loved and undeserving of that love at the same time.

She pulled on her cotton robe and slippers. When she got to the kitchen door, she stopped and leaned against the door frame. Wyatt, in his gym shorts, T-shirt, and bare feet, was turning a piece of bacon in the skillet. His arms, a deep caramel from the summer sun, moved with confidence. He was as much at ease in front of the stove as he was a roomful of rowdy bar patrons, which made her love him all the more.

"Glad to see you up," he said when he noticed her standing in the doorway. "I was about to come get you. Breakfast is almost ready." He flipped another piece of bacon as a faint breeze came through the screen door. Kat noticed the table on the porch was set, and Luna was fast asleep beside it.

"It's such a pretty morning, I thought we'd eat outside," Wyatt said.

"Sounds wonderful." She gave him a quick kiss on the cheek. She pulled a mug from the cabinet—the blue one she had made when she was first learning to throw pottery. The sides were a bit uneven and the handle was slightly askew, but she was proud of the mug anyway. She poured coffee and cradled the mug in her hands, letting the earthy smell of the coffee drift upward.

"How was your gig last night?" she said.

"Okay." He shrugged.

"Just okay?"

"They had technical difficulties, so we were an hour late getting started—threw our whole set off. You'd think a place in Knoxville would be better equipped, but honestly, Smokey's does a much better job with live music than they did. Incompetence just pisses me off."

"I'm sorry it wasn't a good night for you." She set her mug on the counter and put her arms around his waist.

"Careful," he said, pushing the skillet to the back burner.

She pressed her cheek against his back. "The truth is, I wouldn't be disappointed if all of your gigs were closer to home. I miss you when you're gone." She squeezed him then let go.

He pulled the bacon out of the skillet and gave the pan a swift wipe with a paper towel. The eggs were already beaten, but he gave them another couple of whisks before pouring them into the skillet. "Would you grab the hot sauce out of the fridge?" he said, concentrating on moving the eggs around the skillet. "The butter and jam are already on the table."

Kat had never seen anyone put hot sauce on scrambled eggs before she met Wyatt. She pulled the bottle from the refrigerator, grabbed her coffee cup, and elbowed the screen door open. Luna, who lifted her head at the screeching of the door, thumped her tail on the deck.

"Good morning, girl," Kat said. Luna stood and rubbed against Kat, a happy tail beating against Kat's leg.

"Hey, babe," Wyatt called from the kitchen. "Can you come get the biscuits?"

Kat leaned inside the door. "Homemade?" she said as she grabbed the basket.

"Only for you," he said, and she knew again she didn't deserve him.

Wyatt was right behind her, carrying the bacon and eggs. As soon as she sat down, Kat grabbed a biscuit and pulled it apart, letting the steam rise. The butter began to melt as soon as she spread it.

"So how was the party last night?" Wyatt dotted his eggs with hot sauce.

Kat knew she would tell Wyatt about Jake and Molly, yet there was something deeply personal about what happened—what it meant to her—that made her want to keep it as hers alone.

She sipped her coffee. "It didn't go quite as planned."

"Really? What happened?" he said.

"Jake got pissed."

"Yeah, he seems like he's always mad about something." He bit off a piece of bacon.

"No, I mean he was *really* pissed. He knocked the cake onto the floor—with the candles still burning. Then he stormed out of Smokey's." She paused, reliving the moment as she looked out at the tall corn stalks shivering in the breeze. "He even shoved Molly out of the way before he drove off. He shoved her hard, Wyatt. I thought for sure he'd hurt her."

"She's okay, though?"

"Yeah. I took her home. I probably shouldn't have, but she insisted."

Wyatt shook his head. "Why was Jake so pissed?"

"He said he didn't want the party, but Molly went ahead anyway."

"Well, she does get a full head of steam sometimes." He pointed his fork in Kat's direction. "Like a bull in a china shop." His playful grin irritated Kat.

"She still shouldn't be treated like that."

"You know I didn't mean it that way." He reached across and took her hand. "Sometimes you're way too sensitive when it comes to Molly. You know, she's human, just like the rest of us."

"Of course she is." Kat could feel her defenses build and pulled her hand free. She had long ago separated Molly from Beth, had realized that Molly was not a stand-in for Beth. Yet Molly's impulsiveness reminded her so much of Beth that she felt she needed to protect her. "I see her flaws, too," she said. "But last night was different."

"I know how you feel about Molly, babe, but you have to admit that she brings it on herself sometimes."

She was surprised by his attitude. "That's really cruel. Jake didn't just push her. He shoved her against another car so hard she fell to the ground."

"Good god, that's terrible. Jake can be pissy sometimes, but I'd never peg him as the violent sort. I'm sure he didn't mean to hurt her. I bet he's embarrassed about the way he reacted."

"I wish you'd stop defending him."

"Oh hell, Kat, I'm not defending him. I just made an observation."

"An observation with a judgment." She looked down at Luna and threw her a piece of biscuit. "There's something else. She's pregnant." She looked back at Wyatt. "She said she was going to tell Jake at the party, before he stormed out. I think she ended up telling him after I took her home. I'm not sure how he's going to take the news—which is why I'm going to check on her this afternoon."

"You need to leave them alone. It's between the two of them to work out. Besides, she's not your child or your responsibility. She's a grown ass woman and you need to let her be one."

"That's not fair. It's just that after last night—"

"You're worried."

Kat nodded.

"Look, I'm sure there's nothing to be worried about," he said, corralling some eggs onto his fork. "Jake's a bit weird, but I bet he'll be excited about being a dad. I know I would be." Wyatt wasn't looking at her, but Kat knew he was forcing himself not to. He had been talking for a year about wanting a family, mostly in vague ways—though she knew what he meant every time. Once, he came right out and said he wanted a child. She told him she couldn't consider it, that it would feel like a betrayal of her daughters if she had another baby. He said he understood, but she knew it wasn't the truth.

She sighed. "Please don't—"

"Goddamn it, Kat," he said, slinging his napkin onto the table. "That wasn't meant as a dig at you. I'm so tired of stepping on eggshells anytime the word 'baby' is mentioned. You said you don't want another baby and I've accepted that. But, damn it, I can't help the way I feel about wanting one of my own." He pushed his plate away and stood. "I'm going for a smoke." He pulled a cigarette pack from his pocket, tapping the pack until a cigarette came out.

He headed down the path to the river, Luna by his side and smoke trailing over his shoulder. His head jerked, as if he was muttering to himself, while he stomped through the grass and disappeared through the trees. Kat should have expected his moodiness, which sometimes came after a bad gig. When he was in that kind of mood, he seemed to mistake everything she said for her being oversensitive.

Kat got up from the table and stood at the porch rail. The thin clouds above the mountains, whose white tendrils stretched toward one another, reminded Kat of Michelangelo's *Creation of Adam*. On clear summer mornings like this, before the heat of the day became oppressive, she and

Wyatt would drink their coffee on the porch, maybe read the paper or listen to gospel music on the radio. Summer had passed in such a slow, pleasant way that she had taken for granted the life she had built here with Wyatt. She had promised herself she wouldn't do that. But seeing the tension between Molly and Jake mirrored at her own breakfast table made her realize that's what she had done.

She shook her head, chastising herself, and began clearing the breakfast dishes. The clink of the plates as she stacked them seemed to reverberate off the mountain, and Kat wondered if Wyatt heard it. Maybe Luna would drag him back, since she loved getting a few scraps from the table as a treat. Yet, it wasn't until Kat was washing dishes that she saw Wyatt strolling toward the house. The river appeared to have its usual calming effect, as Wyatt was laughing and throwing a stick for Luna to fetch.

"It's already getting sticky out there," Wyatt said when he came in the door. "I'm going to take a shower." His voice didn't have any anger left in it, but he still threw his cigarette pack and lighter on the kitchen table before disappearing through the door to the living room. As Kat finished washing the final plate, Luna sat at the edge of the cabinet, her eyes still anticipating a crumb that might drop on the floor.

"I didn't forget about you, girl," Kat said. She listened for the sound of the shower. When she heard it, she lifted a paper towel with a couple of strips of bacon and biscuits on it. Luna jumped up, her whole hind end wagging as Kat carried the treats to the back porch.

"You better eat out here," she said. "I just swept the kitchen floor." She watched Luna scarf down the food in a few quick bites. When the big chunks were gone, Luna began licking the crumbs from the deck floor. "I'm glad someone is enjoying breakfast this morning," Kat said before going inside.

Wyatt's baritone carried through the house as he sang in the shower. Kat paused at the bedroom door, listening to the sensuous tones of his voice. From the first time she saw him at Smokey's, Wyatt had awakened a desire in her she had rarely felt before. She remembered the sway of his body and the curve of his hips. Whatever else happened between them, passion was always their way back to each other. When Kat opened the bathroom door, steam billowed past her like a ghost. She slipped off her robe and hung it on the back of the door. She let her gown and panties drop into a soft puddle on the floor and eased the shower curtain back. Wyatt, just rinsing the shampoo from his head, slung his hair back and looked at her.

"You joining me?" Hints of suds were streaming down his chest. He moved aside, reinforcing the invitation.

Kat stepped into the tub and brushed past him until the hot water cascaded over her head and down her body. She turned back to Wyatt and pulled him to her. When she pressed her body against his and let her hands follow the curve of his ass, she felt his response. She searched his lips for the forgiveness she knew she would find there. He pressed his lips hard against hers, as if he feared she would evaporate with the steam. He reached behind her and turned off the water, then backed her up against the cool tile. He kissed her neck and down her shoulder before finding her mouth again.

"Let's take this to the bed," she said. Wyatt pulled the shower curtain back and stepped out of the tub, still holding her hand. She followed him to the bed, where he stretched out on the crumpled sheets. She stood a moment, remembering the first time she saw him naked, how the desire for him burned through her, a fire out of control. But she had been awkward, knowing he was also seeing her naked for the first time, knowing he would see the effects of three full-term pregnancies on her body, now rounder and marked with soft pink scars. But he hadn't even noticed, whispering to her how beautiful she was. She grew into those words, into the confidence they brought, into the freedom she now felt in her own body.

The gauze curtains fluttered from the faint breeze and cast a yellow square of light on the bed and across Wyatt's chest. She slipped on top of him, raising her body into the sunlight. Water dripped from her hair down her back and over her breasts. Wyatt cupped her breasts then raised up to move his mouth over them. He lay back down and Kat moved her body with his, until their breathing became a syncopated rhythm, until she felt him release inside her. She leaned toward him, kissing him between his rapid breaths. He rolled her over and moved his hand between her thighs. She let the cool air tingle against her body as the thrill of his touch rose to completion.

Wyatt kissed her, then lay back against his pillow. "You have no idea the kind of power you have over me," he said. He had said it before, and she had always taken it as playful banter, but now she wasn't as sure.

He sat up, threw his legs over the side of the bed, and sat there for a second. She watched the yellow shadows play on his back. Finally, he stood up and found his gym shorts on the floor. He didn't seem angry when he put them on, but he walked out of the room without looking back at her. She didn't know if she should follow him, but when she heard the screen door bang shut, she got up and pulled the cotton robe around her naked body.

Wyatt was sitting on the porch steps, Luna's head nudged between his knees and resting on his leg. Kat sat down beside Wyatt and touched Luna's head. The dog licked her hand then nudged Kat to keep petting.

"Are we okay?" Kat finally said.

"Yeah," Wyatt said, staring into the yard and still mindlessly stroking Luna.

"You sure? You're kind of freezing me out."

"I just get frustrated sometimes." He put his hand on top of hers but didn't look at her. "Sometimes I feel there's a gulf between us—like I'm not free to speak my mind and at the same time like sometimes you're intentionally keeping things tucked away from me." He looked at her. "I just want an honest relationship with you."

She laced her fingers in his and laid her head on his shoulder. "I never want you to feel we can't talk about anything." The words, no matter how sincere they were, felt hollow in her mouth.

17

THE AFTERNOON SUN HUNG JUST LOW ENOUGH to blind Kat. She pulled the visor down but still had to use her hand to block the sun. Molly had sounded fine on the phone, in fact had said she didn't want Kat to come. But Kat was determined to go anyway. She didn't tell Wyatt that part when she said she was going to Molly's. He was already aggravated enough that she was going, and he was likely to accuse her again of obsessing over Molly. It never occurred to her that she was.

Kat was relieved that Jake's car wasn't in the driveway. Molly said Jake would be at his studio to finish a painting, but Kat had still been nervous about running into him. She was probably making too much of last night. The scene replayed in her mind countless times, each time focusing on a different sequence. Jake's face when he came into the bar had been free of visible emotion, but had she really detected the slightest bit of anger in his eyes? Molly pulling out the ridiculous party hat and letting the elastic band snap under Jake's chin. Were Jake's lips pulled tight with rage or was he getting ready to blow out the candles? She wasn't sure.

But the cake hitting the floor and the shove in the parking lot. She hadn't mistaken those bursts of anger. She *had* seen Jake's arm jerk forward just before Molly stumbled back against the car, and she *had* heard the thud as his hand struck Molly's chest and the involuntary discharge of air that came from Molly at impact. Neither Wyatt nor Molly would be able to convince her that she was worrying for nothing after she witnessed that. Maybe she was meddling where she didn't belong. Maybe there was nothing she could do to fix this. But she had been forced to relinquish her anxiety when Beth was in danger, even by Beth herself. She would not let that be done to her again.

Before getting out of the car, Kat stared at the house, which always looked smaller in the daylight. They had only lived there a couple of months. She had been to the house a few times, to pick Molly up or drop her off, since Molly never seemed to have use of her and Jake's only car. But Kat had never actually been inside Molly's house—Molly seemed to always have an excuse for not inviting her in. It was a slight brick ranch built into a hillside, with scrawny shrubs under the picture window. Even though it was farther from Jake's new studio than their apartment at Rusty's was, it was also farther from Rusty, and that's what Jake wanted. Kat figured that the rent for the house was more than for the apartment, but that was one place she was not willing to meddle.

The yard was a bit overgrown, and she remembered Molly saying something about saving up to buy a push mower. Kat wondered if she should ask Wyatt to mow it for them, but she knew Jake would think he was being treated like a charity case. Kat climbed the three steps to the small porch, careful to avoid the missing chunk of concrete on the second step. The front door was open, so Kat knocked on the metal frame of the screen door. When no one answered, she opened the door and poked her head in.

"Molly?"

"Be there in a minute," she called from down the hallway. "Come on in."

Kat stepped in and looked around the room. The curtains on both windows were drawn, making it much darker than it should have been on a sunny afternoon. A lamp on the end table beside a recliner and a floor lamp in the corner were both lit, which gave the room an artificial yellow glow. Behind the recliner hung a painting of Molly, and she moved closer to it. Kat studied it. She was struck by the hair that fell over one eye so that the eye was obscured beneath the swath of orange-red strands. The other eye stared from the canvas in a way that was both inviting and defiant at the same time. The closed mouth, with full lips that echoed the color of the hair, was parted just enough to give the impression they were keeping some secret—or maybe ready to reveal it. A hand, fingers extended and lightly touching the bare neck, held tension in it but was also oddly relaxed. The painting was filled with contradictions of light and dark.

"You like it?" Molly said, as she came up beside Kat. She was wearing gray sweatpants and a Fleetwood Mac T-shirt.

"It's beautiful. One of Jake's?"

"He painted it last year."

"He's truly talented," Kat said.

"I've always thought so." She motioned for Kat to sit on the couch. "I was going to get me some tea. Want some?"

"Sure, if it's no trouble." The Southern manners slipped out of her mouth as a matter of instinct. Kat sat on the couch, something her Grandma Turner would have loved, with big red and pink flowers.

"You know, you didn't have to come today," Molly said from the kitchen.

"I know. I appreciate you indulging me."

"Not that you gave me much choice," Molly said as she came into the living room with a couple of glasses in her hand, the ice clinking as she walked. "It's sweet tea. I hope that's okay."

"No other way for us Southern girls to drink it." Kat took the glass from Molly and took a sip of tea. She searched for a coaster on the end table but set the glass on the bare wood when she couldn't find one.

Molly set her glass down on the table by the recliner and plopped down, sitting crisscross style. She didn't seem to be in any pain from the night before.

Kat cleared her throat. "I know you said on the phone that you are okay, but—"

"I *am* okay." Molly leaned forward. "Damn it, Kat, I love you like a sister, but you really have to stop hovering over me." She pulled her hair back like she was making a ponytail, twisted it, let it fall, then twisted it again. Molly's unconscious habit of playing with her hair always flustered Kat. Beth had the same habit.

"That's what Wyatt tells me." Kat shifted in her seat and picked up the glass to give her hands something to do.

"Well, he's a smart man. You should listen to him." Molly fell back in the chair again.

"But Jake—"

"Jake and I are *fine*—just like I told you we would be. Last night just got a little out of hand, that's all. Jake told me for days he didn't want a party and, well, you know me, I was hell bent on making a fuss over his thirtieth birthday anyway."

"But he didn't have to—"

Molly put up her hand. "Just stop. I won't listen to anything bad about Jake, not even from you. He told me he was sorry about the way he acted and promised he'd never do it again—and I believe him. So, you either drop this subject or you can leave."

Kat had never heard Molly be so forceful, and she sat in stunned silence. She took a drink of tea and set the glass on the end table.

"That's pretty," Kat finally said, pointing to a pastel green woven blanket lying across the arm of the recliner.

Molly picked it up and laid it in her lap. "Jake got it for me this morning. Slipped out after I went back to sleep and went over to Geneva's as soon as the store was open. He wanted to be the first to get the baby a gift." She rubbed it against her cheek then looked at Kat. "That's the real Jake, you know. He's more thoughtful than you give him credit for."

Kat nodded, as if she agreed with Molly, but it sounded like Molly was trying to convince herself. "He's happy about the baby, then?"

"He is. We both are. It wasn't planned or anything, so I'm a little worried about the finances. You know, one more mouth to feed."

"But Jake's studio—"

"It's taken longer to get off the ground than he hoped."

"An artist's life is hard, even one as talented as Jake." She motioned to the painting above Molly's head. "That's why Wyatt does construction work, too."

"Jake wants to devote himself to his art. Honestly, I think my dad's comments keep rolling around in his head. He's determined to prove to my dad that being an artist is a *real* job." She set her glass on the end table and leaned forward. "Damn, if marriage isn't harder than I thought it would be. I mean, I didn't expect it to be Ozzie and Harriet or anything, but I guess I thought it would be—"

"More spontaneous?"

"That was my word, wasn't it?" She laughed and leaned back in her chair. "Back then, I thought it was romantic following Jake on his adventure."

"But now?"

"It's still an adventure—just not the one I thought it'd be." Molly wiped a tear from her cheek. "Damn these pregnancy hormones. My emotions are all over the place."

Kat smiled. "I remember those days—and the morning sickness. I didn't have much with Jenny and Kris, but with Lizzie I was sick all day. I lived on saltines and 7Up."

Molly held up a couple of crackers. "I know what you mean. These are saving me right now."

Kat picked up her tea again and clutched it with both hands, but the ice jingled no matter how tightly she held the glass.

"Kat?"

"Huh?" Kat realized she had become lost in thought. "Oh, sorry. Sometimes the memories are just so painful. They remind me of how much I've lost."

"I still don't understand why you just don't go to Lexington—just show up there. If it was me, I'd be banging David's door down."

"Well, it's not you," Kat snapped back. She was immediately sorry and calmed her voice. "I can't just show up, since I'm the one who chose to leave."

Molly leaned forward again. "You chose to leave because he made you."

"And who knows what he's told them about me. I'm sure they hate me by now."

Molly scooted forward in the recliner and put her feet on the floor. She leaned far forward now. "We're friends, Kat, and you know I love you, but if you're not going to do something about your situation then you have got to stop this pity party of yours."

The words plunged deep, and Kat stared at Molly, trying to decide if she was going to say anything in response. "I think I'd better go," she finally said as she stood up.

Molly rose to her feet as well. "I'm sorry, Kat. I didn't mean to hurt your feelings."

When Kat got to the door, she paused. "I came here because I was worried about you. I can see now that you're alright."

Out in the hot August sun, Kat took a moment to breathe in the humid air. If the words had come from anyone else, even Wyatt, they wouldn't have hurt so much. But coming from Molly, it was as if Beth was speaking from the grave. Kat shook her head. She had to stop comparing Molly to Beth—and she had to stop wearing her feelings on her sleeve. Just as it was back home, her grief—this time for her children—made people uncomfortable.

She looked back at the house, and Molly had closed the front door. Kat took one more deep breath, and headed to her car. She froze when Jake's dark blue Pontiac pulled into the driveway. The car stopped behind hers then swerved into the grass beside it.

"Hey, Kat," he said as he got out of the car. He looked toward the house. "What are you doing here?"

She stuffed her hand in her pocket to hide its tremble. "Just visiting my friend."

"I guess she told you the good news." A smile spread across his face then disappeared.

Kat nodded. She wasn't going to let him know that Molly had told her last night before even telling Jake.

"Look, Kat, about last night—"

"It's okay," she said. "It was a little tense there for a minute, but I've already forgotten about it."

"Good," he said. Kat wondered if his tone was harsher than he meant it to be. "It was just a bad night."

"No problem." She edged toward her car, fumbling for her keys in her purse. "Well, I really need to go. Lots of errands to run. Good seeing you, though, Jake."

As soon as she was inside her car, she exhaled the breath she didn't realize she'd been holding and gave him a hesitant wave. As she backed out of the driveway, she kept an eye on Jake, who stayed rooted where he stood.

18

My dear Kat,

So much has been happening here that it's been hard to find time to write. They tell us the peace talks are progressing, and that Kissinger is in Paris to supposedly hammer out the final details. Since I'm not an eternal optimist like you, I'll believe it when I fucking see it. In the meantime, the war marches on here. So, our routine is pretty much the same. Lots of visits to refugee camps and villages, as well as our work at the clinic.

Hey, do you remember Gian, the boy I mentioned in my first letter? Well, he's back with his family now and doing so well. It was bitter-sweet sending him home—such a precious boy. When he was at the clinic, he was usually up at dawn and trailing behind Carrie or me, wanting to know what he could do to help. It didn't matter what it was. He especially liked to sweep, even though the broom was about twice as tall as him. It was the funniest and sweetest thing I've seen in a long time. I know he's back where he should be—where he needs to be—but I sure do miss that boy.

Probably the biggest news in the last two weeks was the arrival of a French doctor and nurse. Marjorie, that's the nurse, is bunking with Carrie and me at the clinic. She has deep brown eyes and dark, dark hair that curls over her shoulders, when she doesn't have it pinned up for work. I probably make her uncomfortable, staring at her so much, but, damn, she is beautiful. I will say that her nursing skills are as good as her looks, so we're lucky to have her on the team.

Dr. Pascale is the French doctor. If Marjorie is beautiful, he is drop dead gorgeous. His eyes sparkle when he smiles. Oh, hell. This is starting to sound like a romance novel. Anyway, I knew I wanted to fuck him the minute I saw him.

A few nights ago, some of us went to a restaurant near here, and I noticed Emile—that's Dr. Pascale—was watching me all night. Besides being gorgeous, he's really a fascinating man. He told us he'd come to Vietnam as a small way of making amends for his family's part in the decades of French colonization of the country—his grandfather fought in the Franco-Siamese War. Oppression of the colonizers, he called it. (I knew there was a reason I liked him.) He said his mother was furious at him for coming here, a sign of disrespect for her father, she thought. I imagine she was even more upset when he basically told her to fuck off—not that he literally said that to his mother, I'm guessing. It took him two more days to invite me to his room. The doctors get their own rooms. You know that I've fucked a lot of men, Kat, and enjoyed every minute of it, but it was different with Emile. It wasn't just that the sex was amazing (and it was), it was that I felt emotionally connected to him. If I was a giddy schoolgirl, I'm sure I'd be drawing hearts in a diary and declaring that he's the one. But you know me too well to hear something like that ever come out of my mouth. No man is ever going to tie me down. So, Emile will almost certainly be a footnote—a damn great one—for my experiences here in Vietnam—one that will always bring a knowing smile to my face and a tingle in all the right places, if you know what I mean. Whew! Just thinking about it makes me hot!

Now that I'm sure you're blushing (you never could take me talking about my encounters with men), just know that I miss seeing that face of yours turn beet red. I do miss you and everyone in the family so much. But I'll be home before you know it.

And don't you dare show this letter to my mother or my brother. Haha.

Lots of love,
Beth

19

GATLINBURG WAS HOME TO SOME THREE THOUSAND PEOPLE, but as a tourist town, it was not the usual small town. It was never truly quiet, never devoid of strangers. The big rush always came on the weekends. From Friday afternoon until Sunday just after the lunch rush, the sidewalks were crammed with people strolling on either side of the main street, stopping to sample fudge or watch a machine stretch and fold taffy, or to buy handcrafted wooden signs or souvenir T-shirts. Some people were there to seek adventure—viewing the town from the space needle, seeing the oddities in Ripley's Believe It or Not!, playing in the arcade, or hiking in the mountains. Some people were there to relax—hang out in a cabin up in the mountains, drive through the national park, or take in one of the shows. Whatever the reason, they were there by the thousands.

The locals, at least those not working in the stores and attractions, stayed clear of the town on the weekends. If they needed anything, they traveled the roads that wound through the mountains rather than become entangled in the traffic that inched along the main road through town. Kat was used to city traffic, but the two miles of the Parkway on the weekends was worse than most big cities.

In her mind, Kat justified her visit with Molly by arguing that she and Wyatt would miss the biggest part of the crowds when they went into town. She didn't say this directly to Wyatt, though he did seem to be in a better mood when she returned from the visit. Their first stop in town was always for a funnel cake, no matter what time of day, which usually ended with confectioners' sugar sprinkled down their shirts or smeared on their shorts or jeans. The funnel cake was usually followed by some kind of activity—Ripley's, the chair lift, or Hillbilly Golf. Hillbilly Golf was their favorite—riding the incline up to the first hole, then playing their way through tractors and moonshine stills. Wyatt usually won, but Kat made sure to gloat when she did pull off a victory.

This Sunday was no different. Funnel cake then Hillbilly Golf. Whatever tension had passed between them in the morning had dissipated. Wyatt teased her when her golf ball sailed over the bumpers on one of the holes and landed in some brush, forcing him to fish it out for her. "Too dainty to get a little dirt under your nails, huh?" he said, handing her the bright yellow ball. And when she was trying to putt through a miniature barn, he snuck up behind her and goosed her in the ribs. "Stop it," she pushed back at him, smacking him playfully on the arm. This was the core of them together. Arguments, when they did happen, passed quickly, replaced by spirited banter and flirtatious touches. They didn't care who saw them flirt and touch each other, not inappropriately, but more intimate than most people seemed comfortable seeing. It was a freedom Kat had never allowed herself—not caring what someone might think or how they might judge her. She decided that she liked this, that she was more like Beth than she had ever dared to be.

After they finished miniature golf and rode the incline back down the hill, they walked to the main strip. They passed a door that advertised psychic readings. Wyatt said she should get a reading, mainly because he knew she wouldn't. In her strict religious upbringing, such things were taboo. Yet even if it hadn't been, she wouldn't have been ready for something so penetrating.

Even though dozens of restaurants lined the main street, Kat and Wyatt always seemed to end up at the Pancake Pantry, if they managed to get there before closing. In the mornings, the line to get into the restaurant often stretched a half a block or more. But right before closing, they could almost always get seated quickly. Kat ordered the Swedish crepes with sausage links, Wyatt the ham and eggs.

"I've been trying to figure out why you obsess over Molly the way you do," Wyatt said after the waitress took their orders. "Is it because of Beth?" The question startled Kat. He must have been thinking on it all day.

"I guess that's part of it," she said, unwrapping the silverware and laying the napkin across her lap. "I guess I felt so helpless when Beth was in Vietnam that maybe sometimes I'm overprotective with Molly."

He leaned forward, rubbing his finger across his chin. "That makes sense."

The waitress came by and poured coffee in their mugs. "Your order will be up soon," she said. Wyatt shook a couple of sugar packets before ripping them open and pouring them into his coffee.

"Tell me something about Beth that's funny," he said after he took a sip of the coffee.

"Something funny?" she said, puzzled.

"Yeah, something funny. When I catch you reading one of her letters, you always seem so miserable. Even when you talk about her, it's always sad. Surely there's something about her that made you laugh."

"Oh gosh, yes," she said. "She was such a free spirit. Didn't care what anyone thought of her, including me." She leaned forward. "I didn't like her at first. She was loud and opinionated and brash—everything that I wasn't. But I grew to like her—not in spite of all those things, but strangely because of them. Don't get me wrong. Sometimes she would infuriate me—her strong opinions about the war and politics. But just when I thought I couldn't stand it, she'd do something that was so outrageous—or she'd drag me into something so outrageous—that I couldn't help but like her."

She looked across at Wyatt and he was smiling at her. The waitress brought the food to the table and left the check. As soon as the woman left, Wyatt's gaze encouraged Kat to continue.

"One time, before David and I were married, she came to my house wanting to go out. I was studying for a big exam and tried to beg off, but she wouldn't hear of it. She wanted to go shopping, which should have been my first clue that she was up to something." She laughed. She could see Beth, in her braids that tumbled over her breasts, the blue jeans and suede jacket, fringe dangling from the sleeves, the brown beads looped around her neck. "She dragged me to this shop near campus, one I'd never been to before—and for good reason. As soon as I walked in, and the smell of incense burned in my nose, I could tell I was in trouble. 'Back here, Mary Catherine,' she said as she led me to a rack of clothes. 'We're going to find a righteous outfit.'"

"Did she really say 'righteous outfit'?"

"She did," Kat nodded. "And that's not even the most outrageous thing she ever said. So anyway, she pulls this extremely short dress off the rack—big orange flowers all over it." Kat held out her hands to illustrate how big they were. "Then she found some moccasin boots—you know, the kind with the fringe on them—and a big floppy hat. I think it was pale pink and had some kind of flowers in the band. And I'm thinking that she's going to try them on, so I get ready to sit on this stool but, no, she hands the clothes to me. 'Go try them on,' she says. Of course, I protested, but there was no arguing with her—at least no winning. So, I go into this dressing area—not a dressing room, mind you, just a little alcove, no curtain or anything—and I'm trying to maintain some sense of modesty while changing into these ridiculous clothes Beth has picked out. Then I move out into the dim light, feeling completely silly. Beth has this very serious look on her face then lets out a long whistle. 'You are one cool cat,' she says. There's a brief moment of dead silence, and then we both busted up laughing. I laughed so hard I thought I was going to wet myself." She paused briefly, as if she was calculating something in her head. "You know, I think it was after that she started calling me Kat."

When she picked up her fork to cut into the crepe, she realized she had barely taken a breath during the whole story.

"Your whole face lights up when you talk about her like that," Wyatt said, finishing off his last bite of ham.

She wondered why she hadn't talked about Beth more often, why she'd been hoarding memories of her. Was she afraid of the pain the memories might bring? Or was she afraid of sharing Beth with anyone else? Was she afraid that doing so would somehow dilute the memories— making them less hers alone?

"I do need to talk about her more often," she said. "Sometimes I forget that telling her story is the thing that keeps her alive."

Kat took a bite of crepe, letting the tartness of the lingonberry butter rest on her tongue until it mingled with the sweet crepe.

Pottery was on Kat's mind the next morning when she waved to Wyatt as he backed down the driveway. Today Pony was loading his kiln and Kat knew she could add the pieces she'd been drying. She loaded them carefully into a couple of carboard boxes, tucking bubble wrap and old newspapers around each piece to buffer them during transport.

When she pulled into the alley behind Pony's studio, she saw that the back door was open. She could see Pony, his wavy locks concealed under a blue bandana, hunched over the kiln. He didn't seem to notice she had pulled up. Sometimes he was like that—so focused on his work that he was oblivious to anything around him. But by the time she had opened the hatch and lifted one of the boxes out of the car, he was beside her.

"Got something for the kiln?" he asked.

"Four pieces. Nice and dry."

"Perfect timing," he said. "I was just starting to load." He took the box from her, and she followed him inside. He lifted a bowl out of the box, carefully removing the protective wrapping. She watched him turn the bowl around in his hand—running his finger lightly along the foot, deftly testing the thickness of its sides, looking for tiny imperfections. She held her breath waiting for his assessment, even though she had never known him to be unkind. "This is good, Kat," he said. "Your technique is really improving."

"I had an excellent teacher."

"Okay, pupil, those vases over there are ready for glazing, if you have the time." He motioned to a shelf with a half dozen of her vases that had already been fired once. She nodded and turned on the pan of wax to warm. It would be a relief to focus on the pottery for a while, to pull herself out of the heaviness that lingered from her conversation with Molly the day before. While Pony loaded the kiln, she found the bucket of blue glaze—her favorite because it reminded her of the winter sky—pulled it to the table and opened the lid. She stirred the glaze, reaching her hand deep into the bucket to pull up the thick clumps that had settled to the bottom.

Sometimes Kat would glance at Pony, who was steadily loading the kiln, while she dipped the bottom of each vase onto the wax. Both remained quiet. Pony seemed to know when Kat wanted to talk and when she wanted to be left to her thoughts. She figured he probably learned that from years of marriage.

"How long did you say you and Gretchen were married, before she passed?" The question was abrupt, but Pony seemed used to being thrown into the middle of her musings.

"Twenty-two years."

"Were they good years—happy, I mean?" She dipped the first vase into the glaze, swishing it around to let the glaze coat the inside as well as the outside. When she pulled it out, she set it on the board that would eventually be placed back on the shelf.

"Oh, like every marriage, there were hard times—times we didn't want to be in the same room together." He stopped and stared into the distance. "But, yes, they were happy."

"No regrets?"

He closed the door to the kiln and checked the temperature. He had told her many times that the temperature determined how the pottery matured. Too low and it will remain porous. Too high and it will become brittle. The same could be said for the amount of time the pottery was subjected to the heat. "I try not to live with regrets," he said, turning to her. "Regrets get you stuck in a past you can't do anything about. So, I just try to enjoy this moment—you know, the now."

Kat lowered the next vase into the glaze. "That would be nice, to live that way." Her voice carried the weight not just of the past couple of days, but of years of regret. "There are so many mistakes I've made that I wish I could undo."

"But you can't undo them, can you?" Pony pulled a couple of mugs, already glazed, from the shelf and sat across from her. "Of course, that doesn't mean there aren't some mistakes you can correct—in the present, in the 'now.'" He inspected one of the mugs. "Ah, a fingerprint. What will I do?" He grinned.

She sighed. "Lightly sand out the blemish," she said, repeating what he had taught her.

"Most of the time that works. Not always, but most of the time." He rubbed the sandpaper gently over the rounded edge of the mug, holding it up occasionally under the fluorescent light before resuming the gentle strokes of the sandpaper.

She lifted the final vase out of the glaze, watching the dark teal drops fall back into the bucket. She placed the vase with the others on the board. Tomorrow they'd be ready to be fired in the kiln.

20

KAT MADE SURE WYATT WAS GONE before she climbed out of bed and slid the drugstore bag from underneath her nightgowns in the dresser drawer. She had wrapped the bag carefully around the contents, as if she was shielding what it contained even from herself. The plastic bag crinkled when she slowly unrolled it and lifted out the yellowish-tan box. She stared at the *e.p.t* on the front of the box. Her finger traced the letters, lingering on the *p*.

P for pregnancy.

She tried to convince herself that she wasn't pregnant, that it was stress or maybe something else that had caused her to miss her period. When she opened the box, her hands felt weighted down as she pulled out the clear plastic rectangle and then separated the test tube, medicine dropper, and plastic vial from it. With her other pregnancies, she had no other choice but to wait for a phone call from the doctor's office. But back then there had been nothing for her to be ashamed of, except for the first time the test came back positive, before she and David were married, when the doctor had looked up from the chart with disapproval in his eyes. At least she thought it was disapproval anyway. Maybe she had only imagined it. Maybe she just saw what she expected to find there.

This time was different—even if she and Wyatt weren't married. Being an unwed mother didn't carry the stigma it did back then, though in a small town it would certainly still stir plenty of gossip. But people had been gossiping about her and Wyatt for a while anyway, so a little more gossip wouldn't make a difference. Yet it wasn't the potential for gossip that caused her hands to shake as she squeezed drops of her pee from the medicine dropper into the test tube. She had been adamant with Wyatt that she wouldn't have another baby now. She couldn't. Not if her other children couldn't be with her. She had been careful, so how could she have let this happen?

She added the contents of the plastic vial into the tube and shook it before settling it into the holder. Two hours. The directions indicated that she would know in two hours—all she had to do was wait. She leaned against the sink, resting her hands a moment to steady herself. She turned the faucet enough for a small stream of water to wiggle its way to the basin below. Her hands broke the stream, and she splashed the cool water on her face, careful not to disturb the test tube perched nearby. She raised her face to the mirror, trying to find the woman she remembered, the one who used to find joy in everything. Instead, she only found the worry lines that formed on her forehead.

She sighed and pulled on her chenille robe and slippers, turning off the bathroom light behind her. She poured herself a cup of coffee and settled on the couch, pulling her legs up under her. The remote was on the coffee table, so she turned on the television. Maybe Jane Pauley or Bryant Gumbel would keep her distracted. But the conversation was about the Tylenol deaths in Chicago and the ongoing investigation. With her nerves already on edge, Kat didn't need to be hearing about some unknown crazy person tampering with medicine bottles. She turned off the television and went to the front window. She took a sip of coffee and let it warm her.

Autumn had not yet settled in the valley, though hints of reds and yellows were visible high on the mountainsides. The early days of

October had been cool, but the forecast predicted summer-like heat for the following week. Today, though, was cold with a steady rain, which tapped against the window like an old-fashioned typewriter. On most days, the sound would have been soothing to Kat, who loved to sit on the back porch, even on a cool day, and listen to the rain falling through the trees or dripping from the eaves. But this morning, the sound was more like the grandfather clock in Grandma Turner's entry hall—a reminder that time would always move at its own pace.

Time had certainly played with Kat. Nearly nine years since Beth was killed. Three years since she'd seen her girls. Two years since she moved in with Wyatt. Everything measured in years. Why, then, did it feel like days, even hours, since her life began to collapse under the weight of her grief and guilt? And now, a pregnancy would further complicate the mess she'd already made of her life.

Luna was asleep on the recliner, her favorite spot, and had not moved even when Kat turned on the television. The living room was muted without the sun coming through the window. Kat scanned the room and saw the familiar objects. The vase she finished at the end of the summer, orange on the top fading into forest green, sunset over the mountain. The basket of pinecones she had collected when she first moved to Gatlinburg. The picture of the girls in the wading pool, now framed and nestled under the lamp on the end table. Beth's letters, tied together with a blue ribbon, safe inside the leather box Wyatt had given her last Christmas just for that purpose.

She *did* have a life here, she realized. How easy it was to forget that, to wallow in her guilt, just as Molly had said. How easy it was to believe she would never again deserve to be happy. Wyatt tried to convince her that there was nothing wrong with her being happy, and sometimes she believed him. Maybe she was wrong to deny him a baby. Maybe if she was pregnant, it was God's way of allowing her to make atonement. Or maybe God was testing her, adding another baby to make the absence of her daughters more acute. Kat wondered if the rest of her life would be caught somewhere between redemption and suffering, and she couldn't bear the thought of it. She wanted to cry, but she was tired of crying. Instead, she eased back onto the couch and pulled the afghan Wyatt's grandmother had made around her. She watched Luna sleep, watched the steady rhythm of her breathing, watched the occasional twitch of her paw. She wished she could be so relaxed.

When the two hours had finally ticked by, Kat rose from the couch and folded the afghan, her movements slow and deliberate. Luna lifted her head but didn't follow Kat into the bedroom. Even before she flipped on the bathroom light and saw the dark brown circle at the bottom of the tube, meaning she was pregnant, she knew it would be there. What she didn't know was what she was going to do about it.

Even after a week, Kat was still unsure how she felt about the pregnancy. She hadn't told anyone—not Wyatt and not Molly. At first, she justified it because she hadn't confirmed the results with the doctor. Then, when his office called to tell her the test result was positive, she convinced herself that maybe it was too soon to tell anyone. So much could happen in the first few weeks. Kat knew that keeping the secret from Wyatt would be a challenge. Then Molly asked her for a ride into Sevierville to look for a cradle.

Kat had agreed to go, although she probably could have come up with a hundred excuses not to, but ever since Jake's birthday party, Kat needed to be with Molly whenever she could, needed to scrutinize her appearance or dissect her words, despite assurances that everything was fine. Would there be any signs that Jake had lost control again? Perhaps Kat was being overprotective, as Wyatt believed she was, or perhaps she was overreacting, as Molly insisted she was, but she couldn't get the image of Jake's shove out of her mind.

Sitting in the driveway, Kat waited for Molly to come bounding down the porch steps. Kat noticed that Molly's stomach was finally beginning to show signs of a baby growing inside. Yet even before the bump in her belly was visible, Molly had been cradling it, a gesture Kat found reminiscent of her own pregnancies. Now, without being fully aware of it, Kat reached for her own stomach. There was a baby underneath her clothes, underneath her skin. The baby was little more than the size of a small berry, the pamphlet at the doctor's office read, but its heart had started beating—though it had no way of understanding that its mother's heart, beating close by, was desperately trying to wring out the wet, heavy burden of the betrayal she felt.

As soon as Molly stepped into the car, she rattled on about the cradle. She had seen a beautiful wooden cradle at Matt Hensley's store, but she couldn't afford it. She knew she wouldn't find anything as grand in the department store, but she hoped it would at least be pretty. She couldn't wait to see her baby in it, snuggled under the blanket Jake had bought at Geneva's.

Kat remembered the joy that was spilling out of Molly. She remembered looking for the perfect crib, remembered collecting cloth diapers in a neat white stack, remembered rinsing out bottles long before the baby would arrive. She remembered the anticipation of seeing fingers and toes, and counting them just to be sure. She thought about the baby inside her now. It was a part of her and Wyatt and whatever else might be roiling inside her, her heart now scraped against the joy that she remembered.

In the store, Molly wouldn't stay focused. Before she even made it to the baby furniture, she stopped when she saw a stuffed rabbit, its long ears drooping down the brown body and a white fluff of a tail on its back. She picked it up and squeezed it against her chest. When she said, "Isn't it so adorable," and held it out for Kat to take, Kat could only respond with a hurried yes.

"I believe the basinets are over here," Kat said and tried to lead her away. But Molly stopped again, this time at a pale blue sleeper with a mother and baby bunny on it.

"You can't tell me this isn't the cutest thing you've ever seen," Molly said, again thrusting it toward Kat. Kat's hesitancy to take it, to hold it in her hand, made Molly pause only for a moment. "I think I'll decorate the nursery in bunnies," she said, keeping both the stuffed rabbit and sleeper in her hands.

When they moved to the cradles, Kat was relieved that there were only two models to choose from. Molly was less likely to spend time adoring each one and slipping into sing-song about seeing her baby asleep in the rabbit-adorned sleeper. Kat wanted out of the baby section, out of the store. Every minute there, staring at cribs or sleepers or rattles, settled into Kat, pushing her one way and then another about her own pregnancy. She was tired of the uncertainty.

Kat could tell Molly wanted the wooden cradle, the one with a cherry finish and an arched headboard and rockers, because her eyes fell when she saw the price tag. The other one, white wicker with a plastic lining, looked cheap—like a little girl might have for her dolls. Kat saw the resignation as Molly pulled the box from the shelf. But by the time they got to the car, Molly's mood had changed. She grabbed the stuffed rabbit from the bag and nestled it against her neck. Sometimes Kat had to remind herself that Molly was still so young.

The October heatwave was as fierce as had been predicted, so they decided to stop at the Burger Pavilion for something cold before heading back to Gatlinburg. Kat rolled down the car windows as soon as they pulled into a drive-in slot.

"Two root beer floats, please," Kat said into the speaker.

"You've been acting strange all afternoon," Molly said. "What gives?"

"I don't know what you mean."

"Don't play coy with me, Kat. I know when something's bothering you."

"Sometimes I hate you," Kat said, a smile curling on her lips.

"I know." Molly laughed.

The sun curved across Kat's lap, and she watched a prism of light jump around on her pant leg as the silver of her wristwatch kept catching the sun. When Kat looked up, a young woman in a bright red T-shirt and jean shorts raced toward the car on her roller skates, somehow balancing a tray on one hand.

"Here are your floats, sweetie," the girl said when she stopped at the car window. Kat took the frosty mugs from the girl, handing one over to Molly, and gave the girl a few bills in exchange. The girl thanked her and skated away.

Kat picked the cherry off the whipped cream and popped it in her mouth, just like she did when she was a girl. Then she sucked the root beer and ice cream up into the straw and let the cold liquid linger in her mouth before swallowing.

"So, are you going to tell me or not?" Molly finally said.

Kat stared at the poster of a hot fudge sundae on the brick wall in front of the car. "I'm pregnant," she finally said.

"Pregnant? No wonder you've been preoccupied today in the baby section. Damn, I seem to always put you in this position."

"It's not your fault. I've just been so torn up since I found out. Sometimes I'm thrilled and then other times I'm just—"

"You're thinking about your girls."

"It's that obvious, huh?"

"It isn't that hard to figure out, hon. It's natural for you to be conflicted. But, honey, loving this baby won't take away any of the love you have for your girls."

Kat wished she could tell Molly the whole truth. Maybe then Molly would understand what was really at stake, why she had been so preoccupied for the whole time they'd known each other. At one time Molly might have accepted the truth, but now that Molly was expecting a baby in a few months, she would never forgive Kat—even if she knew that Kat couldn't forgive herself. No, Kat knew it was too late for truth-telling.

Molly leaned against the car door, making her belly appear rounder. "What does Wyatt say about it?"

Kat moved the straw up and down, gathering bits of ice cream along the sides of the straw, then licking it off—another habit from her childhood. "I haven't told him yet," she said, keeping her focus on the straw.

"You haven't told him yet? Why wouldn't you tell him?" Molly's voice rose uncharacteristically high. She leaned forward. "You're not thinking about—"

Kat shook her head firmly. "No. Absolutely not." She remembered making a similar response to Beth fourteen years before, when Kat was wrestling with another unexpected pregnancy. "I could never do that, especially since Wyatt has wanted a baby for a while now."

"So then why haven't you told him? It seems a bit selfish to keep the news from him."

Kat kept her gaze firmly on the ice cream at the bottom of the glass. If she had looked at Molly, she knew she would betray the hurt she once again felt from Molly's words. "I'll tell him in my own time" was all she could say, but she knew her voice still carried the hurt.

"Good God, Kat. I didn't mean anything by it."

Kat should have confronted Molly's comment more, but she didn't want a repeat of the last time they had a similar conversation. Maybe she should have pushed past the messy part of their friendship, to not skip over the parts where they would have screamed at each other. Maybe she should have been more willing to have a relationship like the one she had with Beth—when Beth would push and push until they were both red in the face before the tension finally collapsed into absurd laughter.

"Sorry," Kat said. "Guess I'm just moody today. Can I blame it on pregnancy hormones?"

"Well, you can, but then that would mean you've been pregnant ever since I've known you." Molly tried to hold back her laugh, but it coughed out of her anyway. Kat laughed so hard she nearly spewed root beer out of her mouth. It felt good to laugh like that again, especially with Molly.

On the way back to Gatlinburg, Kat kept the windows down and turned on the radio. "Up Where We Belong" was playing and she and Molly sang along, moving their arms in dramatic fashion. When they stopped at a red light and the woman in the car next to them looked at them like they were crazy, they broke out in laughter again.

"You know, if someone saw you this afternoon, I don't think they'd recognize you," Molly said when they turned into her driveway. She added quickly, "I meant that in a good way."

"I know." Kat unbuckled her seatbelt and stepped out of the car. She *did* know exactly what Molly meant. She had lived the last three years as if she had been trying to breathe underwater. Any urge to break through to the surface and fill her lungs with air had been overpowered by fear— fear that the only way to survive was to keep holding her breath. Even when her body had fought to breathe, even when she felt the blackness fill her mind, she had resisted finding a way to the surface. But now, she was finally ready to come up for air.

Kat stood by the car door and let the sun soak into her skin for a moment before moving to the back of the car. "I'll help you carry this inside," she said, as she lifted the cradle out.

"Excuse the mess," Molly said, as they navigated around shoes and boxes from the living room back to the nursery. "I was going to clean before you picked me up, but I ended up sleeping longer than I intended."

"I remember those days, when I was so tired I could barely keep my head upright," Kat said, pulling the cradle out of the box and unfolding the legs. "I see you're doing the nursery in green and yellow." She pointed to a baby quilt nailed to the wall like a picture.

"I guess I have to add bunnies now."

Kat moved closer to the quilt. "Did you get this at Geneva's, too?"

"LuAnn gave it to me—something she made, I think." Molly looked nervous, but Kat didn't know why.

"I had no idea LuAnn quilted like this. Look at the stitches, how tiny they are." When she lifted the corner of the quilt to check the backing—a good indicator of craftmanship—she saw only the edge of the hole at first. She lifted the quilt higher. Underneath, a round section of drywall had been punched back, the jagged edges of the hole white with dust. Kat looked at Molly. The question didn't need to be asked; it was already in Kat's eyes.

"I was trying to hang the quilt and slipped," Molly said. She laid the stuffed rabbit in the cradle, avoiding Kat's gaze as she did so.

"That's a lie, isn't it? It was Jake. He did this, didn't he?" The bottom of the quilt was now bunched in Kat's fist, but she loosened a finger to tap against the hole for emphasis.

"It was an accident," Molly said. Her eyes pleaded with Kat to stop the inquisition. "He wasn't trying to hit me. I don't think he was even trying to hit the wall—and he certainly didn't mean to hit it that hard."

"He shouldn't be hitting anything at all." Kat let the quilt drop from her hand, letting it fall back against the wall. She grabbed Molly's hand. "When are you going to stop making excuses for him, Molly?"

Molly yanked her hand free. "He doesn't mean it."

"He never means it, does he? No matter how often he does things like this—and I'm guessing he does it more often than you want to admit."

"Don't blame him. It was my fault. I was going on about the cradle in Matt's store, how beautiful it was, but how expensive it was. You know how I am."

"Molly, don't let him—"

The back door slammed, causing both women to startle.

"Goddamn it, Molly. I told you to get this mess cleaned up. Where the hell are you?" Something crashed in the kitchen, which made Kat jump again.

"Back here," Molly called, keeping her eyes on Kat. Her face grew pale.

"Honestly, woman, I don't know what you do all—" Jake stopped when he saw Kat. The tension in his jaw released. His voice changed, as if he was no longer the person who had charged his way down the hall. "Kat. I thought that was your car out front. What are you doing here?" He tried to lighten the tone in his voice.

Kat started to answer, but she saw him clench and unclench his fist. She noticed the bandage across his knuckles.

"We went to Sevierville to get a cradle," Molly said. "Remember, I told you we were going to do that today."

"Sure, sure," he said. He leaned his body against one side of the door frame but put one hand against the opposite side, his outstretched arm creating a barrier. "It's just that I expected the house to be clean when I got home." He was talking to Molly but he kept his gaze on Kat. He was watching her, as if he expected her to say something.

"I'll walk Kat to her car," Molly said as she stepped closer to Jake. She placed her hand on his chest. "Then I'll come back and get the house cleaned up." She nodded at Kat to come with her. At first, Jake didn't move, but then he let out a half laugh and dropped his arm. When Kat edged past Jake, she heard him whisper something, but she was relieved she didn't understand it. Once she was at the front door, she heard Jake pound the door frame before he slammed the bedroom door shut.

"Thank you for taking me today," Molly said as they stood by Kat's car.

The sun reflected off the hood of the car, and Kat raised her hand to shade her eyes. "You know you can always call on me," she said.

She wanted to say more. She wanted to gather Molly into her arms and beg her to leave. She wanted to load her onto a bus and send her back to her parents, anything to get her away from Jake. She knew Molly would never go—and certainly not to her parents. She had said before that she'd never go crawling back to her father, not after the way he'd treated Jake before they married.

"Molly, I'm afraid for you," Kat whispered. Molly bit her lip. She looked at Kat, then looked past her.

"He's not a bad man, Kat." Her words were quiet, drifting past Kat like dandelion seeds carried on the wind. She turned and walked toward the house. Her shoulders were drooped, as if they had melted in the sun. When she reached the front porch, she pulled her shoulders back and opened the door. Kat stood, staring at the empty porch, barely aware of a nearby bird calling out for its companion.

For the first time in three years, Kat's tears, which fell down hot cheeks, were not for her own troubles.

21

"WHEN YOU DISAPPEARED FROM YOUR 'WALK', I figured this is where you'd be," Wyatt said as he stood in the door to Kat's make-shift pottery studio. "You know it's only an hour until we meet the justice of the peace. You're not getting cold feet, are you?"

Kat looked up from the clay she was turning. Wyatt was leaning against the door frame, his arms hanging loosely by his side, one hand tucked casually into a pocket. The late October sun made a gray halo behind him.

· "Looks like you're the one getting cold feet," she said, nodding toward his bare feet.

"I'm thinking about going to the chapel this way. What do you think?"

"I think it's too late to become a hippie."

Wyatt stepped fully into the studio, his movement fluid, as if his body was always hearing music. It surprised Kat how much she loved him, how she had given over to her feelings for him. The fact that he rarely took himself too seriously had finally given her the ability to unchain herself from her past decisions. To be sure, the weight of those decisions had not disappeared, would never disappear, but she believed she was finally able to move forward without being tethered to the past.

Wyatt came up behind Kat and kissed her on her neck. "So, you didn't answer my question." He walked around to the other side of the wheel. "You having second thoughts about marrying me?"

Kat let the damp clay slide through her fingers. "No. No second thoughts. Maybe a touch of nerves, though."

"Nerves? Isn't that the same thing as cold feet?"

"Don't go twisting my words, smarty pants." She flung a little glob of wet clay at him. "But you know what my track record is. I'm so afraid I'll hurt you the same way—"

"Okay, I'm going to stop you right there." He pulled her hands away from the clay. For a moment, the clay wobbled below her, until she lifted her foot off the pedal. "I won't let you keep playing the martyr. Whatever happened before is the past. It isn't now and it's certainly not the future. All I need to know is if you love me." He lifted her clay-covered hand to his lips and kissed it. "Because I love you."

"I do love you."

"Then trust me. I'm going to be okay." He put his hand on her cheek. "*We're* going to be okay. I promise." She reached up and placed her hand on his. She was not surprised by the strength she found in his hand, but she was startled by the strength she found in her own.

"I suppose we need to be getting ready to go," she said. He nodded and his hand slipped off her cheek. "Give me a few minutes to clean up in here," she said.

"And in there." He motioned toward the house and grinned. "I'm afraid I got clay on your face. You're a mess."

"Well, you better take a look in the mirror yourself, bud." She laughed at the smudge of clay on his lip.

"Sorry for ruining today's project."

"There will be other projects." She waved him off and he disappeared out the door. She looked down at the wheel. What was supposed to be a flowerpot was now an unrecognizable lump. Kat pushed the clay together and cut it free from the wheel with the wire. Once she had dropped it in the bucket of clay scraps and scraped the wheel, she began the process of washing the clay from her hands and arms. If she hadn't already had her hands on the cool, damp clay, the cold water might have been a shock. But this was what she loved about autumn: everything was sharper. Every sound was crisp and clear: water splashing, leaves crunching, birds calling. Every sight was vivid: dappled mountainsides, foggy mornings, scampering animals. She marveled that so much life could be in a season that was all about dying, a season strangely plump with hope.

———————

The chapel was a little red-brick building sitting on a hillside and nearly obscured by tall pines and oaks. Vibrant yellow and orange mums lined the gravel path to the chapel's door. Wyatt gripped Kat's hand, and she wondered if he was afraid she would slip away from him again if he didn't hold her tight. Inside of the chapel, a dark green carpet formed a *T*, down the aisle and across the front. Candles flickered in the two candelabras that were draped in white roses and leafy green tendrils. In between the candelabras was a single unlit candle on a small wooden table. When they came in, a man in a black suit moved down the aisle to greet them.

"You must be Mr. Jenkins and Ms. Turner," he said as he held out a hand to Wyatt. "I'm Anthony Shepard, the justice of the peace who will be officiating today. It's a beautiful day for a wedding, isn't it?"

"I've been waiting for this day for a long time," Wyatt said, looking at Kat. "It was going to be a beautiful day regardless."

Kat watched the expression of the justice of the peace, as if he expected that answer from the prospective bride rather than the prospective groom.

"You're expecting two witnesses?" Mr. Shepard said.

"Yes, our best friends," Kat nodded. "They should be here any minute."

"You have time to freshen up, then, if you like," a woman, who came up beside Kat, said. "I'm Jules. We talked on the phone when you scheduled the chapel. I'm here to help make sure everything goes smoothly this afternoon."

"Oh, yes. It's nice to meet you." Kat looked at the door in the back of the chapel with a picture of a bride on it. "I do think I'll freshen up. I'll be right back," she said, squeezing Wyatt's hand.

In the room, she stopped at the full-length mirror to adjust the lace on the neckline of her ivory dress. She smoothed the A-line skirt and made a quick half turn to check the back. Up close to the mirror, she pinched her cheeks, even though she had already applied blush. Her bare finger caught her eye, which made her check once more for the gold ring in the lacy sachet around her wrist.

The door opened, and Molly stood there in a belted burgundy dress that accentuated the small curve in her belly. "Hey, sweetie. You look beautiful," she said, holding the door open. "They're ready for you. Are you ready?"

Kat took a deep breath and nodded. Wyatt and Gregg, the drummer in his band, were at the front of the chapel next to Mr. Shepard, and as Kat walked to meet them, her mind settled. Somewhere in the background, a tape of instrumental music was playing. When she recognized the song was "Up Where We Belong," she glanced at Molly, and the two stifled a laugh. Mr. Shepard again seemed confused, but Wyatt grinned at Kat. When she was finally standing before him, he reached out for her hand.

"We are here today," Mr. Shepard started, "to celebrate the love of Wyatt and Kat. Love is the necessary foundation of a marriage. So is trust. So is hard work." Kat pressed her feet hard against the floor to keep her knees from buckling. "There will be many times of joy, of growing together, of unity. But it is in the times of challenge and heartbreak, the times that push your love to the limits, that you will find what is truly beautiful about marriage."

Kat focused on the green and peach light cast on the wall behind Wyatt from the stained-glass window at the front of the chapel. She had noticed the lilies in the stained glass when they first entered the chapel, but now she was captivated by the fairy-like images they created in the cast-off light. As she brought her attention back to Wyatt, she saw that Gregg was staring at her, like he often did, as if he was trying to solve some mystery.

Kat thought she had prepared herself for the vows. Love and cherish. Sickness or health. Richer or poorer. Those were straightforward, uncomplicated. But there was Wyatt, repeating the vow from Mr. Shepard. "I take you with all your strengths and weaknesses, just as I offer you myself with all my strengths and weaknesses." She had been weak ever since she came to Gatlinburg, maybe for her whole life. How could Wyatt have any idea what taking her with all of her weaknesses really meant?

The ceremony was short. The vows, the rings, the kiss. Then they were husband and wife. Molly kept hugging Kat, as if she herself was the one just married. "I'm so happy for you," she whispered in Kat's ear. Kat was happy, too, but every time she caught sight of the gold band on her finger, her thoughts were of Jenny, Lizzie, and Kris. Kat wondered if embarking on this new life with Wyatt meant she had given up on the old one for good.

———

Kat leaned back against the bucket seat and watched the white lines slide by the car. When Wyatt told her he wanted to take her to Chattanooga for a honeymoon, she didn't think much about it. Yet as the mile markers ticked by, she realized that she hadn't been farther than Sevierville since she'd come to Gatlinburg. She had forgotten the liberation that cruising down the highway gave her.

"You're awfully quiet, Mrs. Jenkins. Don't tell me that now we're married you've got nothing left to say."

"You aren't that lucky," she said with a laugh. She stared out the windshield at the green highway signs passing by. "I was just thinking that I haven't been this far south on I-75 since Jenny and Lizzie were little. I think Lizzie was about three when we went down to Daytona Beach."

He reached over and patted her leg. "I'm sorry if this is difficult for you."

She took his hand in hers. "It's always going to be difficult. There's nothing either of us can do to change that. But it's okay. Really it is."

"Well, we'll at least make new memories. I promise you that. And maybe when our little one is old enough, we'll take him to the beach."

How could she tell Wyatt that she didn't want to spend the rest of her life trying to recreate her memories with her girls or to replace them with other memories?

He pointed to a barn off to the left, with "See Rock City" painted in big letters on the roof. Kat remembered seeing these barn signs when she and David went to Florida with the girls. "I'm going to take you there," Wyatt said. "You can see seven states from up on Lookout Mountain. We'll go to Ruby Falls, too—unless you're squeamish about caves. I want to show you the whole world." The excitement in his voice made him sound like a lovesick teenager, but there was something endearing about that.

That excitement reappeared as they drove into Chattanooga. He had kept the hotel a secret from her, but when they stopped in front of The Read House, he looked over at her and smiled. The hotel, he said, was historic—beautiful with incredible views. He had stayed there with his parents when he was thirteen, and it was that thirteen-year-old boy that had become fascinated with the haunted room on the third floor.

"We're not staying in the haunted room, are we?"

"It was already booked," he said, his face not betraying the fun he was having with her. She studied his face a moment before realizing the joke, and they both laughed. "You're such an easy mark," he said.

"Don't make me regret marrying you."

He grabbed her hand and kissed it. "Never—and always."

The room was standard—a king bed with a crisp white bedspread, night tables and tall lamps on either side of the bed, a walnut desk with a padded chair tucked under, a dresser with a TV perched on it, a squat brown wing chair under a floor lamp. Wyatt flung the suitcase onto the bed, but Kat's first instinct was to look out the window. She loved the way a window framed whatever was on the other side. The way it concentrated the view to a specific object, and anything that fell on either side of that object took movement and intent to see it. From the sixth floor, Kat thought she could glimpse the Tennessee River just beyond the city's concrete and blacktop.

They went down to the lobby for dinner, but realized their jeans and sneakers were too casual for the hotel restaurant. They had seen several restaurants down the street as they came in, but when they stepped through the door, they were surprised how cool it had become once the sun had gone down. Kat sat in one of the plush wingback chairs in the lobby while Wyatt went back up to the room to get their jackets. She appreciated the richness of the wood and marble surfaces, as well as the chandeliers and the wrought iron balusters on the mezzanine above. For a few days, she would enjoy the luxury, mainly because she was with Wyatt, but she already missed the simplicity of the rocking chairs on the back porch and the bees buzzing in the honeysuckle that clung to the porch post.

After dinner, they walked to the river. The streets had come alive with people strolling in and out of restaurants and bars, music spilling out into the street every time a door swung open. They passed three young women standing outside a bar, their hair teased high and spiked like Madonna's, the red ends of their cigarettes dancing wildly in their hands as their laughter carried over the music coming from the bar's patio. At a crosswalk, they saw a man rummaging through a trash can, stopping only to ask them if they could spare some cash. Wyatt dug in his pocket and pulled out a couple of dollars and handed it to the man. In front of them a couple walked, their arms around each other's waists, the man occasionally leaning into the woman for a quick kiss.

The river, once they reached it, was streaked with long yellow, lavender, and red lines as the city lights cast their reflections on it. The city noise muted the sound of the river, but if Kat listened hard, she could hear the water's movement, the way it lapped against the concrete platform.

"We always find our way to water, don't we?" Wyatt said. "I guess that's our destiny."

Kat watched the streaks of light wriggle with the water's current. "Do you believe in destiny?" she said. "I mean, that something's inevitable."

"Not really destiny. I guess, more like sometimes certain things just feel right, like they fit together in a way that nothing else would be as perfect. I don't believe in love at first sight, either, but the first time, there at Smokey's when I saw you, I could imagine us together just like this."

Kat loved the idea of Wyatt, three years before, imagining them together at some future moment. Back then, it was hard for her to imagine any future at all. But here she was, newly married with a future stretching before her. She turned to face the city, with a mosaic of white and orange lights against a black sky. City lights drown out the stars, not like back in the mountains. With her back to the water, she became more aware of the rumble of the nearby interstate, the sirens and horns among the buildings just ahead of her, and the music blaring from some bar down the street.

"Would you have ever married me if it wasn't for the baby?" Wyatt said. He had turned away from the river as well. His hands were shoved into his pockets. His question was casual, not angry or full of complaint, but Kat felt the weight of accusation anyway. The answer was complicated, but she knew Wyatt needed a decisive one.

"Of course, I would have," she said. She would have, too, she knew that. She loved Wyatt—not the effusive love a teenager might feel or the saccharine love she'd read in dime store romance novels. No, it was a tender and comfortable love. But would love ever be enough to sustain a marriage? Yet she knew the answer, even if she had never voiced the question. She knew that truthfulness and trust were also fundamental—and that terrified her.

Without being fully aware of it, she pulled the edges of her jacket together, her hands touching just under her chin.

"You cold?" Wyatt said.

"Maybe a little."

"We can head back to the room."

She dropped her hand and laced her fingers into his. They walked back to the hotel, chatting about what they saw along the way, planning what they'd do tomorrow. This is what she would fasten herself to—the uncomplicated, ordinariness of their life together. She would not allow herself to dwell on what would happen if truth began ripping everything apart.

22

January 20, 1973

My dear Kat,

I only have time for a quick note, but I couldn't wait to tell you about a girl I met in one of the camps today. Her name is Thao and she lives in a camp about thirty miles south of here. When we first arrived, she was hiding behind her mother, which was amusing because she is almost as tall as her mother, so she wasn't hidden very well. Of course, it's not uncommon for people in the camps and nearby villages to be shy the first time they see us. I think they know we're trying to help them, but we're still foreigners. Frankly, I don't know why they would trust us. Years of experience with combatants, no matter what side they claim, have taught them to mistrust everyone.

She must be sixteen or seventeen, so it made me sad that she clung to her mother. I mean, what must she have seen in her life to make her that afraid? I tried using some of the Vietnamese I've been learning to show her I was a friend, but she avoided eye contact with me. I could tell, though, she was curious about what I was doing. At one point, I saw her watching as I used a stethoscope on an old woman. Thao's gaze was fixated on the metal disk I placed on the woman's chest. I showed the woman I wanted her to breathe deeply in and out by doing it myself. Then I noticed Thao, still half behind her mother, imitating my breaths as well. When I finished with the woman, I turned to Thao, who quickly slid behind her mother again. When she peeked out, I held out the stethoscope to her. "You try?" I said in my broken Vietnamese.

I could see in her eyes that she wanted to, but she was still hesitant. "It's okay," I said as I motioned for her to come. Finally, she let go of her mother's arm and came to me. I put the stethoscope on and put the disk against her chest, then I took the earpieces out of my ears and motioned for her to put them in her ears. When she did, I put the disk on my chest. Her eyes grew wide and she looked from the disk to me.

"You're hearing my heart," I said, lightly tapping against her chest, where her heart is. "Tim."

"Tim," she repeated, with the most beautiful smile I'd ever seen spreading on her face. I think I made a friend.

I miss you terribly, but Thao is one of the reasons I know I'm where I'm supposed to be. There's talk of peace here. I don't know if I fucking believe it. These people haven't seen peace in decades.

I know you must be getting anxious for your newest little one to arrive. How many days now?

Loads and loads of love,
Beth

February 14, 1973

My dearest Kat,

Well, the Peace Accord was fucking useless. I knew it was too much to hope for. The U.S. soldiers are starting to leave, but the People's Army broke the Accord the next fucking day. The next fucking day! So, our days here haven't felt much different than before. The refugees are still the ones suffering and we're doing what little we can to try to make it more bearable for them.

I did get to Thao's camp yesterday. I can't believe the change I've seen in her. I told you in my last letter that I thought she was sixteen or seventeen, but I found out she's barely thirteen! That explained the super shyness the first time I met her. But I have to tell you that yesterday, she ran to meet us.

"Bác sĩ," she was calling as she came to me. She was calling me doctor, and that was damn fine with me. There was no need to correct her, although Dr. Winslow certainly would have if he'd been there. That asshole thinks all nurses have penis envy, as if only people with dicks can be doctors. Thank God Dr. Michaels isn't like that. He just smiled at Thao and pointed at me. "Da, bác sĩ," he said.

There was no hiding behind her mother yesterday. Thao followed me everywhere I went. Even more than that, she was acting as my aide. She stood close to me as I tried to give medicine to a little girl who had been vomiting the night before. When the girl wouldn't take it, Thao told the girl something in Vietnamese, nodding and pointing to me, then the girl reached out and took the medicine. Thao listened to the translator, Chua, tell an old man that I wanted him to go to the clinic to have a wound debrided. When the old man resisted, Thao spoke to him, gentle but firm, and he finally agreed to go. Later, she watched intently as I changed the bandage of a woman whose arm had been injured by part of a tin roof falling on her. When I was ready to leave, I thanked Thao for her help. I wanted to hug her, but I figured that might be too much too soon.

But today, when I went back to the camp, she was helping me take temperatures and removing bandages to check wounds. I told her she would make a good nurse, or even a bác sĩ.

I'm not sure yet when I'm coming home; it's possible I'll be there in time for the birth of my new niece or nephew. How many days now?

Love to you on this Valentine's Day,
Beth

June 8, 1973

My dearest Kat,

I've been putting off writing this letter because I'm pretty sure I know the impact it's going to have on you. You have no idea how many times I've started this letter only to wad it up and throw it away. Of all the things I thought I was, I never figured to be a coward. But I dreaded telling you the truth.

I know you counted on me coming home after the Peace Accord was signed. Hell, for a brief moment, I gave myself room to hope it would be the end. But even back in February, when I wrote that I might be home in time for Lizzie's birth, I knew in my heart that I probably wouldn't leave. It's not just that the war hasn't stopped—despite the U.S. withdrawal—it's that the reason I came here hasn't stopped either. The U.S. involvement in the war was never why I came here anyway. Innocent families have been devastated by decades of war, and just because the U.S. troops are gone doesn't mean the war is over.

So, you've probably guessed by now that I've decided to stay in Vietnam. For how long, I don't know—probably another year. Please don't hate me. Believe me, Kat, I thought about coming home. I wanted to meet my new niece. I wanted to hug you tight and promise never to go away again. But once I tell you more about Thao, I think you'll understand why I can't come home just yet.

I hadn't seen Thao in a couple of weeks. We'd been busy with a couple of the other camps, as well as treating two of the amputees at the clinic, getting them ready to move across the compound for rehabilitation. In fact, I was just walking back to the clinic after helping a young Vietnamese soldier make his way to the rehabilitation center when a truck drove through the gates to our clinic. The brakes squealed as it came to a stop. The driver climbed down from the cab and motioned me to the back of the truck, where a body lay crumpled. When I got closer, I could see it was a woman, her clothes barely hanging on her body. Though the bruise on her cheek and under her eye and the dried blood around her nose and mouth made her otherwise unrecognizable, the round face was familiar to me. It was Thao.

"I found her in the brush a mile or so from here," the driver said. "I don't know how long she's been there. I wasn't even sure if she was alive, but I thought I should bring her here. She hasn't moved since I picked her up."

I checked for a pulse. It was weak, but she was alive. After we brought her into the clinic, Dr. Michaels confirmed that she had been raped.

No broken bones, but she was beaten pretty bad. "I'm not sure if she'll make it, Beth," Dr. Michaels said, pulling off his gloves. "Keep an eye on her and take her vitals every hour. If she makes it through tonight, she may have a chance." He put his hand on my shoulder as he was leaving the room. "You might want to say some prayers, too. It's probably her only hope."

Kat, you know I've never been into the religion thing—at least not that formal stuff you grew up with. But as I washed the blood off Thao's face and moved the wet cloth down her bruised arms and legs, I found myself pleading with God. "If you save her, I'll stay and watch over her." I sat by her bed all night. Sometimes I dozed off listening to her shallow breaths, then I'd wake in a panic, my own breathing rushing through my lips until I could assure myself that she was still alive. Sometime during the night, I noticed she was shivering despite the thick heat that crept in through the open window. I placed another blanket over her and stroked her hair. Then I found myself humming "Hush Little Baby," just like you do with Jenny. When her body finally calmed, I sat back on the chair by her bedside and wept. All of the tears I'd been holding came at once. I guess I was praying—nothing formal, or even coherent.

By morning, Thao was breathing better and she was even starting to become alert. When she finally opened her eyes, I saw her initial panic ease when she finally realized that it was me standing next to the bed. "Bác sĩ," she whispered. I nodded and squeezed her hand.

It took her a few weeks for her to regain her strength. The bruises were gone but the scars of her attack were still there—in the way she wouldn't let any man near her, not even the doctors. In the way her smile never found her lips again. In the way she refused to go back to her village because of the shame she feared would follow her there.

I tried to comfort her, and I think she wanted me to. Then we realized she was pregnant, and I could see that the darkness was more firmly entrenched.

"She can't ever go back home," Chau told me. "She believes they won't accept her, not with a bastard child. Unfortunately, she may be right." When I protested that it wasn't Thao's fault, Chau just shook her head. I told Thao she could stay with me. I told her that we would take care of the baby together. I told her that everything would be alright. But it wasn't.

I had only left Thao for brief times, to spend a half day in a camp or to tend to other patients. But we needed supplies from Da Nang, and Carrie had already gone twice. It was typically an overnight trip, and Carrie knew I wasn't ready for that. But Thao was doing better—or we thought she was—so I went to Da Nang with one of the Vietnamese men who works in clinic.

When I got back the next day, Dr. Michaels told me that Thao had hanged herself the night before. Chau said she wasn't surprised. It was a heavy shame she carried. Dr. Michaels wouldn't let me see Thao, even after I screamed at him and tried to push past him. It wouldn't have made a difference, though. I was so fucking angry— angry at God, at Chau, at the bastard that did this to Thao, at her people and their culture, even at Thao. But I was mostly angry with myself for not being there. All I wanted to do was go down to the river and sink to the bottom. Just stay there until my mind was free of the pain.

Then your letter came with the picture of my sweet chubby-faced newborn niece. I knew that I had to keep going. For her. For you. For Thao.

At first, I thought that meant I needed to go home. In fact, Carrie and Dr. Michaels tried to make me go. They didn't say it, but I believe they thought I'd gone crazy—and why the hell wouldn't they? For a time, I was. I was inconsolable—raving at the fucking world one minute and in a sobbing heap on the floor the next.

Finally, one night, a few days after Thao's death, I was sitting outside feeling so lost. I looked up at the moon, which was a brilliant white. Its light fell on my face, and I held my hand up in front of me, turning it from side to side, watching it move between light and dark, and I realized, that's all we can do in this fucking life—try to win the tug of war between light and darkness. I came over here hoping to pull the rope farther to the light and, for a time, I think I was doing that. But Thao's death yanked me into the darkness and almost left me there. But I know now that I have to make it right. I have to find my way to the light again. So, I hope you see why I have to stay.

Please don't be too disappointed in me. I promise that I'll make every effort to be home before Lizzie has her first birthday.

Until I see you again (and with all my love),
Beth

23

THE AROMA OF TURKEY AND MULLED CIDER filled the house. Potatoes boiled on the stove, waiting to be mashed, green beans from last summer's garden were simmering, with just a hint of bacon, and a pumpkin pie was cooling on the counter by the stove. Kat had been cooking since early that morning, long before Wyatt got out of bed. She hadn't cooked like that since the first year she was married to David. After that, Betty insisted on cooking most of the holiday meal, leaving Kat to only make a pie or cake, even when she was hosting the dinner at her house. Her own mother had given up on fixing a meal, since no one was particularly hungry for another big dinner, instead opting for a few trays of hors d'oeuvres. So, Kat was enjoying cooking like this again.

As she smoothed the white linen tablecloth and set out the plates and silverware, she thought about holidays. Traditions had been important in her family, even the hors d'oeuvres at her parents. Since she left, Kat had been disconnected from tradition, especially since she had to force herself not to think of Thanksgiving as the day she agreed to give up her children. But this year, since she was expecting a baby in the next year, Kat longed to be reconnected to holiday traditions. She pictured Betty setting her table with the orange and brown plaid cloth she had used ever since Kat had known her. Even when the dinner was at Kat's house, Betty wanted to use that tablecloth. Kat never minded. It was part of being a family, at least part of Beth and David's family.

She hadn't spoken to her parents since September, not even to tell them about the baby she was expecting or about marrying Wyatt, because the last time they had spoken, her mother made it clear that if Kat refused to come home and face the consequences of her decision, they no longer wanted contact with her. What should have hurt was strangely liberating for Kat. Her parents were the final thread to her past, and it had now been cut, so she had no choice but to start new traditions. When she told Wyatt she wanted to fix a big Thanksgiving dinner this year, she suggested inviting Pony. She thought about Molly and Jake, too, but it had become awkward socializing with them as a couple. Anyway, Wyatt and Pony were her family now.

As Kat set the stuffing and green beans on the table, she peeked into the living room. A football game was on the TV, but neither Wyatt nor Pony seemed to be paying much attention to it. Wyatt was reading the newspaper and Pony was talking to Luna, who sat in front of him, ears relaxed and eyes focused on Pony. It was a perfect scene as far as Kat was concerned.

"Dinner's ready," she called as she set the turkey on the table amid all of the other dishes.

"It looks wonderful," Pony said, sitting down at the table and spreading his napkin across his lap. "You really didn't have to go to all this trouble. I would have been fine with a peanut butter and jelly sandwich." Kat had been around Pony long enough to know that he didn't like a fuss made over him. But she also knew that he was lonely, even if he would never say so.

"I wasn't going to let you go another Thanksgiving at home by yourself." She passed him the bowl of mashed potatoes. "I'm still mad at you for not telling me that you didn't go anywhere for the holiday, not even to your sister's. I had to find it out from LuAnn."

"She does like to stick her nose in other people's business." The comment, coming from anyone else, would have sounded snippy, but Pony said it without any hostility. "The truth is, I kind of like spending the day by myself. Gives me time to relish in the peace and quiet."

"And then I go and spoil it by insisting you come here," Kat said, taking the basket of rolls from Wyatt.

"She like that with you, too?" Pony said to Wyatt.

"Pushy?" Wyatt laughed. "Yeah, she pretty much gets her way all the time."

"I do not," she said, swatting at Wyatt's shoulder. "Don't listen to him."

"Okay, I know when to step out of an argument," Pony said, throwing his hands up in surrender.

They laughed and moved in and out of the casual conversation that is the heart of family gatherings. Listening to Wyatt and Pony lament about how much Gatlinburg had changed in the past ten years reminded Kat of her grandfather—the way he and his brother would talk about how much better life was when they were growing up. Back then, women were at home tending to their families, not working in a factory—although after the war, most of them left the factories to go back home. But it changed the way women thought about the home, her grandfather said. And the music, Uncle Jack would chime in. Back in their day, there were no hip thrusting gyrations the likes of Elvis Presley, singing nonsense songs like "Hound Dog" and "Jailhouse Rock." No, the smooth tenor of Billy Murray was more dignified, Uncle Jack confirmed. To a twelve-year-old, their musings were mildly entertaining, but they were just two old men who didn't understand that the world had changed. As she listened to Wyatt and Pony, though—their nostalgia mixed with concerns over the destruction of the natural beauty of the Smoky Mountains—Kat wished she had paid more attention to what her grandfather was saying underneath his words.

After they ate, they lit a small bonfire in the backyard. As the sun set, the fire crackled and popped while Wyatt and Pony drank beer and shared more stories of growing up in the mountains. Gatlinburg was mostly farmland when Pony was a small boy, which Kat had a hard time imagining, since the tourists now were the mainstay of the community. Pony's mother was a weaver, working as a Pi Phi in the settlement school at Arrow Craft. At night, when Pony was done with his farm chores and she was home from the school, she would sometimes weave at her small loom and tell him stories of her younger days, like the day the granny woman came to help birth his mother's sister. "Watching Granny Pellum's hands, her knuckles bent with age, caress her mama's hair while she was suffering the birth pains was like watching an angel, my mother would tell me." Pony remembered when the streets in Gatlinburg got paved and when the electric poles began to line the streets. Wyatt remembered the chair lift being built and the first time he got to ride it. Nothing beat going up into the mountains, though, they both agreed. Being in the old growth forest, seeing deer and chipmunks, catching enough of a glimpse of a black bear to make the heart pound faster. That was the life, they mused. Kat envied their stories. Growing up in the city had its own beauty, its own charm, but hearing the men talk about the mountains made her grateful that her child would be growing up here, too.

"I'm glad we had Pony here today," she said when she climbed into bed that night. "He'd never say it, but I think he gets pretty lonely without Gretchen."

"He's a great guy. I wonder why he never remarried," Wyatt said, yawning.

"I don't think he's ever gotten over losing her."

"I get that." He rolled toward her and pulled her into him. "I'd feel the same way if I ever lost you."

She touched her lips against his forehead, his hair still smelling of smoke. Then she found his mouth and kissed it in a way that told him she wanted more. She felt the warmth of his skin against hers. Breathed in the lingering scent of Stetson. His hands moved down her back, her skin awakening to his touch. As he moved on top of her, his breath heavy in her ear, she thought about loss—about the casualties love leaves in its wake. She pressed her hands against his shoulder blades, pulling him closer, and promised herself that their love would not be one of those casualties.

Kat knew something wasn't right. She had been feeling it since the morning after Thanksgiving when she noticed a spot of blood on her panties. The doctor told her to stay off her feet and Wyatt fussed over her, making her stay in bed all day. Even Luna seemed to sense something was wrong, not willing to leave Kat's side. For a week, Kat stayed in bed, but she could still see the spots of blood when she made her only trips out of bed to the bathroom. When a pain tore through her belly so bad that she doubled over, Wyatt scooped her up and took her to the Fort Sanders Medical Center in Sevierville.

"I'm afraid we can't detect a heartbeat, Mrs. Jenkins," the emergency room doctor said. Kat knew what the doctor was saying, even if Wyatt didn't understand right away. The doctor described what would happen next—sending her up to the maternity ward, inducing labor, most likely performing surgery to clean everything out—but she heard nothing except a buzzing in her ears. She remembered only fragments. The thumping of the wheels as she watched the ceiling move above her like a freeway. The bright lights of the operating room. The warm blanket the nurse laid over her in recovery. The coolness of Wyatt's hand clasped in hers when she was back in the hospital room.

At home, she walked through her life as if she was present in it. She smiled at Wyatt, accepted Molly's offer of sympathy, told Pony she'd be back at work soon, listened to LuAnn tell her she could have another baby. But she felt disconnected from it all. Everything around her seemed out of focus, and she had to concentrate to make sense of anything. When Wyatt asked her if she wanted him to put the Christmas tree up this year, she vaguely remembered saying yes. But when she saw the multi-colored lights in the corner of the living room, she wondered where the tree had come from. She remembered staring at the baby Jesus in the nativity scene on the coffee table and thinking about her babies—all of them.

She plucked the plastic figure from the scene—the manger cradling a baby with outstretched arms, a small halo around his head. With his eyes opened wide and his curly golden head of hair, he didn't look like a newborn. But, then, he was also God.

Still holding the baby in the manger in one hand, she picked up the Mary figurine in the other. Mary had one hand clutched to her breast, the other was reaching out for the child. The child that was no longer beside her. Kat studied Mary and tried to put a name to Mary's expression. Was it awe? Or maybe fear? Did Mary already feel the ache of loss, as if she already knew? When her son was taken brutally from her years later, was she angry with God for letting it happen? Did she blame God?

Kat stuffed the two figurines, Mary and the baby Jesus, between the couch cushions so that they were out of sight.

When Wyatt accused Luna of taking the nativity pieces, Kat didn't correct him. Later, when Wyatt found the figures between the cushions after he'd already packed the Christmas decorations away, she didn't have an answer for him. She recognized the terror in his eyes and knew that he didn't believe her when she insisted nothing was wrong. He didn't pursue it then, but at her six-week follow-up appointment, he talked to the doctor about the way she'd been acting. Kat sat on the exam table in her blue paper gown in stunned silence—the two men talking about her as if she wasn't in the room.

She said nothing on the drive back home. She knew Wyatt was glancing over at her every now and again, but she just watched the buildings slide by her, covered as they were with a fresh blanket of snow. It had been snowing all morning but now had stopped. Winter was the season of death—the flowers and trees barren for a time. She could feel the grief buried under the snow. She had tried to bury her grief, but she knew it would be inevitably exposed.

When they got home, she still wasn't talking. Instead, she listened to the coffee maker gurgle as it sputtered out a fresh pot while she put away dishes that had been drying by the sink. Wyatt moved in and out of the room, but she wasn't focused on what he was doing. When the coffee was ready, she poured herself a cup and sat down at the kitchen table. Through the window, the gray sky promised more snow. Wyatt came into the kitchen again, poured a cup of coffee, and sat down across from her.

"You're upset because I talked to the doctor," he said.

"I really don't want to talk about this now."

"This is what you always do. You shut me out. Anytime the conversation gets the least bit uncomfortable, you just shut me the hell out." He pushed his coffee cup away from him, black liquid spilling over the top and dripping down the side.

"And you always push and push. Sometimes I just don't want to talk. Sometimes I just want to figure it out on my own."

"That's just it. We're supposed to be a team. Work through all the shit together. Isn't that what marriage is all about?"

"Marriage doesn't mean I have to do it your way."

"You're twisting my words. All I'm saying is that I want you to trust me. Maybe I can help."

"Nothing can help, don't you get it? I wrecked my life and now I'm wrecking yours."

"I don't understand."

"Of course, you don't understand." She got up from the table and looked out the window. She wished it was summer so she could be out there, back among the trees, where she could watch the river move, so she could feel its urgency to find its beginning—or its end. It didn't matter to the river. It was destined to move along its course.

"I want to understand, Kat. I'm *trying* to understand." Wyatt's voice sounded desperate, almost frantic.

She didn't turn to look at him. "How could you understand?" she said, talking to river. "It's my fault. Everything is my fault. I've lost all of my babies and it's my fault."

Wyatt's chair scooted across the linoleum. "It's not your fault," he said, and his hand slid around her shoulder. "The doctor said—"

She rolled her shoulder back to push his hand away. "You're not listening," She backed herself into the corner of the room. "I left my babies three years ago and I'm being punished for it."

"David made you—"

"No," she yelled. She looked at Wyatt, at his bewildered expression. "No," she whispered. "No, David didn't do anything I didn't push him into. I'm a liar, Wyatt. I've lied to you and everyone else around here."

She pushed a kitchen chair out of her way and went into the living room, where she collapsed onto the couch. Wyatt followed her and sat at the other end of the couch, his body twisted so he could see face her. He was silent, waiting for her to continue.

"I lied to you about what happened when I left Lexington," she finally said.

Wyatt's face was lost in the dimness just beyond a single ray of sunlight that streamed through the window. She was glad she couldn't see his face. Maybe it would make it easier to finally tell the truth.

"So, if you've been lying to me all this time, what *did* happen?"

She drew in a breath and let it seep out slowly as she gathered her courage to speak the truth. Each piece of her story came out chaotically, floating about the room like the tiny dust particles made visible in the sunbeam. The girls asleep in their beds. Leaving them all in the middle of the night. Grief over Beth. Failed attempts to reach out to her children. David coming to Gatlinburg on Thanksgiving Day. His threat to have her charged with abandonment. Everything spiraling out of control.

Regret.

Regret.

Regret.

When she finished, the only sound in the room was Luna's light snoring.

"So, let me get this straight. You walked out on your family? And you let me believe everything that happened before and after was David's fault?"

"Yes," she said.

Wyatt rose from the couch, and for a second, she could see his face before she turned her own face away. Though his steps were muffled by the carpet, Kat could hear every one of them as he paced back and forth behind the couch. He stopped and planted his hands on the back of the couch. She could feel him staring at her.

"I don't know what pisses me off more," he finally said. "The fact that you abandoned your children or that you've been lying to me about it this whole time."

"I wanted to tell you."

She had convinced herself that she had wanted to tell him. She *had* thought about it so many times—had imagined what she would say and how he would react. Sometimes, she had imagined it might be like her Catholic friends described the confessional—she would confess it all to Wyatt, ask forgiveness, and he would grant her absolution. But it was never going to happen that way and she knew it.

"I was afraid of losing you," she said.

He was quiet for so long that she wondered if he had left the room. She looked up and saw him staring down at her.

"Well, you may have been right about that," he said. "But not for the reason you think. You never have trusted me, have you? I mean, really trusted me."

"Trust has nothing to do with it."

"Like hell it doesn't." He threw up his hands in exasperation and marched into the bedroom. Kat didn't move at first, even though she knew she should follow him. When she finally did, she saw the dark gray duffle bag sitting on the bed and a pile of shirts next to it. Wyatt didn't look up.

"You're leaving?" she said, sitting on the edge of the bed.

"I need to get out of here for a while."

"For how long?" She knew she didn't have a right to ask the question.

"I don't know."

She was quiet for a while, staring into the light coming from the bedroom window. Sometimes she would look his way and watch him stuff clothes into the duffle bag or grab items from the bathroom cabinet.

"I should be the one to go," she said, still not looking at him. "This is your house."

He stopped. "That's the difference between us, Kat. Once we got together—even before we were married—I never saw this as *my* house."

"I just meant—"

"I know what you meant." He pulled a few jeans from the closet and stuffed them into the duffle bag before cinching it closed. He flung it over his shoulder before reaching down to stroke Luna's head. "She should stay here," he said to Kat, "at least until I get settled somewhere."

"Where will you be?"

"I'm not sure. I'm not sure of anything anymore." He gave Luna one more pat and then left the room. Kat stayed on the edge of the bed until the back door slammed shut. As she heard Wyatt's van back down the driveway, she slipped off the edge of the bed and sank to the floor. Luna whimpered and nudged up against her. They sat there together until the late afternoon shadows stretched across the carpet. Then Kat lifted herself off the floor. She moved through the house as if she was walking in a dream. She should have stopped in the kitchen to get something to eat, but instead she pulled on her coat and boots and slogged through the snow, past the now-hidden garden and through the barren trees, her breath trailing in white puffs behind her, until the dark water was finally in view.

24

DURING THE WEEK AFTER WYATT LEFT, Kat spent most of her time in bed, the covers pulled tightly around her. The curtains were drawn, and lifting herself out of bed to do anything was like pushing against a stiff wind. If it hadn't been for needing to let Luna in and out or to feed her, Kat wasn't sure if she would have made the effort at all, or if she would have ever known that night had passed into day.

When the phone rang in the middle of the afternoon, she considered not answering. No one had called her since Wyatt left. She was certain that word had spread, not only that Wyatt left her but why he had done so. She had called Pony the day after Wyatt left, only telling him that she needed some extra time before returning to work. She let him assume her absence was related to complications from the miscarriage, and she had not heard from him since. But she was afraid a phone call might mean something was wrong with Wyatt, so she rolled over and pushed herself up in bed.

"Hello," she said, clearing her throat.

"Hello, Kat." Wyatt's voice sounded tired.

Kat sat up straighter. "Wyatt. It's good to hear your voice."

"I just called to let you know I'm still at Gregg's, so I'll have to wait a bit longer before I can get Luna."

"Oh. Okay." She wanted to mask the disappointment. "She's doing okay. Luna, that is."

"That's good." He paused. "Okay, well, I won't keep you. Just wanted you to know."

She had barely gotten 'goodbye' out of her mouth when she heard the click. Hearing his voice was devastating, but still, she wouldn't have minded keeping him on the phone longer, just to listen to it.

The receiver stayed in her hand for several seconds, the dial tone still buzzing. Finally, she hung up the phone and threw back the covers. The room was hot, and she vaguely remembered turning up the thermostat a couple of days before. She couldn't seem to get warm, even when she was under the covers, but now the air was stifling. She stumbled around the end of the bed and noticed for the first time that Luna wasn't in her usual spot on the bed. Every afternoon, Luna would sit by the back door, waiting for the sound of Wyatt's steps. Every afternoon, she would finally whimper and lumber back to the bed.

Kat shuffled through the living room, her bare feet scooting against the carpet. She briefly shaded her eyes until they adjusted to the light streaming through the kitchen windows. The room seemed too bright, as if it had forgotten that it was part of a house that had been forced to keep any light from coming in. Luna whimpered by the door, and Kat opened it to let her outside, shivering when the cold air hit her face. As soon as she shut the door, she started a pot of coffee. She knew she needed to eat, but she wasn't hungry. All she had eaten for days were dry toast and crackers, and that wouldn't sustain her for very much longer.

She opened the refrigerator and found little there except leftovers from before Wyatt left, which had begun to spoil. Nothing looked or sounded appealing, so she closed the refrigerator door. The bread bag was on the counter. It was almost empty, but she wrestled with the twist tie, took out a piece of bread, and popped it into the toaster.

Only the heels, the pieces that never got eaten by either her or Wyatt, remained in the bag. She might be forced to change that practice if she didn't feel better soon.

Luna barked at the door, and Kat braced herself for another blast of cold air. Once Luna was inside, Kat leaned down to the plastic tub of dog food and scooped some into Luna's bowl. The dog food was almost gone, too. Even if Kat could still subsist on crackers after the bread was gone, Luna needed more. Kat owed it to Wyatt to take good care of his dog.

Kat had put off going to the grocery as long as she could because she was sure she'd see someone she knew. Gatlinburg was a small community, and she rarely went anywhere without seeing at least one person she knew. The artist community was even smaller and particularly tight knit. They would all know her secret by now, and even if they didn't say anything to her, she would see the judgment in their eyes.

On the table by the door, Kat found a notepad and jotted down a quick grocery list while she finished her coffee and nibbled on the toast. When she tore off the list and put the pad back on the table, she saw the calendar by the phone. She had lost track of the days, but using her finger to tap the boxes on the calendar, she counted the days from her doctor appointment. It must be January 25 or 26, she finally determined. Then she saw the red star on the Thursday block for that week, below the 27. Her birthday. When they purchased the 1983 calendar, Wyatt had made a production out of putting the star there because he had missed her birthday last year and she had teased him about it for months. He wasn't going to miss this one, he said.

She tossed the half-eaten toast to Luna and went to the bedroom. It would have been so easy to crawl under the covers again, to shut out the world. To sleep past her birthday. But she had to find a way to shake the grief that again was consuming her. Getting out of the house was the first step, and she knew that. So, she pulled her gown over her head, the one she'd had on for a week now, and stuffed it into the hamper. It was time to awaken her spirit, even if she didn't feel like it.

She stepped in the shower, and at first, the hot water tingled like pin pricks against her skin, but gradually the warmth was soothing. She let the water stream over her head and trickle down her back. Her life had turned in so many unexpected ways, but every way it had turned seemed to lead back to the young woman she met on a college campus nearly two decades ago. The woman who chipped away at a foundation Kat believed was unbreakable. The woman who was brassy and bold, obstinate and opinionated. For a time, Kat despised the woman for it, only to eventually fall in love with the empathy she learned drove her friend's passionate outbursts.

Only to fall in love with the woman.

Kat had never allowed herself to admit that what she felt for Beth was love—not what a sister feels for a sister, but what a woman feels for a man—the same love she felt for Wyatt. She had never allowed herself to reveal the depth of her feelings to either of them.

Now they were both gone.

Now she understood her love for what it was.

Now her grief knew why it had traveled its lonely path—why it had not been able to share itself with anyone. Why it had hidden its source, even from Kat.

But she knew now, and because she knew, she finally let the tears come in great, heaving sobs.

25

FEBRUARY WAS PROVING TO BE COLDER and snowier than January. The wipers pushed a thin line of snow from the bottom of the windshield to the side. The snow wasn't heavy enough yet to cover the road, but Kat clutched the steering wheel as if it was. She was headed to Frank's Diner, which was about halfway toward town, to meet Molly. The only time she had spoken to Molly since Wyatt left was a brief phone call nearly two weeks before, when Molly asked if it was true that Kat walked out on her girls. As soon as Kat said yes, the phone clicked and then a dial tone. Kat wasn't surprised by the reaction. It was everything she expected, everything she feared.

She took a risk by calling Molly. A risk that Molly wouldn't hang up immediately. A risk that Molly would now have the words she didn't have two weeks ago to say that Kat was a horrible person. A risk that the friendship would be irrevocably broken. But it was a risk she had to take. She missed her friend and the easy-going relationship they once had. So, when Molly agreed to see Kat, Kat was both surprised and relieved.

When Kat turned into parking lot at Frank's, she expected to see Molly's car—the one she shared with Jake. When it wasn't there, she wondered if

Molly had changed her mind. Kat stepped out of her car and snowflakes fell on her face. She brushed them away with her hand, the wool of her glove scratching against her cheek. Under the eaves of the diner's roof, she waited, occasionally blowing into her gloves to warm her face. The longer she waited, the more she was sure Molly wasn't coming. But then the dark blue Pontiac came into the parking lot and stopped directly in front of Kat. She hadn't been expecting Jake to come, so when she saw that he was driving, she felt the tension spread from her face, down her back, and to her legs.

Jake got out of the car, the motor still running, slammed the door shut, and stepped closer to Kat. She involuntarily flinched but tried to quickly regain her composure. If she could help it, she wouldn't let Jake see her afraid of him.

"Well, if it isn't Kat Jenkins. Or maybe it's Kat Turner again." He was in her face now and she could smell the alcohol on his breath. "Seriously, girl, how are you doing?" His voice was thick.

Molly, who had been watching this from the car, finally emerged. "Jake," she said as she rounded the front of the car. "Pick me up in a half hour, like we agreed."

"Yeah," he said. He looked at Kat again. "Yeah, sure."

He turned and went back to the car, squealing the tires as he drove away.

"You really shouldn't ride with him when he's been drinking," Kat said.

"Please don't lecture me—not today. Besides, he's the one who convinced me to meet with you."

Molly's cheeks were turning a bright pink, and Kat hoped it was only from the cold. "Let's go inside," Kat said. "It's too cold to be standing out here for long."

Inside the diner, red and pink hearts dotted the walls. Kat hadn't realized it would be Valentine's Day when she suggested they meet at the diner on Monday. Just one more way she thought the universe was taunting her.

Molly took off her coat, revealing how much her belly had rounded in the two months since Kat had last seen her. Kat tamped down a surge of jealousy as she pulled off her own coat and gloves, folding them neatly and laying them on the seat beside her. She waved off the menu the waitress was handing her.

"I'll just have a piece of apple pie and some coffee," she said.

"Same here," Molly said, handing the menu back to the waitress. She stared at Kat, and Kat wondered if the meeting was a mistake.

"Thank you for agreeing to see me," Kat said.

"I felt I owed it to you."

"Owed it to me?"

"As your friend, I guess I should be willing to hear your side of the story."

The snow was fluttering outside and beginning to stick to the parked cars. Kat was already regretting coming here. What did she think it would accomplish?

"My side of the story," Kat repeated. "I'm sure it's not much different than what you've heard already." She paused when the waitress placed the pie in front of them and poured the coffee.

"I've heard a lot," Molly said. "They say you left your girls while they were sleeping in their beds. That David didn't have anything to do with you walking out. That he didn't force you to stop seeing your children. You just made that up so people would feel sorry for you and wouldn't see you as the monster you are."

The words pricked Kat. She wondered if Molly believed all of that or was just repeating what she had heard. Kat poured creamer in her coffee and stirred the spoon slowly as she watched the coffee turn a caramel color. She didn't look at Molly. "Is that what Wyatt's telling everyone?"

"Wyatt? God, no. He's too decent a man to say anything bad about you, no matter what you've done. No, Gregg had to explain why Wyatt was staying with him. Word got out pretty quickly after that."

Kat twisted her fork and flaked off a piece of crust. "I'm not surprised. Gregg's never really liked me."

"Damn it, Kat. Do you ever think of anyone but yourself?"

A woman at a nearby table laughed. Kat turned her head to see an older couple sitting side by side in their booth. The man was telling some story and the woman occasionally laughed at something he said. Something about seeing them there caused an ache in Kat's chest, but also a strange sense of hope.

When Kat turned her attention back to the table, Molly was glaring at her.

"From the first second I found out what you'd done," Molly said, "I have been furious. I can't imagine any mother walking out on her children, and I certainly can't imagine ever doing that to my own child." She moved her hand across her belly for emphasis. "So, why'd you do it? What possible reason could you have?"

"I doubt any explanation will be satisfactory to you. But I'll try." She stared out the window, at the snow that was falling harder now, before looking back at Molly. She tried to explain about Beth, about the grief that overwhelmed her. She tried to explain how lost she felt, how she had stopped being a mother—emotionally—to her daughters. She tried to explain how she felt herself slipping into a darkness that terrified her. "Something disconnected in me, and I had no idea how to reconnect it."

"So that's why you left. That's it? But they say you didn't tell David or the girls that you were going—that you left without saying a word, without even leaving a note."

"I wasn't thinking straight at the time. I didn't know what else to do. I really thought I was doing it for them, for the girls—that if I went away for a while, I'd figure out what was wrong and fix it. I thought it would be just for a few days, maybe a couple of weeks at most."

"It's been three years. Three years without seeing your girls, talking to them, holding them, putting them to bed at night with a kiss. How have you…"

"I know." Kat felt a lump rising in her throat. She held back her tears and pushed her plate away, only a few bites of pie eaten. "David really did give me an ultimatum—give up custody or be charged with child abandonment. That part's true. But if I'm being honest, I think I was relieved when he gave me the ultimatum. I probably could have found a lawyer to fight him in court, but the truth is, I was scared of going back home. Nothing in me had changed. I was still as broken then as when I'd left home." She looked out again at the snowflakes drifting by the window. "There isn't a day that goes by that I don't wish I'd made a different decision."

Molly was quiet. The older couple finished their meal and paid at the counter. When they opened the door to leave, Kat could feel the cold air on her neck. She watched them through the window as they stepped carefully on the thin layer of snow that had accumulated in the parking lot—the man touching the woman in the small of her back and reaching across with the other hand to grasp her arm until he safely deposited her into their car.

"Do you think you'll ever go back? Try—at least—to correct your mistake, to make up for it with your girls." Molly finally said.

"I don't know." The answer was honest and raw. "I just don't know what's best for the girls anymore. I've been out of their lives for more than three years now. How fair would it be for me to just pop back in and disrupt their lives now just to satisfy my need to be with them?"

"But what if that's what they need? What if that's what they want?"

"David's mother doesn't think it is. I asked her once. Even my own parents think it's too late."

"What if they're wrong?"

"And what if they're right? What if I did more harm to them by going back than by staying away?"

Molly thought for a moment without saying anything more. "Well," she finally said, "I'm no expert on that, but I do believe all children, no matter how old they are, need to know their parents—their mother— love them. You should find a way to show your girls you love them. If not now, someday. And for now, you should at least tell people here your side of the story."

Kat shook her head. "It won't make a difference."

"It did to me." Molly scooted her empty plate to the edge of the table, then took a sip of her coffee. Kat gripped her own mug, not sure what to say. Molly leaned forward and touched Kat's hand. "You need to know something. LuAnn's been gossiping a whole bunch about you and Wyatt. She even tried to talk Pony into firing you."

"I should have expected that from someone," she said. "Just not from LuAnn."

Actually, that wasn't the truth. The more Kat had been around LuAnn, the more she understood that the motherly concern she exuded masked a woman who thrived on gossip. But Kat had never guessed that she would go as far as to try to get Kat fired.

Since Kat had started back to work, she and Pony avoided the subject of the miscarriage and Wyatt leaving. It was like Pony to not bring up anything unless Kat did. That was the nature of their relationship—he waited on her to talk, or not talk, about what she wanted to share of her life. So, she was not surprised that Pony hadn't mentioned a conversation with LuAnn. She hadn't even been sure if he knew about her secret, until now.

"Just watch your back," Molly said. They were both quiet, watching the cars on HWY 321 inch along, a sure sign that the roads were starting to cover over with snow.

"They're saying we could get up to six inches of snow tonight," Molly said. "Looks like it's starting early."

Then that was it, Kat guessed. The conversation moved from the weather to how Molly was feeling with the birth of her baby only a month away. They talked like they used to talk, except now they were friends who knew each other's secrets. She knew Molly probably still didn't understand the choices Kat had made—perhaps she never would.

———

At closing time, Kat locked the front door of the pottery shop then headed to the back to get new stock for the front room. She picked up a box of recently cured pieces, and Pony picked up a box, too. They worked quietly, pulling pottery from boxes and setting them on the shelves. The standard pieces—uniform plates, bowls, mugs, and the like—were placed under signs like: *All mugs $7.00.* For the unique pieces, the ones that showed off Pony's creativity, a special price tag was placed on the bottom, depending on the particular technique Pony had used. These were placed on the table in the center of the room.

"This is beautiful, Pony," Kat said as she lifted out a serving bowl with multi-colored glazes spiraling out from its center. "You'll have to teach me this glazing technique."

"I'm always happy to teach you anything you want to learn. Have you been making any pieces lately?" This was as close as he would come to asking how she was doing.

"Actually, I *have* been in my studio a bit in the past week. For a while there, I didn't much feel like it." She glanced at Pony. "Especially after Wyatt left."

"I'm glad you're working your wheel again. I've always found it therapeutic to work with clay."

Kat thought about how the cool wet clay twirling beneath her fingers calmed her spirit. She looked at Pony, who was rearranging some pieces on the table display. "I understand LuAnn had a conversation with you— about me," she said, keeping her attention on the pottery she was putting on the shelves.

"She did stop by," Pony said. "As you can see, nothing came of it."

"I still have a job, and I'm grateful for that. But what she said didn't shock you?"

"Actually, I already knew about everything by the time she came."

"This community is full of gossips," Kat said as she picked up the empty box to carry to the back.

"I didn't hear it through gossips. I don't listen to gossips, anyway." Pony placed his final piece on the shelf. "Wyatt told me."

"Wyatt?" She stopped and turned toward Pony. "Wyatt talked to you?" She couldn't hide the tremor in her voice.

"He came a few weeks ago—not long after—"

"After he found out what a horrible person I am." She turned and walked into the back room. The thought of Wyatt being in this room, telling Pony everything, made her ill. She dropped the box to the floor and sat on a stool staring at the pottery drying on the shelves in front of her. She barely heard Pony come into the room.

"We talked for a while," Pony said, sitting on the stool across the table from her. "But he never once said you were a horrible person. He was confused about what you did, sure, but he was mostly hurt."

"I should have told him the truth a long time ago. I should have told all of you the truth."

"'Should haves' are important for reflection, but you can't stay there. You have to be in the moment."

"Well, in the moment, my husband is barely speaking to me."

"He misses you."

She leaned forward. "Do you think there's hope for us?"

"I don't have the answer to that. The only thing I can say is don't give up. Your marriage is worth fighting for."

She knew he was right, but hadn't she already proven that she was a coward when it came to fighting for what she wanted?

"You're going to be alright," Pony said when he put his coat on then held hers for her while she slipped her arms through the sleeves. When they stopped at her car, he patted her shoulder and looked at her. "Take care of yourself, okay?"

Even with his face half in shadows from the floodlight overhead, she could see the crinkle at the corner of his eye. He turned and began the climb up the hill to his house. She watched him until he disappeared into the night. As she lowered herself into her car, she realized that he had never commented on what she had done to her children, and she knew he probably never would. Whatever he felt about her actions, she knew now that he wouldn't let it change the way he treated her. He would be one of the few people in town who would be that way, but for the first time, she felt ready to face whatever would happen next.

26

THE EARLY MARCH NIGHT WAS COLD—a sharp reminder that winter was not yet finished with the valley. The rain from earlier in the day had changed into light, fluffy flakes that melted as soon as they touched the warm ground. From the kitchen window, Kat watched the snow, visible just beneath the flood light above the garage. She yawned and saw that it was nearly midnight. Johnny Carson would be on, but she wasn't much in the mood to watch television. She moved to the back door and locked it, something she never did when Wyatt was home.

"Another day is behind us," Kat said to Luna, who was stretched out on the sofa. "Time for bed." Kat tapped her leg, and Luna hopped down from the sofa, following Kat into the bedroom. While Kat was changing into her nightgown, Luna jumped onto the foot of the bed as usual, as if she was still expecting Wyatt to show up.

Kat folded her jeans neatly and placed them on the back of the chair in the corner of the room. She slipped on her nightgown, then she crawled into bed. She turned off the light and rolled over. She reached out, just as she had done every night since Wyatt left, to the empty spot where he should have been, as if she expected that once the light was out, he would magically appear. Her hand lingered in the spot, until the sheet was warm under her palm. She exhaled slowly then rolled onto her back. The only noise in the room was the slight rasp of Luna's breathing, which finally lulled Kat to doze off. Sometime later, the sudden ringing of the phone woke Kat from a deep sleep. She fumbled for the phone on the nightstand and pulled the receiver to her ear.

"Hello?" she said, sleep still heavy in her voice.

"Kat?" Molly's voice was barely audible. "Kat, are you there?"

"Molly?" Kat sat up and slung her legs over the side of the bed. She felt her blood pulsing in her fingertips as she gripped the phone. "What's wrong?"

"Can you come get me? I'm scared." Molly's voice faded into a desperate whisper. "I think he's going to kill me."

When Kat stood up, the phone cord twisted around her body and her knees buckled, pushing her to the floor. Luna came down to the floor, licking Kat's hand and cheek. Kat ran her hand down Luna's back as she spoke. "You need to call the police."

"I can't. I don't want to get Jake into trouble."

"If he's threatening to—"

"Just please come get me, Kat. No questions. No lectures."

"Of course, I'll come get you. Are you at your house?"

"No. I'm at a phone booth in front of the market close to our house."

The market was nearly a quarter of a mile from Molly's house. Kat wondered how she had made it there in the dark, just weeks away from giving birth. "I can be there in fifteen minutes. Will you be okay until then?" Kat stood again, untangled the cord from her waist, and was already slipping off her nightgown. The yes on the end of the line was faint, but Kat recognized the terror that lived in it, which made her heart skitter in her chest.

She found her jeans on the chair and pulled them over her hips. After flipping through a couple of sweaters hanging in the closet, she pulled a light gray crewneck out and slipped it over her head, flipping her hair out from under the sweater. She glanced at the clock before she left the room. It was twenty after one.

Luna was close at Kat's side, whimpering as if she, too, felt the tension. Kat grabbed her coat and purse from the hook by the door, feeling for her keys in the coat pocket. When they weren't there, she quickly checked her purse, but she couldn't find them. The keys had to be somewhere amid the piles of papers on the kitchen table. "Where did I leave my damn keys?" The curse word slipped out unexpectedly. "Sorry about that, girl," she said to Luna. She anxiously glanced at the clock while she lifted a stack of mail. "There they are," she sighed. Her hands shook as she grabbed them and stuffed them into her coat pocket. "It's alright," Kat said into the air. "It's got to be alright."

The sound of the screen door slamming behind her echoed into the night. Snowflakes landed on Kat's lashes, causing her to blink them away. Once she turned on the headlights, she realized it was snowing heavier than she thought, although most of the flakes were still not sticking anywhere. Kat thought about Molly huddled, alone and afraid, in a cold phone booth and backed out of the driveway with a reckless haste.

The car cut through the snowflakes, which rushed toward the windshield. The roads were virtually empty, given the hour of night, allowing Kat to push the car and herself faster toward the phone booth. She was relieved when she finally saw it in her headlights, but she didn't see Molly at first. Had she misunderstood where Molly was? Had Jake found Molly and dragged her away? A thousand thoughts jumbled in Kat's mind at once.

She climbed out of the car, the motor still running and the headlights still focused on the phone booth, her eyes watching the shadows for any movement. When she neared, she saw Molly crouched in a corner of the small booth. Kat tapped on the glass, causing Molly to startle. But when Molly looked up and saw it was Kat, she pressed her hands against the wall and pushed herself to stand again. She was in her nightgown and no coat or shoes. She struggled at first to open the door, as if in her panic she had forgotten how. Finally, the door slid open and she nearly collapsed into Kat's arms. She tried to speak, but only heavy sobs came out as her whole body trembled.

"I'm here. It's going to be okay," Kat said, tightening her grip around Molly. The shivering in Molly's shoulders reproduced itself throughout Kat's arms. "Let's get you in the car. It's freezing out here and you don't have a coat or shoes."

Molly hobbled to the car with Kat's arm providing support. When Molly was settled into the seat, Kat pulled off her coat and laid it over Molly then went around to her own car door, which was still open. Inside the car, Kat looked at Molly, who was leaning against the door, her body still trembling. If there were the right words to say, Kat couldn't find them. Instead, she put the car in drive and headed toward her house. She didn't know what had happened, but this time she was determined to convince Molly to get away from Jake for good.

Luna was at the back door when Kat came bounding into the house in search of house slippers or any pair of shoes that Molly could put on to walk across the gravel and wet grass and into the house. When she found something, she hurried outside and returned a minute later with Molly at her side. Kat helped Molly lower herself to the sofa then reached over to turn on the lamp, and for the first time she got a good look at Molly's face. Her cheek was bright red, with a bluish-purple rim just below her eye. Her lip was swollen on the same side of the face, with a trickle of dried blood on her chin.

"Oh God, Molly, what did he do to you?" Kat sat down beside Molly and brushed her hair behind her shoulder.

"He didn't mean—" Molly stopped herself before Kat could say anything. "He was drunk. He's been drinking a lot lately." She put her hand on the cushion to help her shift position then rested the hand on her round belly. "The studio isn't doing well, and what little bit he's making and what I bring in goes right back out for doctor visits and food."

"And booze?"

Molly nodded. "I thought it would be okay because he's never gotten too physical with me—just hitting stuff or throwing dishes. But tonight, he was—Kat, I've never seen him like that. He was furious. He kept saying that everything was my fault, that he could've made it work if it hadn't been for me and the baby."

"You know that's not true, don't you?"

"I do, but—"

"There is no but, Molly. It's not true."

"I know," she said, looking away from Kat and blinking back tears. "The first time he hit me tonight, I thought he did it by accident—that he meant to punch the wall. But when I fell back and landed on the bed, he pulled me up and hit me again. I pushed him as hard as I could and he fell back and hit his head on the dresser. I think I may have knocked him out." She took a deep breath. "I may have killed him. I was so scared that I ran out of there as fast as I could." She was sobbing again.

"Shhh." Kat let Molly's head rest on Kat's shoulder. "I'm sure he's not dead, but we need to call the police anyway."

Molly pushed away. "No. No, we can't."

"We have to." She placed her hands gently on Molly's shoulders. "We have to, just in case. Do you understand?" Molly nodded. "I'm going to go call, but first, let me get you an ice pack. That bruise is starting to come up." She rose from the couch, her eyes still locked on Molly. Luna, who had been pacing before finally settling on the recliner, followed Kat into the bathroom. Kat rummaged in a drawer for the ice pack and also found a washcloth. Her hands shook as she ran the cloth under the water. She took a moment to catch her breath, to fill her lungs until they hurt, and then wrung out the cloth. Molly was slumped forward, her head in her hands, as Kat came back through the living room to the kitchen to fill the ice bag. She had just put the cubes in the bag and screwed the cap shut when she saw the headlights in the front window and heard the brakes screech. Her body tensed, knowing they had not yet called the police.

"Molly!" Jake was yelling as he slammed the car door shut. "Molly, I know you're in there."

Luna growled, her ears pricked back and her eyes focused on the front door. Kat rushed to Molly, who was now sitting upright, terror filling her entire face. "Come here," Kat said, helping Molly stand. "I want you to go into the bedroom. Close the door and don't turn the light on, but there's a flashlight in my nightstand drawer. Find it and then call the sheriff. As soon as you hang up, lock yourself in the bathroom. Take Luna with you."

"But, what about—"

Jake banged on the front door, sending Luna into a barking fit. "Kat. Open up. You can't keep her from me. I need to tell her something. Come on. Open up."

"Listen to me," Kat whispered as she pressed her hand against Molly's arm. "Do as I tell you. You have to protect yourself and the baby. I'll be alright. Now go."

Kat watched Molly lead Luna, who was still barking, by the collar and disappear behind the bedroom door, then she focused on the front door, where Jake was still banging, still calling out for Molly.

"Go home, Jake," she called through the door. "Go home and sleep it off. You can see Molly in the morning."

"Damn it, Kat. You can't keep her from me." His voice carried more panic than anger, but Kat knew that didn't lessen the threat he posed.

"Go home," she repeated. She slowly stepped back toward the kitchen, her heart pounding with the rhythm of his fists against the door. When she made it into the kitchen, she turned off the light and felt her way to the back door. She had forgotten to lock it when they came in earlier. She twisted the lock to secure the door then felt her way up to the chain latch, which rattled as she searched for its slot.

The pounding on the front door stopped, and she waited for the sound of the car driving away. Instead, she heard the aluminum garbage can beside the house clatter as it hit the ground. Jake continued to wail, moving between cursing Kat and crying out for Molly. Kat backed away from the door when she heard Jake's heavy steps on the back porch. The light filtering through the window from the floodlight created monstrous shadows out of ordinary objects: the toaster oven, the coffee maker, the canisters. Then she saw Jake's shadow loom against the wall on the other side of the kitchen table. Kat slid her hand along the countertop, steadying herself, until she reached the knife block on the far side of the sink.

"I'm going to tear this place down if you don't open this door," Jake yelled from the porch.

Kat fumbled through the handles until she found the one in the middle—the chef's knife with the long blade. She pulled it out of the block, then crouched against the wall, the cabinets of the galley kitchen towering on either side of her. Her breaths were coming hard, and she wondered if she might pass out if she couldn't get them slowed. A loud thud on the deck seemed to be Jake overturning the table, then something came crashing through the window, glass shimmering in the stream of light as it hurtled across the room. Kat pushed herself against the wall and gripped the knife in her hand. If Jake managed to get inside, she wasn't sure what she would do, but she knew she wouldn't let him get to Molly.

She waited for more glass to break, for Jake to climb through the window, but instead an unsettling silence filled the room. Was Jake hurt? Or did he pass out on the porch? She leaned forward, thinking it might be safe for her to check on Molly and Luna, but Jake's footsteps on the porch made her stop. She listened as his steps came near the door again, then moved away. Maybe he finally decided to go home.

Keeping the knife in her hand, she reached for the countertop to pull herself up. Cold air was rushing into the room from the broken window. Cautiously, she peeked out the window over the sink. The yard was dark. If anything was moving out there, she couldn't see it. Then she saw a thin ribbon of light coming from the side door to the garage—her studio. She had not left the door open or the light on, she was sure of that. Though they were faint, she could hear noises coming from the studio.

Jake hadn't left.

Kat stared at the light coming from the studio door. In that moment, in her mind, she saw everything in the room: the wheel tethered to the foot peddle, the clay Pony had recently dug, the bucket for scraps, the stool Wyatt had made her the first month she'd moved in. Then she imagined Jake—his hands gripping the stool and smashing it against the floor, tipping over the wheel and watching it break apart.

The light shifted as a dark silhouette appeared in the doorway of the studio. When he took a step into the yard, Kat strained to see him, but his face was obscured in the darkness.

"This is just the beginning, Kat," he yelled. "I'm coming for you now."

She stumbled backward, bumping against the counter behind her. Her hands were numb, so she used both hands to grip the knife. Even in the dim light, she could see her breath pumping out of her mouth.

"Do you hear me, bitch? I'm coming for you."

Kat steadied herself as she heard Jake step onto the porch; his steps were slow, as if he was trying to increase the terror. He wasn't likely to try the door again, so she watched the window while she counted his steps. One. Two. Then they stopped. Through the darkness, Kat saw the blue lights flashing. That must have been why Jake stopped. She dropped the knife and ran to the front door, unlocking it and throwing it open before the officer could even knock.

"He's out back," Kat said when she opened the door. She pointed behind her to the kitchen.

"Okay. Stay here, ma'am, and get down." He motioned to her as he spoke, then he signaled for the other officer to go around the house. Kat dropped to the floor and scooted on her belly to reach the couch. The flickering blue lights were visible through the open front door, but instead Kat concentrated on the blue swirls they made on the carpet. The blood pulsed in her ears, but she heard the officer move into the kitchen just as glass was breaking. He hollered at Jake to stop, then the other officer was telling Jake to do the same. The back door opened.

"This is bullshit," Jake yelled. "I just came here to get my wife. This bitch won't let me see her." Kat couldn't hear what the officers said in return. "Come on, man, I was only trying to tell her I'm sorry." There was another pause in Jake's rambling. "If you're going to arrest anyone," Jake yelled, "you need to arrest my wife. Can't you see this hole in my head? That's what that whore did to me."

Kat wondered if Molly could hear Jake. She wished she could crawl her way to the bedroom and see if Molly was alright. She probably should have never left Molly alone, but she had no choice.

"It's okay, now, ma'am." The officer was standing over her. "He's been taken into custody and can't terrorize you anymore. Deputy Tinsdale is taking him to the station."

"Thank God," Kat said as she raised herself off the floor.

"He said his wife is here. Is that correct?"

"Yes, sir. She's hiding in the bathroom. Do you want me to get her?"

"Yes, ma'am. I need a statement from you both."

Kat hesitated at the bedroom door. Less than thirty minutes had passed since Jake first showed up, but for Kat it had felt so much longer. How would Molly, already shaken from her earlier encounter with Jake, have managed not knowing what was happening outside that room? Kat opened the door. The room was dark and quiet. She turned on the overhead light and softly tapped on the bathroom door.

"Molly?" She waited for a response, but none came. "It's Kat. You can let me in. The police have taken Jake away."

The door opened slowly. Molly's cheeks were wet with tears, her lip now very swollen, and her bruise growing more bluish-purple than red. Her hands shook as she took Kat's outstretched hand.

"An officer wants to talk with us," Kat said. She gave Molly a robe and then led her into the living room. Kat moved through the next few minutes as if she was watching a dream play out in her mind. She was answering the officer's questions, but everything that had happened was playing again in her mind. Not in sequence, but in small clips, like a movie that had been spliced together in the wrong order. She wondered if it was the same for Molly, who seemed like she was in a trance as she answered the questions. Even when the officer used his Polaroid to take pictures of her face and arms, she stood blankly, as if it was someone else standing in front of the officer, not her.

"I think I have all I need," the officer said as he lowered the Polaroid. "We'll contact you if we need to follow up."

"How long will he be in jail?" Molly said, pulling a strand of hair down over her cheek. Kat was startled at how much it reminded her of the painting Jake had made of her.

"It will be at least two to three days before he'll be able to be bailed out. You'll be safe tonight." He seemed to understand the reason for the question.

When he left, Kat insisted that Molly go to bed. She doubted that either of them would actually sleep, but it was all Kat knew to do. She followed Molly to the guest room.

"I hope the guest room is okay. I'm going to stay up for a while longer—clean up a little." Molly nodded, a hint of panic still registering in her eyes. "Here's an extra blanket," Kat added as she handed it to Molly. "You'll probably need it, with the broken window in the kitchen. I'll just be in the other room. Will you be okay in here alone?"

"I'll be okay," Molly said. "Thanks, Kat, for tonight. I had no idea he'd come here. I would have never—"

"I'm glad you called me. If anything had happened to you or the baby—" Her voice trailed off. "Try to get some sleep," Kat said as she closed the door.

She collapsed onto the couch, pulling her knees to her chest. Luna curled up beside her, nudging her nose against Kat's legs. Kat pulled the afghan around her and her eyes became heavy. The room looked strange to her, as if she didn't belong there. She closed her eyes and wondered if she ever had.

At some point before dawn Kat woke up and moved from the couch to her bedroom. Luna followed her and found her spot on the end of the bed. Kat, still in her clothes, crawled under the covers and reached over to the empty spot where Wyatt would have been.

27

WHEN KAT OPENED HER EYES, the light coming through the window was golden. She rolled onto her back and rubbed her eyes, but it wasn't until she saw the gray sleeve of her sweater that everything fully came back to her. Luna had moved next to Kat and whined as she pressed her cold nose against Kat's cheek. Luna was never demanding—never barked to get her way or pressed too hard to get someone to notice her. She usually waited until the attention came to her naturally.

"I guess you must be miserable," Kat said, stroking Luna's long nose. "You're such a good girl to be so patient. It's way past time for you to go out, isn't it?" Kat threw back the covers, and Luna jumped down. When Kat emerged from the bedroom, Molly was huddled on the couch, her head resting on the back cushion and a blanket pulled tightly around her shoulders.

"How long have you been up?" Kat said as she followed Luna to the back door, watching the floor for any stray pieces of glass that might have been in Luna's path. She forced herself not to look at the jagged shards of glass still dangling in the window or the fragments of glass scattered across the table and the floor. Eventually she would have to do something with all of it, but for now it would have to wait.

"Not long, maybe fifteen or twenty minutes," Molly said, her voice lifeless.

"I'll fix us some breakfast."

"I'm not hungry."

Kat knew the feeling well. Knew the emptiness of hollowed-out insides–stripped bare by the pain—and the insufficiency of anyone or anything to fill that emptiness. Yet, she also knew that it *could* be filled, in time. She placed her hands on Molly's shoulders. "You have to eat something, honey. If not for yourself, for your baby." Molly snaked a cold hand from under the blanket and put it on top of Kat's, which Kat understood to mean agreement.

"After breakfast, I'll put some plastic over the window. Maybe then the heat will stay in here instead of escaping outside," she said over her shoulder as she went to the kitchen. The chef's knife was still on the floor, just where Kat had dropped it. She picked it up, the handle now icy, and wondered if she really would have used it on Jake. The thought of it, of plunging a knife into human flesh, made her sling it into the sink, the hollow clanking of the metal against metal sounding eerily like breaking glass.

"It's supposed to warm up outside this afternoon," Molly said, her voice still flat. "I think the weatherman said yesterday it's supposed to be around seventy today."

"That's March for you. Snow last night and summer today." She tried to make her voice light and airy. She laid slices of bacon in the skillet. As the bacon sizzled, she picked up the broom beside the door and began sweeping around and underneath the table. She would deal with the top of the table later. When she had a pile of glass in the corner of the room, she went back to the stove to turn the bacon. Luna scratched at the back door, and Kat let her in before scrambling the eggs and popping bread into the toaster. She set up two TV trays in the living room, one in front of Molly on the couch and one in front of the recliner, before bringing out the plates of food.

"It's not much, but it's better than nothing," Kat said as she set the plates on the TV trays. She nudged Luna from the recliner and sat down to breakfast.

"It's more than enough," Molly said. She lowered the blanket from her shoulders and scooted forward to eat. The pale blue nightgown, the same one she was wearing when Kat picked her up, was noticeable above the neckline of the flannel robe Kat had loaned her. A thin line of red stained the lace bodice.

"We need to take you home and let you change clothes. Get a shower."

"Take me home?" Molly nearly dropped her fork.

"It's okay, hon. He won't be there. Remember the sheriff said he'll be in jail a couple of days at least."

Molly pushed the eggs around on her plate, moving them from one side to the other. Occasionally, she lifted a forkful past her swollen lip. Kat watched her eat and wondered if she should say what was on her mind.

"I know it may feel too early to talk about this," she finally said, staring at the blue and purple bruise, now fully blossomed on Molly's cheek. "But you need to decide what you're going to do, long-term, I mean."

Molly pushed her plate away, the food only half eaten. She pulled the blanket around her again. "You mean whether I'm going to stay with Jake." Molly ran her fingers through her hair, as if she was studying hard on the situation.

"You can't stay," Kat said. "You know that, don't you? Not after last night."

Molly leaned her head back so that she was looking at the ceiling, and a tear fell onto the blanket. "You make it sound so easy," she said. The sunlight streaming into the living room from the kitchen made Molly's breath visible as it moved past her lips.

"I know it's *not* easy," Kat said. "And it won't be easy. But if you stay, it will only get worse. Whoever Jake was when you ran off with him three years ago, or whoever you thought he was back then, he isn't that man—maybe never was."

"How could I have been so wrong about him?"

"Some people are really good at fooling other people," Kat said. The words, as soon as they slipped from her mouth, mocked her. Even though the secret she had packed around for three years had been exposed, Kat still carried the burden of it. Molly seemed willing to overlook the irony, or maybe she didn't even notice it. She had buried her face into the cushion.

Kat picked up the dishes as quietly as she could. In the kitchen, she scraped the remaining food into the trash and laid the plates in the sink. The sun had begun its climb above the mountains, which were now mottled with the greens and purples of early spring. Sometimes she looked at the mountains and believed they had always belonged to her. But today they were unfamiliar. Today they made her homesick for the vibrant green fields of Kentucky fescue. For the contours of white fences protecting chestnut-brown thoroughbreds. For the cars streaming in both directions on New Circle Road, nose to tail, like horses on a carousel. For the two-story house, built nearly two-centuries ago, at the end of a tree-lined driveway. For the girls—Jenny, Lizzie, and Kris—whose only image she could conjure was from the final time she saw them.

When Kat came back into the living room, Molly had moved to the front window, the blanket still snug around her shoulders and dragging the floor like the train of a bridal gown.

"I'm going to call my parents," she said without turning around.

"That's good."

"I don't know if they'll even take my call."

"Of course they will. You're their daughter." Kat wanted to believe that, but her own experience was example enough that relationships, even parental ones, could be damaged beyond repair.

"I haven't spoken to them since last summer—right after I found out I was pregnant. Jake got so mad that I called them." She pushed back the curtain. Jake's car was still out front, where he stopped it in the front yard. "He said I was being disloyal to him. I didn't call them again after that. When Mom tried to call a couple of times, Jake made me hang up on her."

"My God, Molly. I figured it was bad, but I had no idea it was that bad."

"How would you? I couldn't tell anyone, not even you. I kept thinking, 'it will change,' 'give it time, it will change.' But it just kept getting worse."

She dropped the curtain and eased back onto the couch, her round belly protruding under the blanket. "I feel like a damn fool."

"You're no fool, Molly. You loved him, that's all. You wanted to believe the best in him." Molly exhaled, her face pressed into the crook of her elbow, her breath sinking into the blanket. Kat rested her hand on Molly's shoulder and held it there a moment before stepping back. "If you want to call your parents, you can use the phone in my bedroom. It will give you some privacy, and it should be a bit warmer in there." She paused. "I need to get the window covered anyway. Will you be okay if I do that?"

Molly gave a slight shrug, then a muffled "yes."

Kat hesitated, but there was nothing more to say. Nothing more to do in that moment. She stepped onto the deck, the overturned table—the one that Wyatt had made with his father a decade before—lay up against the porch rail. The ceramic flowerpot—a housewarming gift from Pony, which was always in the center of the table—was broken into three large blue pieces on the porch floor. A crowbar lay just under the window, amid shards of glass.

The air carried the scent of the river. A somewhat acrid smell as the waters rushed to sweep away decaying leaves, preparing for the coming spring. Already the air felt warmer than yesterday's chill—not quite to the summer-like warmth coming in the afternoon, but enough to make Kat push up the sleeves of her sweater.

She stepped through the door to her studio as if she still expected Jake to be inside. In the corner of the room, Wyatt's amp lay untouched. The pottery wheel was still upright—too heavy to overturn—but Jake had taken the crowbar and beaten the wheel and the kick wheel, leaving them warped. The motor had been ripped off and had been flung against the wall, a hole in the drywall indicating where it had hit. Buckets and mounds of unused clay were in a pile near the wheel. Pottery that had been drying on the shelf was now pulverized into a grayish brown heap.

If she had the time, Kat would have sifted through the remnants for anything that could have been salvaged. Instead, she found the plastic sheeting, still folded neatly on the shelf. Wyatt was all the time bringing scraps of materials from job sites just in case they might find some usefulness at home—that's what he'd say, anyway, when she'd tease him about it. When she pulled the plastic cover from the shelf, she felt the tears coming. She had every reason to cry over what had happened the night before, over everything that had happened since she lost the baby, but it was this stupid plastic sheet that finally brought the tears. As soon as Kat was in the kitchen, she laid the plastic over a chair and then flushed her eyes with cold water. She didn't want Molly to see that she'd been crying. The living room was empty, though, when Kat went to the coat closet for the step stool. She hoped Molly was calling her parents.

Kat pushed the kitchen table against the wall to give her better access to the window. She climbed on the stool, pulling a corner of the plastic sheet with her. Only by pressing her body against the window casing, trapping the plastic between the window and her body, was she able to squeeze the handle of the staple gun. After every three or four staples along the length of the casing, she climbed down, moved the stool, and climbed back up again—always mindful of the jagged shards left in the window. She had just finished stapling the plastic to the sides of the window when Molly came in. The blanket was no longer around her, making her belly more noticeable. She leaned against the refrigerator.

"They're coming to get me," she said. She had been crying. "Mom was shaken up when I told her what happened—when I told her everything that has been happening. But it was Dad's reaction that tore me up. He was so—so broken."

"Broken?"

"He blames himself—for the way he treated Jake. I told him that no one was to blame but Jake, but I don't think it made a difference. He was crying." She pulled a Great Smoky Mountains magnet off the refrigerator. "I don't think I've ever seen him cry."

"They love you," Kat said. She began to staple the bottom of the plastic to the window casing in an effort to shut out thoughts of her own parents. "When are they coming?"

"This afternoon. They should be here about four."

"Let me shower and change. Then we'd better get you home and packed."

Even though Jake's car was still parked in her front yard, out of habit Kat craned her head to look for it before turning into Molly's driveway. When she shut off the motor, Kat looked over at Molly, who had her head leaned against the window. She still wore Kat's robe and slippers.

"You ready?" Kat said.

"As ready as I'm ever going to be."

The house was uncomfortably dark and quiet. What little light penetrated through the open front door and the kitchen window revealed broken lamps and overturned tables. In the middle of the room lay the mangled remnants of the painting of Molly that had been above the recliner. The strands of red hair across a pale cheek were the only part still recognizable.

"He must have done that after I left," Molly said, pointing to the painting. It didn't seem to bother Molly to see the painting crumpled and broken, but Kat was shaken by the sight of it. "This is where the fight started. I tried to lock myself in the bedroom, but he came after me."

"It's okay. You're safe now." It was a superficial comment, the kind made when no words are adequate but saying something seems the only thing to do. "Why don't you shower first, then we'll work on packing?"

Molly headed down the hall to the bathroom, stopping at the linen closet door to get a towel. When Kat heard the water running, she went into the kitchen. Dirty dishes were stacked in the sink and a loaf of bread, the bag still open, and a jar of peanut butter were on the counter. Kat wondered if that had triggered the fight. A nearly empty bottle of Jack Daniels was on the kitchen table.

Kat pushed the dishes aside, plugged up the sink, and began running the water. Perhaps someone else might have thought it was pointless to clean the kitchen, with Molly getting ready to leave and Jake in jail, but Kat needed something to do with her hands. While the water was running and the suds started to obscure the dirty dishes, Kat closed the bread and tucked it away in a bread box that was sitting on the counter. She opened cabinet doors until she found where the peanut butter should go and set it among the chips and boxes of cereal and crackers. She turned off the water and as she picked up a plate and began washing, she watched a rabbit through the window.

The phone rang, and Kat started not to answer it, fearing it might be Jake. She shook her head and realized it was not likely to be him, so she picked up the receiver. It was Molly's mother saying they had stopped at the Tennessee welcome center, a little over two hours away. They'd call again when they got closer, to get directions to the house. Kat could hear the worry in Molly's mother's voice, yet that voice reminded Kat of Betty, gentle and determined. She realized how much she missed Betty.

She was back at the sink when she heard Molly. "You don't have to do that."

"I know I don't. It gave me something to do." She glanced back at Molly, who was dressed in navy blue slacks and a plaid tunic and drying her hair with a towel. "Besides, I just finished." She pulled the stopper and sprayed the suds from the sides of the sink. "Your mother called. They'll be here in a couple of hours."

"Is it strange to say I'm nervous?"

"Not strange at all." Kat dried her hands on a towel and then folded it neatly and laid it on the counter.

They worked in silence as they packed Molly's clothes into a suitcase and grocery bags. Her toiletries and prenatal vitamins were stowed in a cosmetic bag. The baby's clothes were stuffed into a diaper bag and the blankets were folded neatly and placed in a stack, and everything was carried to the front door. When Kat folded the legs of the cradle, she noticed that the blanket Jake had bought for the baby was lying on the changing table. She picked up the cradle and carried it to the living room. Everything else in the nursery—the crib, the changing table, the dresser—would have to stay.

"Is there anything else?" Kat asked, surveying the small pile by the door.

"Nothing," Molly said. "Most of the stuff is Jake's. I don't want it anyway."

Kat cleared a place on the couch for Molly to sit. When the phone rang, Kat answered and gave Mrs. Fisher directions.

"They'll be here in about twenty minutes," she said when she hung up. She pulled the recliner away from the broken lamps and sat down.

Molly was staring at the pile of bags by the door, then looked at Kat. "Come with us," she said. Her voice sounded more like the first time they'd met.

"What?"

"Come with us. With you and Wyatt—" Molly stopped herself.

"I think we both know that I've never been as spontaneous as you," Kat said. They both smiled. "Besides, I don't think your parents need someone else to take care of. They're going to be pretty busy with a grandbaby in a few weeks." Molly cradled her belly at the mention of grandbaby.

An arc of light traveled along the living room wall, signaling a car was pulling into the driveway. As soon as they got in the house, Mrs. Fisher embraced Molly and held her there, until Mr. Fisher made her stop. Kat stood back, just inside the kitchen, pushing back the resentment she didn't want to feel as she watched the reunion.

As they loaded the Fisher's car, Kat thought back to the night she met Molly—the night Kat had packed her own suitcases and left a home with her babies tucked in their beds. She had often wondered why she made the decision. Often wished she would have made a different choice. But it had been a house of grief for her. Overwhelming grief. A grief that had pushed her out, then followed her. A grief that along the journey had transformed. Softened. Sweetened.

Kat stood in the yard and watched the car back down the driveway. As the car turned to head toward town, Molly waved from the back window. The face, framed by the long red curls, was reminiscent of the face she had grieved for so long. Kat's friendship with Molly had been genuine, but she knew now that the expectations she had placed on Molly were unreasonable. Molly would never have been able to be Beth, and while Kat knew that in her head, her heart had still pulled Beth from her memories and sculpted them into a Molly that never was and never would be. Now, only as Molly was leaving, did Kat feel the regret of never fully seeing the real Molly. The one that was not Beth.

It was a painful realization.

Yet it was the face of Mrs. Fisher, looking back at her daughter, whom she had thought was lost, that made Kat collapse to her knees when the car disappeared from view.

28

HIS VAN WAS PARKED IN FRONT OF THE GARAGE when Kat arrived back home. She wasn't sure what that meant. He had only come home twice since he left—to pick up some clothes or tools—and they barely spoke each time. His visits left her and Luna despondent.

Now, seeing his van, she was oddly nervous. Everything had changed overnight—what she feared, what she valued, what she wanted. More than ever, she knew she wanted her marriage to work. But she didn't know if that's what Wyatt wanted anymore.

She shut the car door, taking a quick glance back at Jake's car sitting in the front yard. As much as she wanted to hate Jake, she also pitied the mess he'd made of his life. Would he ever come to realize what he had and what he threw away? She knew how painful such a realization could be.

When she got to the back porch, she saw that the table had been pulled upright. The pottery and glass shards were gone. The rocking chairs were back in place. Plywood covered the window.

"Hey." The voice came from behind her. She turned. Wyatt was in the doorway of the garage.

"Hey," she said.

"I came as soon as I heard."

She stepped down off the porch but didn't go beyond the step. "How did you hear about it?"

"Pony called me," he said. Kat nodded. Pony knew what had happened because she had called him to let him know why she wouldn't be in for her shift.

"I'm glad he did," she said.

Clouds had nearly obscured the sun, which would soon disappear behind the mountain anyway. In the gray light, Kat could see only an outline of Wyatt's face, not the expression in his eyes or the curve of his mouth. She could only guess by the way his words sounded what his face might have revealed. She wondered if he could see her face.

"Where's Molly?" he said. "Is she okay?"

"Her parents came to take her back to Louisville."

"Is she going to stay there for good?"

"Don't know. But she won't be going back to Jake."

"That's good."

They stood in awkward silence, as friends but also as strangers. As wounded lovers.

"It's a mess in there, isn't it?" she said to break the silence.

"I'm sorry," he said, but his words seemed to carry a meaning beyond what was in the garage behind him. "I'm trying to clean it up."

"I'll help." She dropped her purse on the porch and moved toward him until his face came into view. She wanted to kiss him. She wanted to feel his lips against hers. To feel the heat of his body and know that they were one body again. She had hated being two—separate and alone. They weren't meant to be alone—not from each other.

Inside the garage, he had set the buckets upright on the bench of the pottery wheel. On the battered wheel was a squirt bottle and several small storage bags, each bag with a cube of clay. He had seen her use this method to revive dried-out clay, when he had accidently left a batch of clay uncovered in the studio. He had cursed himself for being so stupid, but she had simply pulled out the storage bag and spritzed the clay with water before sealing it in the bag. "All is not lost," she had said then, turning to him with light dancing in her eyes. "And even if it were, I'm sure I could find bigger things I could be mad at you for."

She missed the way they would tease each other.

"We'll get you a new wheel," he said, scooping up the dust from the broken pieces of vases that had been drying and were waiting to be fired in Pony's kiln. "We'll make your studio even better than it was. And I'll sit out here and play guitar and watch you create art out of a lump of clay."

"Does this mean you're staying?" She wasn't looking at him, afraid of seeing too much—or not enough—in his eyes under the stark florescent light.

He came up behind her and slid his arms around her waist. She placed her hands on top of his and felt the cool metal of his wedding band. She heard his breath, just above her ear, and, in the distance, she heard the river rushing past the boulder.

THREE

29

THE MOUNTAINS WERE GREEN AGAIN, as most of the trees were now fully leafed out and ready for summer, replacing the patchwork of white, rose, and pink of the magnolias, redbuds, and dogwoods of early spring. But looking up into the hillsides, Kat could still see remnants of the spring color hiding in the green of mid-May. She heard the rush of the river, rippling with snow melt and fresh spring rains. She pushed the edge of the hoe into the rich, black soil, creating a furrow deep enough to set out the tomato plants. She knelt in the dirt and pulled a plant from the tray. The warm soil, as she gathered it around the tomato plant, reminded her why spring was her favorite season.

The garden was the connection between her previous life and her current life. Every spring, from the first spring she had moved into the centuries-old house in Lexington until now, she had planned what would be planted and where in the garden it would go—mindful of rotating her crops to keep the soil healthy. Then she went about the task of planting—some from seed and some transplants from the nursery down HWY 321, but always the same gentle smoothing of the soil with her fingers. Tending the garden was such a spiritual act for her that she sometimes wondered if Adam had really been cursed by God after the fall from paradise.

"I don't think I'll ever grow tired of watching you in the garden."

Kat shaded her eyes and saw Wyatt standing at the gate. "You're always welcome to join me," she said, holding out a tomato plant toward him.

"We both know that would be a disaster, with my black thumb. Anyway, I have something here that might actually pull you away from that tomato plant." He held up an envelope. "It's a letter from Molly."

"From Molly?" She quickly laid the tomato plant in the furrow and pulled the soil around it, gently patting it down, before she jumped to her feet. She wiped her hands on her jeans then grabbed the envelope from Wyatt when she reached the gate. It had been five years since Molly left Gatlinburg.

Years that welcomed a child—a boy that had the same narrow face as his father.

Years that returned that father to his freedom, but also took away his prison-enforced sobriety.

Years that dissolved one family and created a new one—a wife and a new husband, a young boy the new husband took as his own, and a baby girl all their own.

Years that healed a marriage, which had been broken by a secret finally revealed.

Years that changed little else in Kat's life, except a few more side glances or outright glares cast her way by people who thought they knew her whole story. But those years had taught Kat that trying to change what people thought of her—or her past, for that matter—was as useless as trying to stop time itself.

Luna was stretched out across the porch, directly in front of the steps. Neither Kat nor Wyatt considered making her move from her spot, since her aging joints made it more difficult for her to get up and down. Instead, Kat sat on the step just below Luna and opened the envelope. When she unfolded the letter, a picture of Molly and her new family dropped out:

Steve, in his light gray polo shirt, with one arm around Molly and one hand on Zachary's shoulder; Molly, her hair now in soft waves, like Kelly McGillis in *Top Gun,* cradling a sleeping Sara Catherine in her arms; and Zachary, whose squinting smile made him look too much like Jake.

Kat rested her shoulder against the rail as she read the letter. Whenever she received a letter from Molly, she devoured every word, as if she was in some way reliving her life as a mother through Molly's stories.

"How's everything with Molly?" Wyatt asked when Kat tucked the letter back in the envelope.

"She and her family are fine."

"You don't sound too sure of that."

"Oh, it's probably nothing," she said, tapping the letter against her leg. "It's just that Jake called Molly's parents last week. He was drunk, but said he'd changed his mind about giving away his parental rights for Zachary."

"Can he do that? I mean, legally, could he contest it this long afterward?"

"I don't think so. Honestly, I don't think he even wants Zachary in his life. I suspect he's just trying to get Molly upset—you know, punish her for the way his life turned out."

"He's a piece of shit alright."

"I guess I was naïve enough to think he'd leave her alone after he moved to Arizona."

"Not a man like Jake."

"Makes me grateful I have a man like you." Kat sat up and gave Wyatt's leg a pat. "Now, before we both get too sentimental, come on and help me plant some tomatoes and squash." She stood up and motioned for him to come with her, but as he was standing, the phone rang.

"Saved by the bell," he said, his grin reminding her why she loved him. She handed him the letter before he stepped over Luna and disappeared into the house. She was still thinking about Molly's letter when Wyatt came into the garden to find her.

"Going to help after all?" she said, not really looking up at his face.

"That was Daniel, over at Pony's," he said. "Pony collapsed while he was loading the kiln. They think it's a heart attack."

Kat dropped the plant she had in her hand and stood. "Pony? Is he okay?"

"He was apparently conscious when the ambulance took him."

"Did they take him to the hospital in Sevierville or on to Knoxville?"

"Daniel thinks it was Sevierville. He was pretty shaken up, so he wasn't making much sense." Wyatt wrapped his arms around her. "I'm sorry, honey," he whispered.

"We have to go there," she said, pulling back enough to look into his eyes. "Pony is like a brother to me."

"To me, too. I don't know if they'll let us see him, but we'll try."

Kat grabbed her purse from the kitchen, and they climbed into the car. She had never been bothered by the road that curved along the West Prong of the Little Pigeon River. Most times, the road, which was a pleasant drive that avoided the traffic of town, allowed her to watch the river bend away from the road and return to it a little further on. But today the road made her sick to her stomach as Wyatt took the curves as quick as he dared. Even so, it still was about a half an hour before they pulled into the Fort Sanders Sevier Medical Center parking lot.

"I'm looking for Robert Vickers," Kat said to the receptionist in the emergency room. "He would have been brought in by ambulance within the last hour."

"Are you family?"

"Not blood family," Kat said, pulling at the corner of her shirt. "We're close friends."

The receptionist checked the computer in front of her. "He's here," she said, looking up at Kat. "They're still working on him. I'll have to check to see if you would be permitted back to see him. You can have a seat over there and wait." She pointed to a row of seats against the wall.

When Kat sat next to Wyatt, she realized that she had left in such a hurry she hadn't changed and was still in her gardening clothes: the plaid button-down shirt, unbuttoned all the way down and sleeves rolled up to her elbows; the once-white cotton T-shirt, now grayed a bit with age; her jeans, streaked with dirt down her thighs and embedded in the knees; her old cloth sneakers, the toe of one shoe frayed. Under other circumstances, she would have been mortified to be seen out looking like that.

She tried to read a magazine while they waited, but she found herself watching the clock above the door. Wyatt occasionally reached over and placed his hand on her thigh, and she would put her hand on top of his. An hour and a half passed before the receptionist called to Kat. "They said you can go back," she said when Kat got to the desk. "But only one of you. He's in Bed 3." Wyatt nodded at her to go.

The receptionist pressed a button and the doors buzzed before opening into a room, partitioned off into treatment bays with long brown curtains. Two nurses were at a desk near the front of the room, and Kat thought about how one of those nurses could have been Beth if she hadn't been killed. A young woman came out of one of the bays carrying a plastic tub with bandages and vials sticking out of the top. Kat walked down the middle of the bays and saw the number 3 hanging from the ceiling in front of one of the curtains. She paused for a moment, then slipped through the curtain.

Pony was propped up slightly in the bed and his eyes were closed. He was hooked up to several machines and an IV pole held a couple of bags that dripped into a tube leading to his wrist. He looked older lying there, with his hair, more gray than black now, jutting wildly from his head. She wondered if she should leave and let him sleep, but he opened his eyes.

"Hey, Kat. What are you doing here?" He was a bit groggy, but he smiled at her.

"I was in the neighborhood and thought I'd stop by."

"If I'd known you were coming, I would have combed my hair." Kat was comforted by his teasing.

"I *am* embarrassed for you." She laughed and moved beside the bed. "How are you feeling?"

"Like I've been rode hard and put up wet."

"You know you gave us all a scare." She touched his hand and smiled down at him. "Let's not do that again, okay?"

"Yes, ma'am." His eyelids drooped and then closed. Kat watched him sleep for a moment, thinking back to the day she met him. She had no way of knowing then that he would become not only a brother but also a father to her, always giving her wise advice. She listened to the cardiac monitor beeping above her head and watched the lines rise and fall across the screen. A nurse came into the bay.

"He'll be groggy for a while," she said. "As soon as a bed is available, we'll transfer him to a room."

"I'll let him rest, then," Kat said.

"Are you his sister?" the nurse said as she checked a monitor.

"No," Kat said. "Just a friend."

"Oh. He said something about needing to call his sister."

"She lives in Ohio. I wonder if someone called her." She looked down at Pony again. "I'll make sure she knows, Pony," she said. "I'll be back soon. You hang in there." She touched his hand again then went to find Wyatt.

———

Kat had met Carol twice before when she had come to visit Pony. She was older than her brother by about ten years, and though they were somewhat close, they only saw each other every couple of years or so. Pony rarely traveled away from his shop, and Carol had raised five children mostly by herself after her husband was killed in an accident.

As soon as Carol heard about Pony, she and one of her daughters were on their way to Tennessee. Kat knew it would be past midnight when they got into town and checked into their motel. She met them the next morning at the hospital with a basket of snacks, puzzle books, and magazines.

"You didn't have to do that," Carol said.

"Sitting in a hospital room all day can be hard. Besides, it was the least I could do if you won't stay with Wyatt and me."

"We couldn't put you out. Anyway, we'll be closer to the hospital at the hotel."

"Of course."

"Have you been in to see him this morning?" Carol asked. Kat could see the worry lines on her brow.

"No. I stopped by last night, after they got him settled in his room, and he was still a bit groggy. I told him you were coming, and he did manage to smile, so I know he'll be glad to see you." She picked up her purse. "I'll let you visit with him by yourselves this morning, then I'll swing by this afternoon."

"Thank you for your kindness, Kat."

For the next three days, Kat moved between home, the pottery shop, and the hospital. Pony's condition stayed the same—no better and no worse. He was sometimes alert enough to talk, but mostly he slept, at least while Kat was there. She could see the weariness in Carol's face as the days dragged on. Kat also felt the weariness in her bones, the worry that never left her body. When she arrived at the hospital on the fourth day, Carol suggested they talk in the waiting room, which was usually quiet.

"Pony's not getting better," Carol said when they sat down. She smoothed her skirt and then let her hands rest in her lap. "The doctor says he's not sure if Pony will make it."

Kat looked at Carol, whose brow was furrowed and eyes wide, and saw what her own face must have looked like. After the first day, on the ride to the hospital, she hadn't let herself consider that Pony wouldn't survive.

"Even if he does get better, he's got a long recovery ahead of him," Carol said. She looked away from Kat, as if she was analyzing something in her mind. "I'm thinking of taking him back to Dayton with me."

"Oh." Kat couldn't imagine Pony could be happy anywhere but his shop. She also couldn't imagine her life without Pony in it. "If you think that's best."

"I don't know what's best. I just know that he can't be here by himself any longer."

Kat wanted to protest, to say he wasn't alone, but she was not family, and family had to make the decisions for him now.

"Pony thinks the world of you, Kat," Carol said, looking straight at Kat this time.

"Well, the feeling is mutual. I'm not sure I would have survived living here if it wasn't for him."

"He wants you to take over the store for him."

"Of course, I'll do whatever I can to help while he recovers."

"No, permanently."

"Permanently?" Kat shifted. "He won't ever be coming back?"

"Not for a long while, at least. Even if he recovers, I don't think he'll ever be able to manage the business. He's coming to terms with that reality." She took Kat's hand, an intimate family-like gesture that Kat didn't expect. "He and I talked about it, and he wants you to take over. He knows you'll treat the shop just like he would."

"I'd be honored to do that," Kat said. She looked out the window at the gray clouds gathering to the west. More spring rains were coming. "But it won't be the same without him."

When Kat stopped by Pony's room, Carol's words were still settling into her mind. She wished Pony was awake. She wished she could tell him that she would take care of the pottery shop. She wished she could tell him what he meant to her. Yet, all she could do was take his hand in hers and whisper her gratitude, hoping he was aware enough to hear it.

The next morning, when the phone rang before seven, Kat sensed it would be Carol and that the news would not be good.

"I'm sorry to tell you this," Carol said, but Kat didn't hear anything else she was saying.

30

IT WAS JUST THE KIND OF SPRING DAY that Pony would have loved. The sky was the brightest blue, the color of his favorite glaze. The clouds, the few that were above, were like puffs of unspun wool. A faint breeze moved through the trees that surrounded the cemetery and rustled the awning above the mourners.

Kat watched the awning ripple in the wind. Even when Wyatt's voice carried the haunting words of "On Eagle's Wings," Kat couldn't look toward him. Seeing the casket beside Wyatt was too painful. It wasn't just that she had to think about Pony being lowered into the ground. The shiny wood and brass box forced her to remember the cold February day that she heard the minister utter Beth's name. *I am the resurrection and the life. The one who believes in me will live, even though they die; and whoever lives by believing in me will never die.* Kat's faith had faltered since Beth died, but she had to believe she would see Beth again. And Pony. She told herself that she would see them both again one day.

After the graveside service, they drove to the River of Life Baptist Church, where the members were providing a meal for Pony's family and friends. Kat had considered not going. It was LuAnn's church, and she had been avoiding LuAnn ever since the secret had come out. Not easy in a small community, but LuAnn seemed to be doing the same. If Kat happened to see her in the grocery, she would turn down an aisle or in the opposite direction. When they couldn't avoid each other, they never spoke. LuAnn always stared at Kat and then moved on.

"It was a beautiful service," Kat said as she and Wyatt drove to the church. "I'm glad so many people came."

"He was loved by this community, even if he probably didn't realize how much," Wyatt said.

She looked down at the funeral program in her hand. "I know I should have been focused on Pony, but my mind kept drifting to the day we buried Beth."

"I can see why you'd be thinking about her on a day like today. I often think about my parents at funerals. In a strange way, funerals connect us to all the people we've lost as well as to the people who are experiencing the newest loss."

Kat thought about it—the way every funeral tries to gather the isolated grief of every mourner and to bind it together through ritual and tradition. For that time, people know what to do with grief, how to share its burden and provide comfort. But once the funeral is over and everyone goes back to their own lives, grief builds walls to protect itself, and few people understand what to do to with it then.

The church parking lot was already full by the time Kat and Wyatt arrived. At the funeral and graveside service, Kat had been spared most of the judgmental glares she was used to seeing. But the fellowship time would be different, and she knew it. If she didn't feel the need to say a final goodbye to Carol, she probably would have told Wyatt to take her home. He gave her hand a squeeze before they walked into the fellowship hall at the back of the church.

The room was full—people in line at the potluck table, people eating at the tables in neat rows across the room, and people gathered in small clutches telling stories about Pony or talking about the upcoming homecoming celebration at the church or simply the fickleness of the spring weather. Kat saw LuAnn in one of the clutches, talking with one hand moving wildly and the other holding a plastic cup, but LuAnn didn't seem to notice Kat. Carol was on the other side of the room, but she was surrounded by several people. Kat found an empty corner and decided to position herself there until she could speak to Carol. She refused Wyatt's offer to get her some food but agreed to a cup of lemonade. Wyatt had barely left her side when she saw LuAnn coming toward her. Kat's chest tightened. The door to the outside was not far, and she wondered if she could reach it in time, but LuAnn was there before she could even take a step.

"Afternoon, Kat," LuAnn said, her voice an odd mixture of southern hospitality and venom.

"LuAnn." Kat wanted to keep any conversation short.

"It's so sad about Pony. He was so young to go like that."

Kat nodded.

"I heard you're taking over Pony's shop," she said, raising her glass of ice tea to her lips.

"Word sure spreads fast around here." Kat wanted an accusation to hang in her words.

LuAnn seemed to ignore any accusation. "You know, you'll never have the support of the other artists here. They all know what you did to those precious children of yours, and it's unforgivable."

"Is this really the place to have this conversation?" It might have been Kat's imagination, but she felt the eyes of everyone in the room on her and LuAnn.

"The church is the perfect place for truth telling. But you wouldn't know that, would you?"

Kat threw up her hands. "I'm not having this conversation with you, LuAnn." She tried to push her way past to the door, but LuAnn grabbed her arm.

"You're good at walking away, aren't you?"

Kat jerked her arm loose.

"You know, I used to feel sorry for you," LuAnn continued. "For what your husband did to you. For what *you* said he did, anyway. I took you in and treated you like my own, provided comfort to you—and all the time you were lying to me."

Kat worked to stay calm. "I truly appreciate everything that you and Rusty did for me when I first came here, and I'm sorry I lied to you. But, honestly, I don't owe you an explanation about my life and my choices." Kat brushed past her.

"Maybe not to me," LuAnn called after her. "But I'm sure God is still waiting for you to explain."

Kat whirled around. "Well, then, that's between God and me, isn't it?" Kat turned and walked away, shoving the door open when she got to it, finally letting out her breath when she stepped into the warm spring air. She stood for a moment, the tension slow to drain from her fingertips after she uncurled her fists.

The door opened, and for a moment Kat feared LuAnn had followed her out to continue the conversation. But it was Wyatt.

"I saw you talking to LuAnn."

"More like her talking to me—or lecturing, really. I can't believe that after five years she chose today to tell me off. I can't believe we were once friends."

"I guess she felt betrayed."

She looked at him, her eyes wide in disbelief. "Please tell me you're not defending her."

"Of course not. What she did was wildly inappropriate—and I'm sure not accurate." He took Kat's hand. "I'm sorry if I made it sound like she had a right to say anything at all."

"I just want to go home."

When they were driving away, she looked back at the church, and she knew that it would always be this way. That she would never be free of her past.

In the few weeks that passed since the funeral, working with pottery was even more of a respite than ever for Kat. She tried to run the pottery shop, to honor Pony's legacy. But she knew that part of her was only keeping the shop going to prove LuAnn wrong, which for a while, seemed important to her. She spent most of her mornings getting the receipts from the day before ready for the bank, if Daniel hadn't already done it, and paying the bills. But as quick as she could dispense of her chores, she would be back to her own studio with a mound of damp clay gliding under her fingers. She was more at home in her studio. That's where she wanted to be, really.

Daniel managed the store for her, and though he never complained about her absence, she knew the store would have faltered if he were not there. He had come from a long line of potters and was more adept at managing the store than she was. LuAnn would probably gloat, but Kat finally urged Daniel to take over ownership of the store, even if it meant going against Pony's wishes. She would keep making pottery and bring it in for Daniel to sell. She would help out in the store if Daniel needed her. Pony's legacy would still live in that store, and her connection to him and the store would remain intact.

Kat's studio had taken over the whole garage now, except for Wyatt's music gear, which filled one corner. Her kiln was tucked in another corner. Shelves lined the back wall for the pottery to dry and the side wall for clays and glazes. A table was in the middle of the space, which she used for general work, such as wedging the clay and glazing. She had placed the new electric pottery wheel near the garage door, so that when it was good weather, she could open the door and look at the mountain rising across the road from the house. She sometimes missed the old kick wheel, the way it made her whole body connect to the clay, but as long as her hands could feel the clay respond to her touch, she was happy.

In her studio, Kat grabbed the apron from the hook and tied it around her. Luna, who had taken her time following Kat, found her spot beside the wheel and eased her way down. Kat hated to see Luna struggle so much with her arthritis, but Kat always appreciated Luna's company. Over the years, Luna had become as much her dog as Wyatt's, not showing a preference between the two.

Kat opened the garage door and saw the blanket of gray clouds moving over the mountains. "Looks like we may get rain today after all," she said to Luna. "We'll see how long this door gets to stay open."

She cut a chunk of clay from the big block and began wedging it on the table. When it was ready to put on the wheel, she sat on the bench and threw the clay onto the wheel, then began to center it. As she pulled the clay up, she saw what it wanted to be. Pony had taught her that sometimes the clay would let her know what it was supposed to be. She pressed her thumbs down into the clay and let it flair toward her hands until she felt the correct thickness on the bottom. She wet her hands again and then pulled the clay up into a cylinder before squeezing in and lifting out until the shape of a bowl appeared. Her fingers continued to guide the clay to stretch out the bottom a bit more until she was satisfied with the form that was on her wheel.

"There," she said as she stopped the wheel and looked down. "Isn't it wonderful, Luna?"

When she heard her name, Luna lifted her head, and Kat noticed a small circle of what appeared to be blood on the concrete floor. "What's that, girl?" she said as she dipped her hands in the water and wiped them on a towel. She stooped down and inspected the spot closer. It was definitely blood and when she examined Luna closer, she saw the blood around her nose. Kat's chest tightened, and she tried to tamp down the panic that was rising in it. She cradled Luna's head and wished she could call Wyatt, but it was impossible to reach him at the construction sites.

The vet's office told her to come in after lunch and they could work her in. She tried to keep herself busy, first cutting the bowl free from the wheel and putting it on the shelf to dry. Then she cleaned the wheel and organized the glazes, something she'd been meaning to do for months. She didn't feel like eating lunch. When the time finally came, she stretched a blanket over the back seat and went to get Luna. She gently picked her up and realized she was much lighter than she had been back in the fall, when they had to wrestle her into the tub to bathe her after an encounter with a skunk. Kat laid her onto the blanket.

"It'll be alright, girl," she said before closing the door.

Kat had to force herself to slow her breathing as she pulled into the veterinary clinic. She lifted Luna out of the back seat and carried her inside. When she was told to sit in the waiting room, she cradled Luna in her lap, no matter how ridiculous it may have looked for her to do that with such a big dog. But a woman sitting close to her with a terrier in her lap just smiled and nodded.

When Kat was called back to the exam room, she paced until Dr. Thompson came in. Kat watched as Dr. Thompson felt around on Luna's body and checked her eyes and mouth, talking to Luna the whole time. Kat wondered if some of the comforting words were meant for her as well. The veterinary assistant drew blood, and then Kat and Luna were alone again in the tiny room.

"Well, Mrs. Jenkins," Dr. Thompson said when she finally came back in the room. "The blood tests are showing a couple of elevated results. Nothing alarming, but I would like to keep Luna overnight and run some more tests."

"What do you think is wrong with her?"

"We won't know, of course, until the results come back, but it may be cancer."

Kat felt lightheaded, just the way she felt when she heard the news about Beth. "Cancer?"

"If we've caught it early, then she has a good chance of survival, so let's not jump ahead of ourselves. I'll call you in the morning—it'll be late morning—and update you."

Kat nuzzled against Luna's face and kissed her on the nose before watching the assistant pick Luna up and carry her through the door. By the time she left the vet's office, the rain was coming down hard. She ran to her car and wiped the water from her face after she ducked in. She was glad to have to concentrate on the road instead of thinking about what might happen to Luna.

When she stepped out of the car at home, the rain had slowed to a steady summer rain. That will be good for the garden, Kat thought. Lost in her own thoughts, she walked to the garden gate and watched the rain soak into the soil and drop from the tender leaves of plants that were just beginning to grow bigger. She didn't seem to notice—or care—that she was now drenched, that her hair was falling into her face. She held out her hands and cupped them, letting the water pool, before pulling them apart and watching the water splash to the ground. Then she dropped to her knees and curled her body toward the ground. When the tears finally came, she couldn't distinguish them from the raindrops. She heard Wyatt's steps squishing through the grass before she felt his arm around her.

"What are you doing out here?" he said.

She looked at him, at the rain streaming down his forehead. "I don't know."

"Let's get you out of the rain."

He helped her up and kept his arm around her until he eased her into a chair on the porch. He knelt in front of her, resting a hand on her thigh. She pushed a strand of hair out of her face and looked down at him.

"What's going on?" he said, not moving to push his own dripping hair from his face.

"It's Luna." She placed her hand on top of his. "I had to take her to the vet this afternoon." His eyes moved across the porch, as he suddenly realized Luna wasn't there. "She may have cancer. It may not be as bad as it sounds. Dr. Thompson said if we've caught it early, she has a good chance. They'll call tomorrow with the test results." She ran her fingers through his wet hair as she stared into his face, trying to bring a look of reassurance to her own.

"Then we'll hope for the best," he finally said.

They were quiet, and Kat listened to the rain hit the roof above her. Wyatt laid his head on her lap, and she continued to run her fingers through his hair. Finally, he raised his head and looked at her.

"I still don't understand why you were out there by the garden in the rain."

"I'm not sure," she said. "I just found myself drawn there when I got home. Something about life being there." She stared out at the garden. "I've been walking in grief for so long that I'm not sure what normal feels like anymore." She looked at him. "Or is this what normal is?"

He didn't say anything, but instead lowered his head back onto her lap. He stayed there until the trembling in her body was finally imperceptible.

31

My dearest, dearest Kat,

I hope you're sitting down as you're reading this, because I'm coming home! It's still three weeks away, but I'm already booked on a flight out of Saigon. I'm sorry I'll miss Lizzie's birthday (barely), but maybe we can celebrate it again after I get back. Surely no one will mind more cake. Haha

I've told you before that losing Thao was so hard on me. There's not a day that goes by that I don't think of her—that I don't wonder about what might have been if she hadn't been attacked. One of my strongest memories has been a conversation we had while she was healing at the clinic, before she knew she was pregnant. She told me that she had a dream the night before. She and her mother were in a big house on the coast, back where her family was from. Her mother had made banh xeo, her favorite meal, and after they had eaten, her mother presented her with a beautiful comb for her hair, which made Thao so happy. It was her grandmother's comb and her mother had never let her wear it before.

Listening to Thao talk about the dream, about the comb, I understood what she had lost because of everything that had happened to her and to her people. But I also saw the peace the dream had given her, the connection to her family it brought back to her.

Just after Thao had first been brought to us, Dr. Michaels and Carrie went to tell Thao's mother. They spared her the details, only telling her that Thao had been in an accident. Carrie told me Thao's mother was upset, but stoic. It's how these people have learned to cope after decades of war and tragedy.

I hadn't been back to that particular refugee camp since Thao's death. It was just too painful. But I finally decided that I had to face it—that it was part of my healing process. I knew I had to face Thao's mother. I think I still blamed her for not accepting what happened to Thao, even though she had never been told about any of it.

So, I went to the camp a few days ago. I didn't see Thao's mother at first, and to be honest, I was kind of glad. But she sent a young girl to get me and the translator. I thought maybe she was sick, so I went, thinking Thao would have wanted me to go.

When I came into the meager house, the woman was sitting at a small table. She motioned for us to sit and I sat down across from her. She didn't look sick, but she seemed sad. We sat across from each other a moment, not saying a word.

"My Thao loved you, doctor," she said—her words coming to me through the translator. She wouldn't look at me. "Daughter would say that your hair is like the sunset over our old village." She reached down into her lap

and set a beautiful tortoise shell comb onto the table. "You to take this," she said in broken English. I knew immediately that it was the comb Thao told me about—her grandmother's comb—the one in her dream.

"I can't take this," I said, trying to push the comb back toward her. "I know what it means to your family."

She shook her head and pushed the comb back to me. "You must take." I nodded and thanked her, wondering if she knew what really happened to Thao. Maybe she knew how I had tried to take care of her daughter. I don't know. It was strange for her to be willing to part with something so precious to her family.

But as strange as it was for her to give me the comb, I knew what it meant for me. It was a sign from Thao. I knew that her dream had somehow been about her and me—and she was telling me now that we would always be connected to each other. I knew that it was time for me to go home—to my family.

I don't regret a moment over here. I've seen more pain than I ever thought possible, but I've seen more resilience, too. These people keep pressing forward no matter what happens around them or to them. I guess they have no fucking choice, but that doesn't stop me from being inspired by them. I mean, my God, if they can keep going on, what excuse could I ever have.

So, I'll be getting off a plane at Blue Grass Airport, wearing a tortoise shell comb in my hair, remembering someone so special to me, and looking forward to spending time with the family that I love. Counting the days until I see you again.

With more love than I can say,
Beth

Sunday Herald-Leader
February 23, 1974

Local Woman Killed in Vietnam

BY SCOTTY WILSON
Staff Writer

Bethany Lynn Hunter, 26, of Lexington was killed by enemy mortar fire near the village of Quảng Ngãi, Vietnam. Hunter had been serving as a nurse for the Refugee Medical Corps (RMC) since November 1972. She was scheduled to return to the States on March 15.

The RMC, based in New York state, is a humanitarian organization, whose purpose is to provide medical aid to refugees throughout the world.

"She was a caring and compassionate nurse," said Carrie Hernandez, in a letter sent to the family. Hernandez served with Hunter in Vietnam. "The world is a darker place without her in it."

Prior to working for the RMC, Hunter was an emergency room nurse at Central Baptist Hospital (Lexington) and served as a volunteer nursing aid in Guatemala while in college.

Hunter's body arrived in Lexington on Thursday. Funeral services are scheduled for Monday at 2pm at Milward Funeral Home. She will be interred at the Lexington Cemetery.

Ms. Hunter is survived by her parents, William David Hunter and Betty Smith Hunter, Lexington; one brother, David (Mary Catherine), Lexington; and two nieces.

32

KAT TAKES THE SLAB OF CLAY AND CENTERS IT on the wheel. She's not sure what she's going to make. Maybe today this clay will tell her what it's meant to be. Sometimes it works that way. Wyatt is at the kiln, loading dried pottery from the nearby shelf. When he has time, he enjoys helping her with the kiln, although he has never had the nerve to try the wheel.

Kat is focused on the clay, but she hears the car coming up the driveway. She looks up, but she doesn't recognize the car. When it stops, a young man with hair the color of a raven steps out of the driver's side of the car. The young woman in the passenger seat is slower to emerge.

"Who's that?" Wyatt says when he comes up beside Kat.

"I'm not sure." Kat dips her hands in the bucket of water and gives them a quick scrub. She picks up a towel and wipes her hands, but some of the clay still clings to them. She pulls off her apron and hangs it on the hook then continues to wipe her hands with the towel. She moves out of the garage and into the sunlight, shading her eyes and squinting toward the car. When the young woman, who's obviously pregnant, moves toward her, threading herself between Kat and Wyatt's vehicles, Kat sees something familiar in the way the cheekbones are raised and the nose sits like a button in the middle of the face. She feels her knees buckle.

"Mrs. Jenkins?" Kat is shaken by the formality in the voice. "I'm—"

"Jenny." Kat keeps her eyes focused on Jenny's face, watching to see if it will soften with the mutual recognition.

"Yes, I'm Jenny Clark," the woman says. "This is my husband, Bobby." Jenny points to the man standing beside her, but with her eyes, she dares Kat to say anything. She is only eighteen. Married and pregnant. Kat wonders if the pregnancy had forced them to get married, a story Kat herself is all too familiar with.

Kat nods at Bobby. "Nice to meet you." The comment is instinctual— the polite response—but it feels out of place in this context. She looks back at Jenny. "I'm so happy to see you, but how on earth did you find me?"

"I saw a card from you at Nana's. I copied the return address on the envelope, in case I ever wanted to find you."

Kat remembers that she'd sent Betty a card on the tenth anniversary of Beth's passing. She never heard anything back, but it provides a small comfort knowing that Betty had not thrown the card away.

"I need to talk to you," Jenny says abruptly. She stares at Wyatt. "Alone."

"Of course," Wyatt says. "Bobby, is it? Why don't we walk over to the river." Bobby glances at Jenny, who nods at him to go. Luna, who has been asleep on her bed in the corner of the garage, has come up beside Wyatt.

"We can sit on the porch," Kat says after the men disappear through the trees. Luna goes back to her spot in the garage, while Kat and Jenny climb the porch steps. Kat motions for Jenny to sit at the table. "Can I get you something to drink?"

"I don't want anything," Jenny says.

The empty chair screeches across the deck floor as Kat pulls it out and she sits across from Jenny. Kat tries not to stare, since Jenny already seems nervous, but she can't look away. The last time she saw her eldest daughter, Jenny was a girl, only nine years old, just beginning to discover her own voice. Now she has bloomed into a young woman, about to become a mother herself.

Kat wants to reach across the table and touch Jenny's arm or stroke her hair. She wants to reassure herself that it isn't a dream. She has a thousand questions she wants to ask, but she is silent. Jenny has come here for a reason. Kat cannot steal this moment as if she is the one who designed it.

"It's strange," Jenny finally says, glancing at Kat, then looking away again. "I've been thinking about this moment for a long time, but I suddenly don't know what to say."

Kat twists the towel that is still in her hands. "It's okay. Take your time."

Jenny stares into the tree line. Maybe she is hoping Bobby will come back and they can leave. Maybe seeing Kat is all she really needs. Finally, she takes a deep breath and lets the air out slowly, as if she has been holding it there for a long time. "For almost ten years now, I've wondered why you left. I thought maybe it was because you stopped loving Dad. Or maybe you stopped loving all of us. But seeing you here, in this cozy life you've built for yourself, I wonder now if you ever loved us at all."

Kat thinks she has prepared herself for this moment, if it ever came, but Jenny's words knock the breath from her body. Her chest heaves to get it back before any words are able to come.

"I suppose no matter what I say, my words will sound hollow to you, and I understand why." She realizes she has twisted the towel into a tight coil. She sets the towel aside. "I did love your father at one time." She reaches her hand across the table. "I still love you and your sisters."

Jenny looks at the hand but does not touch it. Instead, she stands and turns away from Kat. She is quiet for a moment, then turns back. "You're right. Your words *are* hollow." She leans against the rail. "Do you have any idea what it was like after you left? Dad fell apart. He was drunk off his ass most of the time, and he brought home a parade of women who didn't give a shit about us girls. Hell, they didn't even care about Dad, and he didn't care about them."

She stares at Kat, her jaw set firm. "Lizzie and I cried for weeks, waiting for you to come home. Then Dad said you weren't coming home. He didn't say why—just that you weren't coming home. Kris was too young to cry for very long. She didn't understand that you were really gone. As she got older, she started saying magical spells, trying to conjure you up. She still does sometimes." She chuckles. "Can you believe that? Magical fucking spells."

"I'm sorry." Kat knows the words are pathetic, but it is all she knows to say. No words can undo what she has done.

"Yeah, sorry." Jenny's voice carries more sadness than anger, although both were there. She sits down again and looks at Kat. "So, why the hell *did* you leave?"

"For a long time, I didn't understand it myself." Kat leans back in her chair, though she doesn't take her eyes off Jenny. "It's hard to explain, but when your aunt Beth died, something broke inside me. You were still young when she died, not much older than Kris was when I—" The word catches for a moment in her throat. "When I left. Do you remember her at all?"

Jenny shakes her head. "Only a little bit. I have a vague memory of her playing dolls with me, and I remember her long red hair."

"She did have the most beautiful hair. It was one of the first things I noticed about her when I met her in college." Kat smiles at the memory. "It's strange. I hated her at first. She was so opinionated, but as I've thought about it, so was I. But somehow, we became friends and then sisters. Maybe deeper than sisters. She always pushed me to think differently about the world, and about myself. I was only beginning to understand that when she was killed."

"But she died years before you left."

Kat looks at Jenny. Looks at someone who reminds her so much of herself that it hurt. "I know. I thought I had put away the grief, like I was supposed to. But the longer it stayed away, the more it demanded to be dealt with. I realize now that I was hanging onto the grief, afraid that if I let go of it, then Beth would be gone forever. In a strange way, feeling the pain of losing her kept her close to me. Back then, when I left, the grief I still didn't understand got tangled up with everything Beth had been trying to tell me for years. I couldn't untangle the two, and I thought I needed time away from everyone to sort it all out."

"You left without saying goodbye. You made us feel you didn't care about us."

Kat's body feels heavy. The pain in Jenny's voice is fresh, but it also carries years-worth of injury. Kat looks at Jenny, then looks away. "I wish I had done things differently—"

"Then why didn't you ever come back?"

"It's complicated." Going into what David did would only cause Jenny more hurt, she knows that. "There were times that first year I convinced myself that I was going to go back, but then I didn't feel less broken than when I left. As more time passed, and I started to sort out my feelings, I worried that it would disrupt your lives for me to come back."

"Well, you were probably right about that. We've moved on without you. It might not have been all good, but I can only imagine the emotional trauma you would have stirred up if you *had* suddenly shown up."

They are silent again. Kat wants to know more about Lizzie and Kris. She wants to hear about their favorite subjects in school or who their friends are or whether they have any hobbies. She wants to know more about Jenny. When did she meet Bobby? Is she going to college in the fall? Kat wants to know everything.

But she is also scared to know.

She looks at Jenny, who has one hand resting on top of her rounded belly. "When's your baby due?" she says.

"We're expecting her sometime in mid-July."

It's a girl. A granddaughter.

"You must be excited," she says. "Maybe after she's born I could—"

"No." Jenny's response is quick, but calm. She leans forward, clasping her hands in front of her. "I came here today because I needed some answers—and you've given me some. But I don't want a relationship with you."

"Oh." Kat feels the breath leave her again.

"Not right now, anyway. Maybe not ever." She stares at Kat, as if she is memorizing her face. "I think I understand better why you left and why you didn't come back. But I don't know if I can ever forgive you for it." She stands again, her chair scraping against the deck. "And I don't want you trying to talk to Lizzie or Kris. You were right not to mess up their lives by coming back. It's maybe the only selfless thing you've done for us in the past ten years."

Kat stares up at Jenny. She wonders if this will be the last time she'll see her daughter. "Will you tell them you saw me?" she asks.

"I don't think so." Jenny turns toward the porch rail and stands silent for a moment. Kat wonders if she should say something, but Jenny turns back to face her. "No, I can't. If they ever tell me they want to find you, then I'll decide if I should tell them."

Kat wants to tell her that keeping such a secret can cause resentment from her sisters, if they ever find out, but it will be foolish to give her such advice.

"Well, I guess I don't need anything else from you," Jenny says. Kat doesn't know if this means for just today or forever. "Would you tell Bobby that I'll be waiting for him in the car?"

"Of course," Kat says as she stands. She pushes back her instinct to wrap her arms around Jenny, who has—whether intentionally or not—taken a step back. "I'm glad you came" is all Kat can say, but she knows it sounds too casual, as if Jenny is a friend who dropped by for afternoon tea. When Jenny's eyes widen in surprise, Kat knows for certain it has been the wrong thing to say. She considers correcting herself, but it will be pointless. Nothing she can think of will sound any less trivial.

Kat takes one more look at Jenny and steps off the porch. She watches the grass underneath her feet as she moves through the yard. Only when she reaches the back corner of the garden does she glance back toward the house. Jenny is gone.

Wyatt and Bobby are standing by the river talking when Kat comes through the trees. She tells Bobby that Jenny is waiting for him in the car, and Wyatt catches her eye, as if to ask her if she's okay. She doesn't know if she is, and she doesn't know if Wyatt understands that from the lack of expression in her eyes.

"I'll walk you to the car," Wyatt says to Bobby. He touches Kat's arm and whispers, "I'll be right back."

The twigs crack behind her as Wyatt and Bobby walk through the trees. She drops to her knees and fixes her gaze at the water. On either side of her, the river rushes, scooting across rocks and around boulders, but in front of her, the water appears as if it isn't moving. But she knows it is, because rivers are alive, traveling from their origins high in the mountains until they join other rivers and empty themselves into larger and larger bodies of water or spend themselves out into creeks and streams in flat lowlands.

She imagines herself stepping into the calm water in front of her. It's not too deep there, maybe just below her waist. The water is cold and she shivers, but she kneels, letting the water cover her chest. She lowers her head under the water, her eyes closed, and she feels the current try to push her body, to carry her to wherever it is going. She thinks about relaxing her body and letting the river take her, but instead, she lifts herself out of the water and onto the bank. She imagines all of this as she stares at the river.

Wyatt is kneeling beside her, his arm around her shoulder. "They're gone," he says.

They're quiet.

"I continue to live out the consequences of my decision," she says, looking at Wyatt. "She doesn't want a relationship with me."

"I'm sorry." He kisses her on the forehead.

"I can't blame her. But I also won't give up hope—on any of them. I'll be here if ever they want me in their lives." She rests her head on his shoulder, and they stay that way for a while—she doesn't know how long. This day will settle in her, joining the other fragments of grief she still carries. The grief will visit occasionally, on days when she doesn't expect it, but she will remind herself that love has also settled into her heart.

Kat lifts her head off Wyatt's shoulder, rocks back on her feet, and stands. She reaches a hand to Wyatt, and he stands, too. They look once more at the river, then turn and walk to the garage.

Kat puts on her apron and sits on the bench before reaching for the small bucket of water. She sprinkles water over the drying clay in the center of the wheel. Wyatt picks up his guitar, sits on a stool, and begins strumming "The River is Wide." Luna settles into her spot by the pottery wheel. Kat turns on the motor, and its familiar humming fills the room. She looks at the empty spot in the driveway, then she dips her hand in the water and brings it to the clay, which moves beneath her fingers, waiting to tell her what it will become.

ACKNOWLEDGMENTS

I am grateful to the faculty and my friends at the Bluegrass Writers Studio/MFA program at Eastern Kentucky University, whose advice and positivity challenged me to revisit pieces of the manuscript for continued refinement. I especially owe thanks to Julie Hensley for her insightful comments and questions that helped shape the format of the book. Thanks to Virginia Underwood for her astute editing, her gracious encouragement, and her support of my narrative vision.

Thank you to Megan Sauter and Les Greeman at Broadway Clay in Frankfort, Kentucky, for showing me the basics of making pottery and talking to me about this art form.

To better inform my understanding of the conditions in Vietnam during the war, particularly the effects on Vietnamese children, I watched the 1972 documentary, "The Gooks," by filmmaker Pierre Gaisseau. The film was produced by the Canadian Broadcasting Corporation (CBC) and distributed by NBC and then PBS.

On pages 15 and 16, the italicized sentences appear in 1997 edition (W.W. Norton) of *The Feminine Mystique*.

As always, I thank my husband, Glenn, and sons—Nathan and Adam—who read or listened to drafts and provided feedback and encouragement.

ABOUT THE AUTHOR

SHERRY ROBINSON, an American fiction writer, is the author of two previous novels, *Blessed* (2019) and *My Secrets Cry Aloud* (2009). She is the recently retired Vice Provost and Professor of English at Eastern Kentucky University, where she spent thirteen years specializing in American Literature before moving into administrative positions.

Robinson is a native of Lexington, Kentucky, where her desire to be an author was also born. From an early age, she became entranced with words, but it took many years and a few detours before the publication of her first novel. Among those detours was the completion of an MA from Eastern Kentucky University and a PhD from the University of Kentucky, both in English. Reading the works of so many accomplished authors taught her the characteristics of quality writing and inspired her to reignite her passion for writing. In addition to studying great works of literature, Robinson spent two summers at the Hindman Settlement School's Appalachian Writers Workshop under the mentorship of Silas House. She completed an MFA in creative writing from Eastern Kentucky University, Bluegrass Writers Studio, in 2021.